MW00656945

Poppy
and the Pirate

ALSO BY ELIZABETH COLE

Poppy and the Pirate

ELIZABETH COLE

SKYSPARK BOOKS

PHILADELPHIA, PENNSYLVANIA

Copyright © 2022 by Elizabeth Cole.

All rights reserved. No part of this publication may be reproduced, distributed or transmitted in any form or by any means, including photocopying, recording, or other electronic or mechanical methods, without the prior written permission of the publisher, except in the case of brief quotations embodied in critical reviews and certain other noncommercial uses permitted by copyright law. For permission requests, write to the publisher, addressed "Attention: Permissions Coordinator," at the address below.

SkySpark Books
Philadelphia, Pennsylvania
skysparkbooks.com
inquiry@skysparkbooks.com

Publisher's Note: This is a work of fiction. Names, characters, places, and incidents are a product of the author's imagination. Locales and public names are sometimes used for atmospheric purposes. Any resemblance to actual people, living or dead, or to businesses, companies, events, institutions, or locales is completely coincidental.

Ordering Information:
Quantity sales. Special discounts are available on quantity purchases by corporations, associations, and others. For details, contact the "Special Sales Department" at the address above.

POPPY AND THE PIRATE / Cole, Elizabeth. – 1st ed.
ISBN-13: 978-1-942316-55-8

Prologue

THE WATERS OF THE LAKE sparkled in the sun, sending glimmering shards of diamond over a wash of deep blue. On the shore, five girls gathered around a rowboat.

"Are you *sure* Mrs. Bloomfield said it was all right for us to take the boat out alone?" asked one girl, the dark-haired Camellia. The headmistress of their school was a kind but firm woman, who didn't want any of her charges to get into trouble.

"We're not alone," retorted Poppy, who had instigated the whole plan. "We're together and we know what we're doing! My goodness, we're all nearly *fourteen*!"

And so the little party set out in the boat. Poppy took the stern, mostly so she could pose dramatically. Rose volunteered to row on the left side, while Heather took the right. In the bow, Camellia and Daisy sat on the narrowest bench, Daisy trailing one hand in the placid water.

Rose was blind (due to a fever that had taken her sight a few years prior), but that didn't stop her from rowing, and she put all of her effort into it, her shoulders, arms, and back working hard. Heather mirrored her in perfect concert, and together they propelled the little boat into the middle of the lake.

"I wish I knew a sea shanty," Rose said. She loved to

sing.

"I don't think we're allowed to know those," Heather grumbled (she did not care for the many restrictions placed on young ladies).

"Aye, they're too salty!" Poppy retorted, laughing.

"Oh, no, the puns again," Camellia said, rolling her eyes. "I may have to jump overboard and swim to safety."

"How's our rowing, captain?" Rose asked Poppy.

"You're doing marvelously!" Poppy called back. "We've got plenty of time before we're anywhere near the opposite shore. But wait, do put up the oars for a moment. We're almost exactly in the middle!"

She looked back over her shoulder, but couldn't see any hint of the grand structure known as Wildwood Hall. The old, rambly building housed the Bloomfield Academy for Young Ladies of Quality, where all of them were students. Today's excursion was a special treat, for, in a week, they'd all go home for the summer. Poppy would miss her friends (besides Rose—the two girls lived together and Poppy helped Rose navigate the world).

Ah, navigate the world! Poppy smiled at the unintended joke, thinking that her brain had definitely turned to all things nautical. It must be the influence of the story Mrs. Bloomfield had read to them yesterday, for it was full of ships and pirates and a brave princess who sailed the seas until she found her lost love at last.

Inspired, Poppy shifted in the boat, which wobbled slightly (but was otherwise stable, for five girls and their picnic lunch made excellent ballast). She pulled a crown out of her bag and put it on her head. As far as crowns went, it wasn't very valuable—being made of an old pasteboard hatbox, then encrusted with stray and mismatched glass beads—but the girls used it in nearly all their make-believe games.

"Listen to me! I am the rebel Princess Judith, and I am searching for my beloved Prince Zev. Do you all remember?"

"Of course we do," Heather replied cheekily. "Mrs. Bloomfield read it aloud from the book of Jewish folktales she just got. I adore how the lovers were separated for so long and then finally got reunited at the end."

"That's how fairytales work," Camellia noted. "It all ends happily ever after, with no loose ends. Life is not so tidy, or so certain."

Poppy waved that off. "Well, Judith's tale had plenty of twists and turns. Here, look at these sticks—they're your swords for when we come upon pirates and thieves in the forests of the island ahead. And now, Rose and Heather, take your oars. Row hard—we'll pretend it's the great storm that Judith sailed through on her way across the ocean."

"Honestly," Daisy said. "The whole story would have been very short if the characters just talked to each other! After all, Judith and Zev were actually already betrothed and would have been married anyway…except their fathers didn't keep their promises very well."

"It's more exciting the way it happened." Poppy brandished her stick in the air. "Remember when Judith's ship got seized by pirates, and she tricked them into following her plan? She was the cleverest of all."

"She got them drunk," Heather said bluntly. "If I learned one thing from that tale, it's not to drink anything an unknown woman offers you."

Poppy ignored that. "Onward, my faithful crew! We'll sail to that dark-forested land beyond, and if there are thieves within, we shall beguile them and steal their treasure."

"Ahoy!" Daisy called enthusiastically, taking up the

cause.

When they landed, the girls played for hours, staging scenes from the story they'd heard, and taking turns being the rebel princess who became a pirate and even a king (she had the foresight to pretend to be man for safety) before finding her true love and revealing her own feminine identity, to the amazement of all.

Poppy jumped and shouted and screeched and wept with the others. When she played, she played with all her heart. And a little part of her knew that these long, lazy summer days could not last forever. Someday, they'd grow up, and move apart, and take on the roles of grown women. They'd all have to find husbands and marry, or work in one of the few acceptable positions for ladies.

What lay in Poppy's future? She couldn't imagine, but she doubted it would be as exhilarating as the tale of Princess Judith, who fell in love, and endured hardship, and encountered pirates, and was sought after by kings, and made her own way thanks to her own wisdom, despite everything life threw in her path.

When the afternoon was done, and their bellies began to hunger for supper, Poppy led her merry crew back to their trusty ship. This time, Camellia manned an oar, and Daisy took the other.

Poppy adjusted the paper-and-foil crown on her head and pointed in the direction of Wildwood Hall, across the lake.

She called out in a voice that carried far over the water, "Come, let us go home!"

Chapter 1

SEVERAL YEARS LATER

Dearest Poppy,

Your mother wrote to me lately, and from her account, I gleaned that you are feeling a bit at odds in London. Not that she complained! She would never, and indeed has nothing but praise for your good spirit and your unfailing help with the family firm. She tells me that you have gained such knowledge about fabrics and the intricacies of the actual import business. Of course, I am not surprised in the least, as you were always a clever child.

You no doubt feel a strong sense of duty to the family, but if you should wish a change of scenery, know that you are very welcome to visit Pencliff Towers in Cornwall. We would be delighted to have you at any time, but the summer here is particularly lovely—which is not a thing I can say for summers in London!

With affection,

"Aunt" Candice Towers

Poppy St George folded the letter back up and replaced it in her reticule. She was no longer a child, but she was still clever. And she could easily read between the lines. It was no secret that Poppy had been feeling at odds lately. Hence this plot between her mother and a long-time friend to pull Poppy out of the city, and out of the doldrums she'd slipped into months ago.

A mewing sound broke her concentration. "Yes, Misty, I shall feed you presently."

When Poppy agreed to come to Cornwall, she'd made a point that she would not go alone. Her cat would be coming along. Miss Mist, named for the soft grey of her coat, was not fond of the traveling basket she'd been placed in for the journey (scratching the interior constantly during her waking hours). But Poppy couldn't stand to leave her behind, and anyway, if travel was healthy for young ladies, surely it was healthy for young cats as well.

"Perhaps you can decimate the Cornish rodent population this summer," Poppy suggested, earning another meow. Miss Mist was a hunter at heart.

The carriage rolled to a halt on the road, which currently ran along the very edge of the headland. The coachman suggested that Poppy step out for a few minutes while he attended to a personal matter. Poppy appreciated the coachman's tact and dutifully disembarked, walking to the cliffside to look out at the sea.

It was a striking sight. Standing on the windswept, rocky cliffs of Cornwall felt like standing at the edge of the world. The fog-grey waters of the sea stretched out to the horizon, and clouds scudded across the sky. A few fat drops of rain pelted her face. She could not imagine a setting further from the busy, built-up world of London. But it also felt terribly lonely here, and Poppy felt a little trill of fear. Was this what the rest of her life was destined to feel like?

"Miss!" called the coachman. "We'll be going now."

Poppy turned her back on the ocean and returned to

the coach. She had been assaulted by the vehicle's seats for days now. Her backside was bruised, her dignity was abused, and she was *still* not to her destination.

"Come along, miss, before the rain soaks you clean through." The coachman, not much more than a boy, helped her climb into the cab. The one good point was that she now—finally—had the coach to herself. The other passengers had disembarked one by one: at Exeter, at Lostwithel, at other smaller towns whose names had already left her. When the final passenger beside her had gone, Poppy seized the chance to stretch her limbs. But even so, she was ready to be done with the journey.

"How much longer, Mr. Kellow?" she asked the driver.

"Only two hours or so, miss, if the road remains good."

This was a good *road?* she thought. Poppy thanked him, knowing he wasn't responsible for the conditions. Only two more hours of grueling pain. How wonderful.

As the coach continued on its way, Poppy wondered for the hundredth time if she'd made the correct decision in accepting this invitation.

Poppy had known Mr. Towers and his wife since she was a little girl, since they were close to her mother and her birth father (long deceased). Once Mr. Towers retired from his work as a barrister, he moved far away from London. Poppy first thought the idea of Cornwall romantic. Now that she saw the rough hills, the grey waters, and the sparse population, she feared the reality would simply be dreary.

Since her cousin and dearest friend had married last year, Poppy was no longer required as her companion, a position she'd gladly held for years. And indeed, she understood that in some way Rosalind, who Poppy always regarded as the more innocent one, had now grown beyond her.

"To think I turned proposals down!" she told herself. True, she hadn't *wanted* to marry any of her few suitors, and particularly not while Rose needed her as a companion. But still…no doubt she'd been presumptuous in assuming her future contained more proposals, especially considering her reduced social status after her mother remarried to a tradesman. Poppy was happy for her mother—her stepfather was a good man who aimed to provide everything his family needed. And Poppy herself had little patience for the complex hierarchy that sorted everyone into little boxes according to their birth names and bloodlines. However, it was an irrefutable fact that English society cared deeply about such things, and Poppy's standing was now lower and less desirable than it had been when she was younger.

Rain now spattered over the glass window. In the faint reflection, she saw the damp air had made the few curls by her temples fall, so her blonde hair looked much darker and straighter than usual. So much for looking presentable! Poppy traced wet circles on the inside of the glass, unconsciously writing the letter *C*. Once she saw the image, she made it into a circle, and then wiped the whole thing out with an impatient gesture. The so-called gentleman belonging to that initial did not deserve a place in her thoughts. A pair of dark eyes momentarily haunted her memory—beautiful eyes that had seemed so sincere, but then proved to be quite the opposite.

Fortunately, being composed of fire more than water, Poppy wasn't a morose person by nature. The clouds and rain blew off within an hour, and the return of the sun and the hints of blue sky restored her usual spirit. Thus she was eagerly watching for the appearance of Pencliff Towers.

The coach turned and passed through a gate onto an even narrower track. When the house finally came into view however, Poppy barely noticed it, despite its scale and grandeur. The horizon beyond was so arresting that mere architecture could not compete. The house perched on a bluff situated above a small, curving bay. Though on the channel side, the waters here seemed as deep and wild as the great ocean to the west must be. Cliffs appeared to enclose the waters below—though a thin line of sandy beach could be glimpsed at the edges of the bay. Poppy hoped there was some way down to the water.

The rock of the cliffs was a dark, streaked grey, with a few trees and shrubs clinging tenaciously to the surface here and there. The top of the bluff was given over to rough, long grasses. In foul weather, the view might be foreboding, but in sunlight it was stunning. Poppy was smiling by the time the coach stopped and the door opened.

"It's beautiful!" she exclaimed. "I never expected it would be so pretty…the land, I mean, though the house is impressive."

"Aye, Pencliff Towers is the grandest estate around," said Kellow. "The only one around, to be honest."

"Is it so isolated?" she asked in dismay.

"Oh, no, miss. The town of Treversey is not more than three miles beyond—my last stop, in fact. St. Mark's Head over there hides it from view," he said, gesturing to a hill to the south. "But the town has everything you'd need, and you'll no doubt see it for yourself soon enough."

"You're from there," Poppy guessed.

The coachman smiled, and she realized anew that he was really quite young, perhaps not older than seventeen, making him three years or so younger than she was. "That I am, miss. My mother runs the tearoom on Greene Street." He ducked his head then. "Excuse me, I'll get your bags."

Soon the bags and the trunk were piled up by the front door, which was just opening up. Before Poppy could offer a gratuity to Kellow, one of the footmen preempted her by doing just that, "with thanks from Mr. Towers for seeing his guest safely here."

Poppy looked at the house more carefully now. Pencliff Towers faced east and had no towers. Strange! She was surprised by both its age and its size. For some reason, she'd thought it would be more rustic.

Kellow tipped his hat to her as she was hustled inside by a maid. She looked with a bit of awe at the grand foyer of the home. In keeping with the outside, it was much fancier than she'd originally anticipated.

"We weren't sure when to expect you, Miss St George," the maid said. "I've just sent word to Mrs. Towers, who will be—"

She didn't even get the words out before Mrs. Towers blew in. She was about sixty years old, with a stout frame. Her hair was completely white, and indeed, had been since Poppy could remember. However, her hair did not predict her attitude, and she moved through life like a ship at full sail. It was not wise to attempt to slow her down.

"My goodness!" she cried. "Little Miss St George is here at last! Though you're not little any longer, are you?" With those observations, any lingering coolness of the house was pushed away.

"Mama sends her greetings," Poppy said dutifully. "It was most kind of you to allow me to stay with you for the summer. And Miss Mist here as well."

Poppy indicated the basket holding the cat, and Mrs.

Towers immediately bent over to coo at the creature, who mewed in her most pitiful and adorable way.

"Oh, you darling!" Mrs. Towers said. "We must find a bit of fish from the kitchens for you after such a journey!"

Poppy smiled. Evidently time hadn't changed Mrs. Towers's doting, motherly attitude.

"It really is wonderful you came," Mrs. Towers said, once she straightened up. "We need more young people about. This place is beauty for the soul…but it can get too quiet. And I thought, Poppy St George was always a clever child. She'll liven up a dull house."

"I'm not the only guest, am I?" she asked.

"Oh, no. We always like to have a number of friends and family to stay. Right now we have Miss Metcalfe and her sister, young Miss Elisa…I knew their mother from school, rest her soul! And there's Mr. and Mrs. Hobbson, and the Ainsworths. Miss Ainsworth is so charming…"

She rattled off more names as they continued through the house to the seaward side (Miss Mist remained in the carrier, to be looked after by a housemaid who would take her upstairs).

Poppy had a vague impression of lushly furnished rooms and vases of flowers in nearly all corners, but keeping up with Mrs. Towers was a task in itself, so she could not linger.

On the way, a young woman in a rather plain gown stepped out of a room.

"Miss Elowen!" the hostess proclaimed. "I was just talking about you!"

"Oh, indeed?" the other asked nervously.

"Yes. Elowen Metcalfe, meet Poppy St George. I insist you two become great friends."

Elowen smiled shyly at Poppy, saying "How can we not, after such a decree?" She possessed very pretty eyes of china blue, striking in contrast to her dark hair. Her eyes held a little twinkle that heartened Poppy considerably.

"I think it shall not be too onerous," Poppy agreed.

Mrs. Towers looked around. "Is your sister about?"

"No," Elowen responded. "Elisa is lying down. The visits to the doctor always fatigue her."

"Poor dear. Well, Poppy can meet her at dinner. There is not any sweeter child than Elisa Metcalfe, dear. You'll see. Now come along, I want you to meet the other guests! I'm sure I've forgotten some names! There's the Hobbsons, who I think you met once in London when you were young. And the Ainsworths are rather newer acquaintances. Oh, talk about a coincidence. Mr. Ainsworth actually wanted to buy this property, when it came up for sale several years ago. Fortunately, Mr. Towers's man of business acted quicker, and we were able to secure the sale before he could. Good thing too, because apparently he was prepared to offer even more for it! Poor man, he lost out. But in all honesty, it was for the best. He's a bit of a parvenu, really,"

Mrs. Towers confided, in a lower tone. "Desperate to make a name for himself and gain the admiration of those he'd like to call peers. Naturally, owning a great house and joining the landed gentry would help. But he'd have regretted it, I'm sure. For all it costs to keep up Pencliff, I might as well have painted all the walls in silver and gold!"

Mrs. Towers herded Poppy onward through the house. Then they stepped out onto a wide, white gravel terrace overlooking the ocean. About six feet below the terrace, a green lawn extended thirty yards to a low stone wall, and beyond that the cliff face fell away to the shore far below. Several people were sitting there, taking advantage of the view. Mrs. Towers hailed them cheerfully.

Poppy's breath suddenly caught in her throat when she saw a certain gentleman with the other guests. He was handsome in an athletic sort of way, and while she should not by rights have recognized him, something in the slope of his shoulders, the way he held his head, took away all doubts.

He was the last to turn and see who had arrived. When he did, he shot up out of his chair. It *was* proper for a gentleman to stand when meeting a lady, but such speed was unusual. His expression was at first astonished, but by the time Poppy reached him, it had grown into a smile.

"If I am not mistaken, it is Miss St George," he said.

"You are not mistaken, Mr. de la Guerra," she returned, in a far cooler tone. "I do wish I'd known you were here. I would not have come."

Chapter 2

ADRIAN —

She's *here*.

—Carlos

Holy hell. What was *she* doing here?

Carlos de la Guerra had first met Poppy St George in the course of a rather delicate situation the previous year. His close friend—the wealthy, rakish Adrian Marsh, better known as Viscount Norbury—had done the impossible and fallen in love. And not with just anyone. Rosalind Blake: a blind woman who was as respectable and innocent as Adrian was dissolute.

Naturally, Carlos did what he could to help his friend win the girl…which led him into the path of Poppy, who served as Rosalind's companion and protector, with an emphasis on *protector*. He discovered that she was defiant and fierce, even to the point of offense. She once threatened Carlos with bodily harm.

Carlos was entranced by her.

To say she was *unusual* was an understatement. He liked her more the next time he saw her, and still more the third—and last—time. Unfortunately, he was forced to leave London almost immediately afterward to return to his home in Santo Domingo, and he was kept away far longer than expected. The complications of his own family's business, his desire to help his island win independence, and the various commitments he owed to friends and associates meant that he was either at sea or embroiled in work constantly for the last year. The few times he managed to get to London or correspond with Adrian, he learned nothing more about Poppy.

He knew he'd missed his chance.

So yes, Carlos nearly jumped out of his chair when he saw Poppy step into the sunlight. True, he hadn't seen her in more than a year, and at that distance, she could have been any young lady. Nevertheless, her face was etched into his brain, and her voice sounded sweetly familiar… right up until he saw her iron hard gaze, and fully realized how she felt about him.

She had every right to be annoyed. He hadn't been as forthcoming with her about his intentions as he could have been. He doubted that Miss St George would still be interested in listening to his excuses.

But she was here, wasn't she? Perhaps fate was offering him another chance.

"Miss St George," he said, keeping his true feelings inside. "You're looking well."

"I am thriving," she returned, eyes narrow. "Not that you would have had the opportunity to notice during your prolonged absence from London."

A young woman seated nearby had twisted around, watching this exchange with avid curiosity. She was dressed in an ensemble that looked distinctly military in style, with a host of buttons and gold braid down the front of her green velvet jacket.

"So you two already know each other?" she guessed,

tipping her head.

"We are only slightly acquainted, through mutual friends," Poppy corrected, keeping her voice even.

"Oh, how wonderful!" Mrs. Towers chimed in, hastily smoothing over the awkward moment. "You have saved me one introduction."

That didn't stop Mrs. Towers from introducing Poppy to the rest of the people sitting nearby. First, there were the Ainsworths, who were both tall and narrow. Then the Hobbsons, who were as round as the Ainsworths were lean.

The young lady in green was the last to be introduced. "And finally, Miss St George, this is Miss Blanche Ainsworth. So many young folk about! This will be a lovely summer, won't it?"

"I foresee much diversion on the horizon," said Blanche. Her soft voice somehow had the opposite force of the words themselves. Carlos was taken aback by it, and he wasn't even the recipient. Blanche's tone seemed threatening.

Poppy looked at her as well, a frown crossing her face. Carlos realized the threat was actually aimed at Poppy, though he didn't know why. The ladies had just *met*, for Christ's sake.

"Diversion! That is the very word, Miss Ainsworth," Mrs. Towers agreed, though in a much warmer tone. "And speaking of diversions, Poppy, I am so glad you can be added to my little showcase tonight. I was rather hoping for someone to play pianoforte."

"Oh, no. You are doubtless thinking of my cousin, who is most accomplished."

Mrs. Towers nodded. "I believe you're right—it was little Rose I remembered playing so well. Is it true that she is married now?"

"Indeed," Poppy smiled as she spoke, and Carlos got a little pain in his chest when he saw the emotion there. "She married Viscount Norbury last fall. And since then, she's hosted several events featuring the finest musicians in London."

"My, she's become a regular patroness of the arts, hasn't she? She made a smart match. And so unexpected, if I may say."

"It surprised many in society," Poppy said in a mild tone.

Carlos had to choke back a laugh. She was understating the case. The announcement of Rosalind and Adrian's marriage was first taken as a joke by members of society who had known the viscount's reputation as a rake.

"They are very happy," Carlos added.

"How would you know?" Poppy asked in a low voice. Before he could reply, she deliberately turned to Mrs. Towers, and said in a much kinder tone, "If you'll excuse me now, the journey was tiring. I really ought to get settled."

Mrs. Towers said, "Our housekeeper, Mrs. Biddle, will show you to your room. We can't have you wandering the halls, or we may never see you again! Pencliff Towers is quite a tangle, as you'll soon discover."

"I'm sure," Poppy muttered, shooting a dark glance at Carlos as she left.

"I don't recall you mentioning that Miss St George would be a guest," he said to Mrs. Towers, in as calm a tone as he could manage just then.

"Did I not? Well, she is staying until the end of the summer. Poor dear, I'd been informed she was quite lonely after her cousin's marriage. The two were closer than sisters! But surely you must know that, Mr. de la Guerra?"

"Only a little. I met Miss St George while Norbury

courted her cousin. The two ladies were always together…almost always, that is."

"There was something of a scandal about it, wasn't there?" asked Blanche, looking delighted at the idea of someone else's scandal.

"Some people will try to stir up rumors about the most inconsequential things," he said. "I assure you there was nothing untoward in their courtship."

"But there *was* talk of a duel." Mrs. Towers supplied that intelligence.

"Duels are discouraged nowadays," Carlos noted, without actually denying one took place. In fact, Carlos had served as Adrian's second for the duel itself. Adrian was one of the most skilled fighters he knew, whether with a blade or a gun. But he'd be damned if he glorified the situation.

"Well, well," Blanche said. "I simply must know all the details of that story. Won't you tell me, Mr. de la Guerra?"

"I'm afraid the story must wait," he said. "Please excuse me."

He walked away from the terrace and across the green lawn to the low wall at the edge of the yard, out of the view of the other guests. Beyond that, the land extended for several feet and then crumbled away, leaving only sheer cliff above the strand far below.

He contemplated jumping in. Not that he was prone to melancholy—but he would like to swim away from the increasing complications surrounding Pencliff Towers. The unexpected arrival of Poppy St George would make things even more difficult than they already were.

Carlos had come to Pencliff Towers at the invitation of the owners, but he had other reasons for being in Cornwall…not all of them exactly above board.

He often ferried goods across the Atlantic under the auspices of his family's shipping business, and his ship was not far away (under the aegis of his always-dependable first mate Valentin). But his real purpose was more personal—he was looking for a killer.

In early spring, he'd learned his closest childhood friend had died. Mateo Vega was a brilliant man, a skilled fighter, and one of the most passionate revolutionaries he'd ever known. Mateo was the sort of person the phrase "full of life" had been coined to describe. Thus, it seemed impossible that he could ever die. And to be drowned in the ocean, when he'd practically lived in the water, swimming and sailing every day of his life—how could fate be so cruel?

The moment he heard the news, he went to Ximena, Mateo's sister, who still lived on the estate next to Carlos's family home in Santo Domingo. He found a house in mourning.

The housekeeper, wearing a black band on the arm of her usual uniform, informed Carlos that Ximena was hardly eating, and she feared for her life.

"She depended on her brother for everything. There's a cousin who inherits the estate, but he's in America somewhere and who knows when he'll take charge of anything? I fear she'll waste away in her grief."

"I'll talk to her," Carlos had promised.

"Please. If anyone can get through to her, it's you."

He was led to a dark room upstairs, where he found Ximena dressed in black, hiding in the shadows. She looked like death, with dark circles under her eyes and a baleful stare. He spoke her name three times before she blinked and seemed to recognize him.

"Carlos," she sighed. "You've heard?"

"That's why I'm here. How can I help?"

"He's dead. He's beyond all help."

"I meant how can I help *you*," he said gently. This Ximena was terrifying to behold. She'd always been a vivacious, laughing girl. The figure in front him was practically a ghost.

"He was murdered," she whispered, her gaze still unfocused.

"What? I heard he drowned."

"The body was pulled out of the sea, but he didn't die in any accident while sailing. He was killed because he knew something he shouldn't."

He sat across from her and took her hand in his. "Tell me everything."

And she did—slowly—because she broke down in tears every few minutes. Evidently, Mateo met a British man claiming to support the cause for Dominican independence. Mateo knew that the Dominican forces badly needed supplies to fight the various colonial powers contesting the island. So he sailed to Britain, bringing back a shipment of rifles (supposedly purloined from French army units fighting in Portugal and elsewhere). On the next trip, it was saltpeter from North America, a key ingredient in gunpowder. According to Ximena, Mateo was ecstatic, feeling that his work would give the Dominican patriots the edge they needed against better-equipped, trained, professional soldiers.

"But he was nervous," Ximena said. "He knew that any naval vessel that caught him would imprison or execute him and his crew—that's always a risk. And he didn't trust the supplier in Britain. Said the man was dangerous."

"All smugglers are dangerous," Carlos said. "Mateo knew that, so what made this one worse?"

"I'm not sure, but I think he feared this man would double-cross him. He was no patriot of any kind, just a leader of some gang."

"And you think he sold out Mateo?"

She nodded. "I know it. He killed my brother out of greed. And Mateo's death means that our people won't get the supplies they require to fight off the cursed soldiers who think this island is a toy to fight over." Her eyes blazed as she spoke. It was the first sign of her returning spirit.

"Let me see what I can find out," Carlos offered. "It won't bring Mateo back, but it may help his soul rest. And it may help if you know his killer faced justice."

"Would you?" she asked, hope in her red-rimmed eyes. "I can't tell you what it would mean to me. I see Mateo in my dreams every night. He's begging me to do something, but I don't know what I can do!"

"You can stay here, get well, and keep the estate running. Ximena, a lot of people's lives depend on you. Meanwhile, I'll sail to Britain and investigate this. Mateo was a brother to me. If he was betrayed and murdered, I'm not going to let his killer go."

"That's all I need to hear," Ximena breathed. "You can avenge Mateo's death."

"Then I need to know details. Where did Mateo sail to pick up the goods?"

"Cornwall. He mentioned a town...Trever-something. But Mateo said the smugglers used a base well outside the town proper. A network of caves."

From what Carlos knew, the peninsula of Cornwall was practically *all* caves. They could be found at nearly any point along the shore, whether on the channel side or the ocean.

"I don't have many contacts in Cornwall," he said. "I mostly use London as my base when I ship goods, legal or not. But I know some people. And if this man is so dangerous, other people will know about him too. Did Mateo ever name him?"

Ximena shook her head. "The man used a code name: Dragon. But Mateo did describe him in a letter to me. He's a big man, with curly back hair and eyes like a demon. Don't ask me what that means—you know Mateo's way of speaking."

"I do. And the gang? How many of them were there?"

"It must be large. Mateo said it was a very efficient operation—and they practically took over some tavern on the waterfront, use it like a private club. He said they moved smoothly, with lots of help.   A signaler on the shore, men ready to move goods at a moment's notice… and he said that local Customs officials always looked the other way when the dragon flew through the night."

"Paid them off," Carlos said. "I'm due to ship some goods to London in a week. I'll arrange to spend some time in Cornwall after that."

"If that man killed Mateo, he'll kill others as well. Oh, Carlos, God watch over you."

Well, something was watching, he reflected now, but probably not God. Would God arrange for Poppy St George to appear at the very same location where he was hunting down a gang of smugglers? Unlikely. He'd have to be careful to keep her from getting any more involved than she already was.

Chapter 3

ROSE —

He's *here.*

—*Poppy*

The note was short and, to anyone other than the two women, it would be meaningless. But as soon as the words were read to her, Rose would instantly know who Poppy meant. (Not that Poppy had discussed Carlos with her after their initial encounters. Indeed, it was more likely that any mention of his name was met with Poppy's stony silence.) But Rose was her dearest, closest friend, and she had sensed how Poppy felt those first few times she met Carlos and the hope she'd briefly harbored. Was it possible that she'd met a quick-witted, good-hearted person who actually liked her attitude *and* didn't mind that she was merely a daughter of trade-class folks? Carlos seemed to fit that bill, and he very much hinted that he'd call on her, which would be the next step in a more formal courtship.

But apparently, he was more interested in other types of ships, because he sailed away on one and she never heard from him again. Until now.

And all she could do was run away! When Poppy made her escape earlier, she didn't look back to see if Carlos was watching her. Either he was, which would be disconcerting…or he wasn't, which would quite destroy her already fragile ego.

The housekeeper walked Poppy to her room, which was located at the far end of the main wing on the upper floor. A peaceful space, it overlooked the sea through one window, and the road toward St. Mark's Head through another. Poppy began to unpack her belongings, hoping that by establishing herself in this room, she could restore her equilibrium.

The one person she had *never* expected to see here was Carlos de la Guerra…which was particularly infuriating because he was the person who was in some way responsible for her being here at all.

Poppy first met Carlos during the scandalous events that brought Rosalind and Adrian together. Poppy found Carlos vexing at first, then attractive, and then vexing again. She wouldn't have given him another thought except for the fact that he'd seemed so interested, so attentive the few times they'd spoken. She felt like a fool for thinking of him so much, and looking at him now, she felt like even more of a fool for not being able to despise him. It made her rather cross.

Miss Mist had also been exploring her new surroundings, and she leapt to the windowsill to look over her domain (all cats perceive the world around them as their rightful domain). The sight of the cat triggered another memory involving Carlos, because he'd climbed up a tree to retrieve the tiny grey kitten that had managed to get herself stuck up there.

After Adrian proposed to Rose, Carlos came to the house once more. Ostensibly, it was a courtesy call, but it was truly a practical provision to ensure that everyone had the same story about what had occurred so that they could stave off the gossips. Poppy nevertheless sensed an interest on his part. Carlos had been incredibly charming and she liked talking with him. He braved her sharp tongue with grace, and told her he was looking forward to seeing her at Rosalind and Adrian's wedding. Poppy knew he was different. She couldn't wait to see him again.

Again never came. She waited. Weeks became months. At Rosalind's wedding, she heard only that Carlos was traveling, but she didn't want to make a spectacle of herself by asking more pointed questions.

Later on, one of Rosalind's dictated letters said, in passing, "Adrian mentioned that he corresponded with Mr. de la Guerra, whom you may remember. He inquired after you, and hopes that you are well."

Poppy had crumpled the letter up. "If he wants to know if I'm well, he can ask me directly!"

And yet…he *had* mentioned her. After some thought, Poppy had un-crumpled the letter and stored it carefully in her little portable writing desk, which was now placed on a table in the guest room, where she'd scrawled her short note to Rose.

Poppy addressed the note and sealed it, then stared out at the sea. Poppy didn't believe in destiny, but what were the odds of meeting Carlos again here, nearly at the ends of the earth?

She decided that she would give him a chance to explain himself, if he cared to. Perhaps it would be terribly awkward. After all, she had no indication he wanted to see *her* again. But maybe…

"Oh, Lord," Poppy muttered aloud. "All this speculation is maddening. No wonder people hurl themselves into the sea!"

Not wanting to brood about Mr. de la Guerra, she decided to get her bearings. She would explore the house and the land, especially the water's edge. She had little experience of the ocean, and none of a coast so wild.

So she changed into a plain blue wool gown, topped it with a cropped jacket in a deeper blue, and put on sturdy walking shoes. On the main floor of the house, she saw a footman in the foyer.

"Is there a way down to the water from the house?" she asked him.

"Of course, miss, but the steps are rough."

Poppy merely lifted a foot to show her shoes. "I am not faint of heart, and I am prepared," she said.

He nodded in cautious approval. "Very well, miss. I'll show you where the steps begin."

The footman, who told her his name was Daveth, led Poppy out a side door and onto the wide lawn separating the house from the sea. Poppy could see guests still sitting on the terrace, but she would need to shout at them to be heard.

The footman headed to the low stone wall that ran the length of the lawn. "The steps begin here, miss," he said, pointing to where a wide step was cut into the earth—the top of the long stairs to the beach. "Be wary. There are loose rocks all the way down, not to mention the grade."

Poppy looked down at the steep descent. Over a hundred yards below, the breakers crashed onto a sand beach, their crashing much muted at this height.

"Thank you," she said as she walked to the steps. She glanced at the house and saw the figure of Mrs. Towers waving at her. Poppy waved back, not knowing if she responded to a friendly send-off or a warning. But she didn't think it looked so dangerous.

A few moments later, she revised her opinion. The

steps, cut into the rock itself, were generally wide enough, but their height was uneven, and little stones made the way more perilous. The stairs moved down the slope in a zig-zag fashion, forcing her to turn sharply every fifteen steps or so.

When she finally got down to the beach, she breathed a sigh of relief. Poppy walked to the water's edge, keeping back far enough so the waves wouldn't get her shoes wet. Up close, the beach wasn't as pristine as it seemed from the top. Fishbones, rocks, and broken shells gathered along the tide line. The mineral smell of the sea mingled with less pleasant odors, including rotting seaweed and a few dead fish.

Still, Poppy didn't mind. The horizon stretched out in front of her, seemingly endless. The bulk of St. Mark's Head cut off the vista to her right, but there was still plenty of sea and sky, enough to make Poppy forget herself altogether for a few moments.

As she listened to the sound of the waves, she smiled, truly calm for the first time since leaving London. In the distance, a fishing boat sailed by, reminding her she wasn't alone. Of course there were the people in the house —what an assortment of personalities. And there was Carlos de la Guerra in the middle of it all. If only she understood *his* personality.

Poppy refused to dwell on him. She walked from one end of the beach to the other, a journey that would have taken only minutes, except she stopped every few steps to pick up an interesting stone, or a shell, or bit of flotsam. At the far end of the beach, she came upon the cliff again, which turned abruptly to jut out into the sea, cutting the beach short. A dark, jagged hole at the bottom of the cliff seemed to be a grotto or cavern. Part of her wanted to explore it, but she had no idea if it was safe enough to do so. She knelt down and peered inside. All was darkness, but she felt a faint but steady breeze on her face, suggesting that there was considerable space within.

"Too bad I didn't bring a lantern," she muttered.

Poppy turned around and walked back to the stairs. This time, she looked up at the cliff face itself, noticing how steep and forbidding it was. Without the stone-cut stairs, the beach would be totally inaccessible to anyone not in a boat.

She climbed the steps slowly, weighted down by her gathered treasures. At the top, she found herself out of breath.

She also found Carlos de la Guerra.

The previous encounter that day had not deceived her. He was just as good-looking as she remembered. Possibly more so. *Oh, it would be so much better if he were not so handsome*, she thought. His nearly black hair and deep brown eyes had haunted her dreams for months. And his smile made her knees just a little wobbly. (No, surely that was the long hike up the stairs.)

He stood near the head of the steps, as if he'd merely been looking out at the water. But something in his stance was too poised, too expectant. Poppy wondered if he had been waiting for her.

"Hello," he said. "What did you discover down below?"

"Nothing much." To make her point, she held up her hands to show the assorted objects.

"You have your souvenirs already?"

"Well, that way I can leave at any time," she said, a bit tartly. (The long climb didn't help her temper, though she reminded herself that she intended to behave in a more lady-like way.)

Carlos frowned slightly. "Mrs. Towers said you were

to stay through August."

"That was before I knew you were here." Poppy began to walk toward the house.

"Am I so offensive to you?" he asked, keeping pace with her.

"Not at all, Señor de la Guerra. In fact, I have no opinion of you."

He said, "I doubt that. If you have no opinion, why are you hurrying away from me?"

Poppy stopped short. "I am doing no such thing."

"You are. And I wish you'd stop for just a moment. I want to have a word with you," he said.

"Choose it carefully," she warned.

"What?"

"*What?*" she repeated. "You wanted one word with me and that's what you chose? How disappointing."

Carlos took a breath. "You're not making this easy."

"Why should I?"

"Are you angry at me?"

She narrowed her eyes. "Is there any reason for me to be angry, considering that I have not seen or spoken with you for over a year?"

"I've been engaged."

Poppy felt her heart skip. "Congratulations."

"Oh, no. That's not what I meant," he said, rather too quickly. "I've been occupied. With family business."

Poppy was overheated, tired, and her arms were full of beach detritus. She wasn't patient by nature, and she had no reserves left.

"Señor de la Guerra," she said, standing up to her full height, which was still considerably less than his. "Contrary to what you may think, your absence has not altered my daily round, nor has it caused me to weep bitter tears. Since we are both staying at this house, there is no reason to avoid each other. But do not expect me to wait upon your next word…if only because it seems to take months for you to think of your next word. Now please excuse me."

She started walking again, and this time Carlos did not follow her. She should feel triumphant at delivering such a dressing-down. But seeing Carlos silenced brought her little joy, even if she was the victor.

Before Poppy could make it to the safety of her room, she was accosted again, this time by Blanche Ainsworth.

"Miss St George," the lady said. "You are a woman of much vigor! You went all the way down to the beach and back already? And you gathered such treasures," Blanche said, with a glance at the rough shells and stones in Poppy's hands. "How…*rustic*."

"It seemed the thing to do."

"I wanted to better acquaint myself with you," Blanche went on, in a sweet tone. "The Misses Metcalfe and I aren't of a feather, of course. So it's good to have another woman from London around. I can't wait till the next Season starts—that's the most exciting time. You must feel the same."

Poppy raised an eyebrow. Did she look like the sort of girl who dreamed about the parties of the Season? She was in fact the sort of girl who sold gowns to the girls who did. She decided to nip any misconceptions in the bud. "Certainly, my family looks forward to the Season. My stepfather imports fabric, you see, and we sell so much for gowns and things in advance of the Season."

"Trade?" Blanche asked, stepping back as if Poppy announced she had the plague.

"Indeed. I often help out in the warehouse and our shop. It is most gratifying to assist my family in their business."

Blanche now looked both appalled and confused. "If you're...but then how could you know a viscountess?"

What a snob. Poppy's eyes narrowed. "You mean Rosalind? Well, she was my cousin before she was a viscountess. And I was her companion before I was a shopgirl. Life is full of changes, Miss Ainsworth. One never knows what's beyond the horizon."

"I see. I wondered why dear Carlos—I mean Mr. de la Guerra—had not spoken of you."

"He has no reason to, I'm sure," Poppy said. *Dear Carlos?*

"So many women who meet him seem to have designs on him, you know."

"Well, *I* have none," Poppy snapped.

"That is wise of you, Miss St George. I always pity ladies who set their caps at men who clearly have no intention of reciprocating. It's just sad, isn't it?"

"Not as sad as a lady who thinks she's far better than she really is. In fact, Miss Ainsworth," Poppy went on, "I think the saddest thing of all is someone who thinks a battle won, when in fact the armies have yet to take the field."

If Blanche heard the new challenge, she didn't show it. "You are a most curious person, Miss St George."

"Curiosity is the least of my traits, Miss Ainsworth." With those words, Poppy retreated to her room. Of course she had no designs on Carlos. She didn't even like him. But she was piqued by the other girl's suggestion that Poppy wasn't *good enough* for Carlos. Perhaps that was true, but Miss Ainsworth was not the arbiter of such things.

And Poppy was not the kind of girl who backed down from a fight.

Chapter 4

Dearest Carlos,

By now you must have been in Cornwall for some weeks, and I hope that you have made some progress in your search. Your visit was a great help to me, and think I may have passed through the worst of the shock, though not the sorrow. Every day, I see objects around the house that remind me of Mateo, and I am so certain that he'll enter a room at any moment, calling my name and ready to tell some exaggerated story from his most recent voyage. Those moments hurt, and yet I do not wish to forget them, because that would mean forgetting my brother.

And that is why I write now. After you left, I recalled a conversation with Mateo, where he mentioned that the leader of that gang had a ship of his own. Apparently, that is not usual. Most smugglers are landsmen who simply work with captains or sailors—you would know better if this is true, of course. But I thought it might help you to identify the gang, and ultimately Mateo's killer.

I pray for your success in this matter, and I pray for you (I know these things are separate, and that the latter is more important than the former).

Fondly,

Ximena

After reading Ximena's letter, Carlos stared out the window for a long moment. Her memory was a significant one. He'd heard mentions of numerous smuggling operations in the area, but he'd had little luck identifying which might be the group working with Mateo. But if he was looking for a gang that actually owned a ship, that would narrow it down to just a few at most. It would be a huge stride forward.

These early summer days were long, but at last evening descended, and that meant the inevitable dinner and endless chit-chat with other guests. Carlos dressed with slightly more care than usual (he remembered that Poppy had strong opinions on fabric and clothing, for obvious reasons). When he was finished, he put on a cross hanging from a gold chain, tucking it under his shirt. This wasn't a matter of style—it was a reminder of his purpose. The cross was Mateo's. Ximena gave it to Carlos when he left, as a token. He touched it through the fabric, feeling the outline of the metal.

"Hermano, los voy a encontrar," he said softly. He glanced in the mirror and decided that he looked about as well as he ever would. Carlos could just barely pass as a gentleman in Britain. He knew how to dress and what to say. But he spent half his life very far from the drawing rooms and upper-crust clubs of this world; placing himself in the role of "unassuming, polite gentleman" was a strain whenever he remembered the freedom of a life at sea, or the more familiar setting of Santo Domingo. Things could be *very* formal there as well...but not always, particularly when he was out among the people.

However, he was here now, and his mission depended on circulating among the upper-class guests at the house, and the locals in Treversey. Carlos had wrangled an invitation to Pencliff Towers from a friend of a friend in London. The ostensible reason was to strike up an acquaintance with another guest at the house. Mr. Ainsworth was up to his neck in the smuggling of French imports. The current war hampered all legitimate trade, with British navy blockading French ports, and privateers taking any opportunity to run down French ships.

Carlos learned that Ainsworth was one of the primary contacts for smugglers looking to get goods through Cornwall and onward into England, including London. Carlos made it known that he was ready and willing to sign on as an occasional partner. After all, Santo Domingo was a thriving port itself, and there was always interest in getting goods from the old world into the new.

Luckily, Ainsworth accepted Carlos's story and he seemed open to the idea of an alliance. But he was still very cagey about the exact operations in Cornwall, which was all Carlos really cared about. It would be suspicious to pry too much. He had to bide his time.

However, no one had told Carlos that Ainsworth's daughter would also be at Pencliff Towers, or that she was marriage-minded. Blanche Ainsworth had apparently decided that Carlos would make a perfect match for her. Why, he didn't know, other than that he'd inflated his supposed wealth and influence as part of his story, and now the Ainsworths thought his family practically owned half of Hispaniola.

It was easy to play along with Blanche at first. She was beautiful and witty (if a little too impressed with her own cleverness), and the flirtation seemed harmless. Carlos was smart enough to avoid any traps she might set. He had no intention of getting ensnared by any woman. Then Poppy's face flashed briefly in his mind, and he shook his head to get her out of there.

He'd hoped that a place called Pencliff Towers would possess multiple towers (it would make watching for smugglers' ships much easier). But he soon learned that the name was merely a whimsy of the current owners, who had changed it from the simpler Pencliff House when they purchased it.

"Took the locals about five years to come round," Mr. Towers said the day Carlos arrived and asked about it. "But they finally call the place by the name we like. Probably helps that I've employed half the town for work or repairs at some point!"

He left his room on the upper floor and walked down the wide staircase to the main level. Downstairs, he saw Mr. Towers holding court in the parlor, where people were gathering before the dinner chime rang.

"Ah, there's the man we were just speaking of!" Mr. Towers said, gesturing in welcome.

"I hope the words were kind," Carlos responded easily.

"But of course, Mr. de la Guerra," Blanche said, with a smile. "We were saying that it's remarkable how well you speak English, despite having grown up in the Caribbean."

"My grandmother is English," he noted, privately thinking that these people were easily impressed. The typical Brit (after admitting that other countries existed) was always astonished to realize that it was possible to speak not only one language, but several. "And she's a very talkative lady."

"Oh, I should just love to meet her someday!" Blanche cooed. It was the most blatant hint she'd offered so far—it was unlikely she'd ever meet Carlos's grandmother unless they got married.

And to be sure, Blanche seemed perfectly content with

the notion. She was beautiful, accomplished, and possessed nearly every quality one could ask for in a proper lady (especially if one overlooked the fact that her family wasn't *quite* as blue-blooded as they seemed). She had the sort of soft beauty that had probably already inspired a few amateur poets to praise her in verse. Carlos could do far worse. One thing he did not like, however, was the concept of being *presented* with a bride.

"What a sweet thought, Blanche." Mr. Ainsworth said.

"Someday," Carlos echoed, again refusing to commit to anything. "Perhaps after I have taken care of some matters this summer."

"Whatever you hope to accomplish, sir, you must call upon me as a friend. The Ainsworth name opens many doors in this part of the country." The implication was clear. What better business alliance than marriage?

Carlos offered some platitudes and accepted the seat next to Blanche after Mrs. Ainsworth patted the couch meaningfully. Blanche leaned forward and began to talk, and he nodded at all the right points, even as he kept watch on the doorway from the corner of his eye.

When would Poppy appear?

* * * *

Poppy spent longer than usual preparing for that evening.

"I'll be proper. I'll be sweet." Poppy repeated these words as she dressed for dinner. Her gown wasn't new, but it was one of her favorites: a soft cotton lawn in a lovely blue, the same shade as a cloudless summer sky. The gown was edged in white lace, and her lace wrap completed the outfit. She bound her hair up carefully and even curled a few locks around her face so that she might look as delicate as possible. Her headdress was a simple band of blue ribbon, looped several times around the blonde strands to affect a careless type of grace.

She put on her gloves and slid her feet into the soft leather slippers she favored. The result was a simple, but she hoped alluring, picture. For some reason, the knowledge that Blanche considered Poppy a sort of threat made Poppy quite keen to *become* a threat. Surely Carlos would at least glance at her!

She didn't take more than five steps into the main room before she saw Carlos. He looked incredibly dashing in evening clothes. His face was animated and earnest...because he was completely focused on whatever Blanche Ainsworth was saying.

And why not? Blanche was a vision. She looked radiant in her gown, which probably cost five times more than Poppy's ensemble. The delicate cloth was stitched all over with embroidery, and beading at the hem and the neckline glittered softly in the light. Her hair was caught up in a pile on her head, save for a few locks that lay loose around her neck. Her eyes sparkled as she spoke, and she smiled at Carlos as if he were the only man in the room.

In turn, Carlos looked enchanted by Blanche, who was the epitome of a proper young lady. *She* probably never collected beach rubble and climbed stairs until she was sweaty. *She* never worked in a shop or counted bolts of cloth in a warehouse.

He leaned in close to her, as if he hung on her every word. Poppy's eyes prickled, the way they did when she wanted to cry. Oh, why couldn't she keep her smart comments to herself, even for a moment? Naturally he would think twice about renewing any acquaintance with her after she'd been so rude to him earlier.

In the room where the guests gathered before dinner,

Poppy saw that her options for conversation partners were the elder Ainsworths, who smiled at her the way tigers must smile at a piglet, the Hobbsons, and the Metcalfe sisters. The decision was an easy one to make.

Poppy strolled directly to the sisters. "May I join you?"

"Oh!" said Elowen. "Please, if you like."

"Well, if I didn't like, I should not have come over."

Elowen smiled at that, then said. "Please meet my younger sister, Elisa."

"Hello, Miss Elisa. I'm Poppy St George." Poppy saw with a slight surprise that Elisa was actually much older than she had first assumed. Mrs. Towers called her a "sweet child" (which Poppy took to mean an actual child of twelve or younger). But Elisa must have been eighteen or so. It appeared she suffered from some defect of birth. Her head seemed a bit small for her stature, and lids of her blue eyes were slightly slanted. But she smiled at Poppy, in no way discomfited by the inspection.

"Your dress is pretty," said Elisa warmly.

"Why, thank you," Poppy said, sitting down near them. "So is yours. Those little rosebuds embroidered onto the fabric are darling. Did you choose the pattern?"

Elowen began to speak, but then halted so Elisa could answer in her own time. Poppy waited as well, pleased she wouldn't have to come up with snappy repartee just to impress her companions.

"My sister makes my clothes," Elisa finally said.

Elowen explained further, "I sew a good part of our dresses, as the sizing is particular for Elisa. I do get pieces ready made for the bodices." She dropped her eyes, suddenly embarrassed. "I apologize. What a quotidian subject."

"Not at all," Poppy said briskly. As before, she wanted

to get the matter of her class out in the open as soon as possible. "As it happens, my stepfather is an importer of fabric, and I've been learning a lot about the seamstress trade as well. I love to hear what other women are doing to make their wardrobes."

"My goodness, how lucky you are to be able to see all those fabrics and notions!" Elowen said, looking intrigued. "I rarely get the chance to look at anything beyond the most common items. Our budget is quite modest," she added, looking down at her hands.

"You do splendidly with what you have," Poppy told her. "I've seen women decked out in silk and lace who don't appear half so well-turned out. But tell me, what brings you both here to Cornwall? Your accent is much more northern."

"Indeed, we hail from York. The Towers were friends of our family from years ago, and were generous enough to let us stay here for a while."

"That is almost exactly my situation," Poppy said with a laugh. "Mrs. Towers does collect friends."

"She does indeed. Actually, my sister is seeing a doctor in the area. We hope he may help her condition."

"Forgive my surprise, but the doctor practices all the way out here? Not in London?"

"In London," Elowen said with a bit of heat, "we are told over and over that there are places where I can send Elisa to live, where she won't be a bother to her family." She reached out and took her sister's hand. "I have no intention of doing that. She is *not* a bother."

Elisa nodded. "Family ought to remain together."

"I've always thought so," Poppy agreed, thinking of how she'd been Rose's companion for so many years. The fact that the girls were cousins was a further bond in their friendship.

"Elisa has a few physical complaints," Elowen noted. "Dr. Drake is eager to test a new treatment to help Elisa strengthen her muscles."

"It hurts me to stand too long," Elisa added.

"Can you not sit, or try one of those wheeled chairs?" Poppy asked.

"I *want* to be stronger," Elisa said. "Elowen takes walks at home, but I can't keep up for long."

"Oh, I am sorry to hear that. It's terrible to be left behind. I was my cousin's companion for years—she was blind from a young age, and she feared the same sort of thing."

Elowen smiled at Poppy. "But you did not let her remain behind, did you?"

"I tried not to. In fact, she is now married, so you could say she left me behind, although of course I want her to be happy."

Mrs. Towers appeared beside them. "I am sorry to interrupt you ladies when you are all getting along so swimmingly, but Mr. Ainsworth would like a word with you, Poppy," she said.

"Me?" Earlier, she'd gotten the distinct impression that the Ainsworths hadn't liked her much.

Poppy allowed Mrs. Towers to lead her over to Mr. Ainsworth, who was standing by the fireplace. As they reached him, Mrs. Towers was approached by a servant, who whispered something earnestly.

"Oh, please excuse me," she said. "A little matter with the supper preparations."

So Poppy was left alone with the man. She said, "Good evening, sir. Mrs. Towers tells me you had a question for me."

He offered her a cool smile that faded instantly. "Not in specific. I thought you might appreciate an escape."

"I don't understand," Poppy admitted, confused.

"From the conversation you were trapped in," Mr. Ainsworth explained. "It was gracious, I suppose, for you to speak to that odd, deformed girl. But really, she should not be here at all. I don't know why someone would bring such an uncivilized creature out among us."

"Her conversation was perfectly civilized," Poppy said tightly, feeling that Elisa's manners far exceeded Ainsworth's.

"She can barely put two words together."

"Why put forth an effort to do so if they will fall upon deaf ears, sir? One might as well read poetry to a stone wall," she snapped, entirely forgetting her earlier vow to act sweet and meek. Thankfully, the chime for dinner sounded just then. "Ah," she said, relieved. "If you'll excuse me, it seems supper will be served after all."

Poppy's arrival that day meant she had the status of honored guest for this evening, so she was escorted into the dining room by Mr. Towers, and seated to the right of him, and to the left of Mr. Hobbson. The following night, she would likely be seated much further down the table. (She resolutely ignored the fact that Carlos escorted Blanche into the room, *and* sat beside her.)

Both of the older gentlemen were delightful dinner partners, and happy to have a young lady to jokingly pay court to. In fact, thanks to them Poppy nearly forgot the unpleasant conversation of Mr. Ainsworth earlier.

After the meal, the gentlemen remained in the dining room to enjoy the customary brandy and cigars, while the ladies withdrew to sip sherry and gossip until the men rejoined them.

In the drawing room, Poppy was soon accosted by Mrs. Ainsworth. "What a fine color that dress is, Miss St George. So charming for your fair coloring."

"It is kind of you to say," Poppy replied. Perhaps Mrs. Ainsworth was not like her husband.

"You'd catch a gentleman's eye in that," the older lady went on. "*If* there were any gentlemen unspoken for in this house, that is."

The implication was clear. Carlos and Blanche were an item. Irritation stirred inside her, but she said, "Oh, I'm not here to catch anyone's eye. I wanted a break from the heat of the city. That is all."

"Well, you look revived already, dear. Not so pinched as Miss Metcalfe. No wonder she cannot even garner a glance from any man."

"I thought Miss Metcalfe looked quite lovely," Poppy told Mrs Ainsworth. "I expect she has more suitors than she claims."

"She has no suitors," Mrs. Ainsworth said, in a conspiratorial tone. "And the reason should be obvious."

"It is not obvious to me." Elowen was darling, and as sweet as Poppy was tart. She knew that most men would leap at the chance to gain a wife of such a gentle disposition.

"The reason is her sister, of course."

"Because she is the guardian of Miss Elisa? It's not unusual to have a ward. As long as her suitor has a modest income, the support of one more family member…"

"Oh, don't be naive," Mrs. Ainsworth said impatiently. "She has no suitors because she comes from quite poor stock. And no intelligent gentleman would risk passing such an affliction on to his heirs."

Poppy's mouth dropped open. Before she could answer, she heard a stifled sound. Turning, she just noticed the hem of a pink skirt around the corner of the doorway. It was Elowen's, proving she had most certainly overheard the remark.

Poppy glared at Mrs. Ainsworth. She'd have gone after Elowen, but she feared she would be intruding. Yet she could not stand there, not with such vile people. Then the gentlemen filed into the room, and she caught sight of Carlos...just as Blanche rose to her feet and went to him.

"Well, I think I need a breath of air," said Poppy, rather more acidly than she meant to. "If you'll excuse me?"

"Oh, but..." Carlos began to say, looking at Poppy as if he didn't have a lady hanging on his arm.

Blanche broke in, "Certainly, Miss St George. You can go outside and pout as long as you like." She said the words in such a gentle tone it took Poppy a moment to register the words.

"Pout?" she said. "*Pout?*" Incensed, Poppy strode to the French doors opening to the terrace, and moved through them before anyone could flag her down.

Outside, the sea breeze made the air much cooler than in the house. Clouds obscured the stars, and far over the water rain threatened. She pulled her wrap tight around her shoulders. "Ugh, such people," she muttered to herself. How was it possible that the Towers could even be friends with the Ainsworths? And why did Carlos have to be here, with Blanche practically glued to his side? (He didn't look at all upset to have the gorgeous woman fawning all over him, either.)

Poppy stormed across the lawn at a most unladylike pace, directly toward the stairway down to the shore. How frustrating! To have spent months...pining, actually *pining*, for a gentleman, only to find that he'd been romancing another woman. And despite her hideous parents, Blanche was far more of a lady than Poppy ever could be.

"I hope they have long, polite conversations forever!" she grumbled into the wind. "I hope she bores him to death."

With no further thought to the wisdom of it, Poppy stormed toward the steps to the beach below, which lay in total darkness.

* * * *

Carlos stared after the figure in blue. He needed to speak to Poppy properly. He'd hoped to do so during dinner, but he'd got stuck escorting Blanche into the dining room and then had to sit by her while Poppy got to enjoy the banter of Towers and Hobbson. The trio seemed to be having the time of their lives, to judge by all the laughter. He reasoned he could talk to Poppy in the drawing room afterwards, since guests were expected to mingle. But the second she saw him enter, she decided to vanish again.

He had to find her. But first he had to extract himself from the silken snares of Blanche Ainsworth. She always spoke so quietly that he had to stand a lot closer to her than he preferred...close enough to smell the cloying rose scent she wore, and to see the stitching on her finely made gown. But if he was to get information from her father about the local smuggling operations, he'd have to play nice for a while longer.

She also had an alarming habit of nearly touching him while she made delicate gestures to accompany speech. "...and they say that this new rage is all over London," she was saying. "With such a to-do over it, I can only imagine what the coming Season will bring. What are your thoughts, Mr. de la Guerra?"

He had no thoughts on whatever she was talking about, because he hadn't been paying attention since Poppy left. "I'm sorry, I got distracted...What was that?"

"I was remarking that the coming Season will surely

be a veritable cascade of wedding announcements. You'd best make your own proposal early, sir, if you wish to be assured of a *yes*." Her tone was coy, and her smile slightly naughty.

"I don't think I'd make any woman a good husband," he said, more bluntly than he meant to. "I'm at sea more than half the year."

"Absence makes the heart grow fonder," she countered, placing her hand on his arm.

"Or it allows a wife to spend her husband's money in peace, or find other companionship while he's away."

Blanche's jaw tightened for just a moment. But then she sniffed, saying, "My goodness, Mr. de la Guerra. What sort of woman would ever dream of such behavior? Only a *shopgirl* would be so gauche."

A clear shot at Poppy, whose stepfather employed her to work in the shop and warehouse.

"You know," he said, struck with an idea for escape. "Miss St George just dashed out in the dark. Someone should tell her to stay near the house. I'd best do that before she tumbles off a cliff or something like that."

Leaving a startled Blanche behind, Carlos strode through the French doors to the terrace, unlit except by the light thrown out from the interior candles and lamps. He looked around, expecting to see Poppy glaring back at him for daring to intrude. Instead, he saw no one at all.

"Miss St George?" he called.

She didn't answer, but Carlos saw a flicker of movement at the end of the lawn. A woman in a blue dress was walking toward the stairs to the cliffs and the shoreline. "Oh, hell," he muttered. What else could he do but follow her?

Chapter 5

❧ ⁊⁊⁊ ❧

THE BEACH WAS A DIFFERENT world at nighttime. Poppy
regretted her decision to come down—especially as the
moon was hidden behind clouds, making everything dan-
gerously dim—but it was too late now. She had just
scrambled onto the top of a large boulder when she heard
footsteps descending the lowest stairs.

"Miss St George?" Carlos called, stopping in front of
her rock. "Is that you?"

"Who were you expecting?" she retorted. "A mer-
maid?"

"You could have been hurt, walking down here in the
dark."

"Well, I wasn't. Proof that women are perfectly capable of doing things by themselves. *Some* women,
anyway."

"May I join you?" Without waiting for her reply, he
vaulted himself easily to the top of the rock and settled
near her.

Poppy was quite conscious of him so close, of his
steady, quiet breathing. She chose to be annoyed by it.
"Oh, please go away," she said finally. "I am not done
pouting."

"You were not pouting, and Miss Ainsworth should

not have said that."

"All the same, I'd rather be alone."

"No," he said simply.

Poppy looked over, curiosity cutting through her frustration. "You realize staying with me is hardly an improvement in terms of my reputation." Indeed, the idea of him alone in such a place with an unmarried woman was borderline scandalous.

He shrugged. "I disagree. A lady's physical safety is always paramount. So you're stuck with me until you're back at the house."

"What do you think could happen? I'll be swept away by the sea? Or kidnapped by a selkie?"

"I doubt you'd let yourself be kidnapped by any mythological creature. You're much too practical for that. Owls, however, are a possibility."

"Owls?" Poppy echoed, confused.

"That's what they sometimes call smugglers around here," he explained.

She frowned. "I know that smuggling exists, but I thought it only occurred in large cities. What's to smuggle out here?"

"It's a link in a chain, and thanks to these lonely shores, Cornwall has more than its share of smugglers. I've heard about a few already. And they're dangerous men." As he spoke, he kept his gaze on the water, and he seemed upset.

"Truly?" she asked, interested in spite of herself.

"It's common knowledge around here. People talk. I listen."

"You didn't listen when I told you to go away."

"I did listen. I simply chose to disregard your request."

"I suppose I should have expected that," she retorted,

suddenly remembering the last time she'd seen him in London. She requested—rather boldly—for him to partner her in one dance at Rosalind's wedding, which he never actually attended.

His eyes narrowed, apparently remembering the same thing. "I'm sorry I couldn't see you at the wedding. In fact, I had to make a voyage back to Santo Domingo. A family matter I couldn't ignore. And then there was more business to deal with. It feels like I've been sailing non-stop for the past year."

"What made you wash up in Cornwall?"

"More business. Mostly. I hope to get some important information from Ainsworth."

"Is he holding out until his daughter has a proposal in hand?" Poppy asked tartly.

He looked over at her, startled. "You think he's that cold-blooded?"

"Based on what I've seen today, absolutely," she affirmed. "Trust me when I say that one thing that makes a father sleep poorly is an unmarried daughter. I've seen it with my own friends." Poppy's own birth father had passed before that was a factor in her life, and her stepfather kept a firm distance from such matters, saying that Poppy's mother knew best. (Poppy cared for her stepfather very much, and this was one of the reasons why.)

"Ainsworth definitely has been encouraging the match, but I wasn't expecting it to be a quid pro quo."

"You may need to reconsider," Poppy said, even though she was absurdly happy to learn that there wasn't any understanding yet. After a moment, she realized that if Carlos had actually offered for Blanche already, the woman no doubt would have said so.

"I like to make my own choices, especially for something so important." He looked at her then. "I'm glad you're here for the summer."

Poppy hoped her emotions weren't evident on her face. What did that mean? It would be easy to be angry at Carlos, to think he'd only been passingly interested in her. But now he was glad? Any rational observer would tell Carlos that Blanche was the better choice for a bride.

"You know," she said suddenly. "You could have simply written to me, if you had wanted to."

"The one time I did send you a letter, you nearly took my head off for the impropriety I took."

"It *was* improper!" she said, recalling the incident. "You invited Rose and me to an illegal duel!"

"Technically, it wasn't an invitation, just an informative note."

"You knew what would happen. Of course I had to tell Rose, and of course she insisted on attending."

"I suppose that's true," said Carlos. "I was very happy to see you, however."

"You didn't even know me."

"I knew you immediately," he argued. "Your spirit was instantly recognizable—provoking, in the best sense."

"You are making things up," she said, but without rancor. In fact, it would be lovely to believe the nonsense he was spouting. Especially as he was so close to her. He could have kissed her, if he tried. Poppy's head tilted in an unconscious invitation.

Carlos leaned even closer. "Poppy…"

A wave suddenly splashed against the boulder, spraying fine droplets over them.

"Oh, bother," she said, startled out of the mood. "Does this mean the tide's coming in?"

"Yes, but we've got another two hours before this beach will be inaccessible."

Poppy blinked at his knowledge. "Why do you know that? Wait, is your ship nearby? The *Agustina*?"

He looked delighted. "You remembered her name!"

There was literally nothing about Carlos that she'd forgotten, no matter how hard she tried. "Well, you remembered the name of my cat, didn't you? So, is your ship here in Cornwall?"

"Yes, as a matter of fact."

"I'd like to see it. Her. Someday."

"She's sometimes in the harbor of Treversey," Carlos said. "When you go into town, I could point her out."

"I suppose," Poppy said, feeling sad all at once, "that I should go back up to the house. Avoid scandal and all that."

"Why would you want to avoid it?" he returned.

"Oh, stop teasing me and help me down, if you want to be useful."

He slid off the rock, then turned. That was when Poppy realized there really was no ladylike way to leap off a four foot tall boulder in a gown.

"What's the matter?" he asked, lifting one arm above his head, just at the height for her to grab for stability. "Just take my hand and jump down. I'll make sure you don't stumble."

"The angle is…rather awkward. You must not look," she warned.

"Take my hand, and then I'll close my eyes," he said.

Poppy did, and then jumped, finding it less demeaning than she feared. But then she was standing toe to toe with Carlos, her hands in his.

He was smiling at her in the way that made her stomach flip-flop. He said, "There. Back on the ground, and your dignity intact. Oh, wait." He reached around her and adjusted the bow on the wide ribbon just below the waist of her gown. "There. You're once again high-tied."

She groaned, mostly to cover her reaction to their near embrace. "If this devolves into puns, I'll have to leap into the ocean to escape."

"Then I'll not dampen the mood further."

"Mr. de la Guerra!"

"Sí?" he asked, too innocently.

"*Stop* it."

"I like you better when you're berating me, rather than when you're silent."

"Don't tease me. I'm all too aware I can't keep my mouth shut."

"You're so diverting it's never occurred to me to wish otherwise."

"Speaking of diverting," she said, pointing to a light on the water she just noticed, "What is that?"

Carlos followed her finger. The odd light bobbed and shook on the water, as waves partially obscured it for a second, then revealed it again as it crested.

"A boat, I expect." His voice became much lower. "A small one."

He was right. The light belonged to a dinghy making its way toward the shore. Their shore. Poppy watched as the boat came closer and closer.

"They're smugglers," Carlos muttered. "And they're going to beach here. We have to get out of sight."

"What?" Poppy shivered. Real smugglers would never appear at the beach directly below Pencliff Towers, would they? And yet, the house suddenly felt as remote as the moon. "Maybe they're just local fishermen, out for a pleasure cruise at night, through eel-infested waters."

"I doubt it," Carlos said.

"Then we should leave."

"It's too late for that. They'll see us." He shrugged out

of his coat and wrapped it around her. "Here. I'm sure you didn't expect to be outside so long."

Poppy pulled the coat around her shoulders. He was correct—her flimsy wrap wasn't enough, and she was grateful for the protection of the coat. "Are you sure we have to remain?"

"I'm sure that we're within pistol range." He glanced around. "But we can edge behind this rock and be much less conspicuous. Slowly, now."

With his hands on her shoulders, he guided Poppy's steps backwards a few feet until they were both in the lee of the large stone. The concealment was partial at best, but better than nothing at all.

The boat continued to edge closer to the shore as Poppy watched in growing concern. It appeared the boat was heading for the part of the beach further from them, yet it would only take one pair of eyes to see them and give the alarm.

She shifted, and felt Carlos's hand on her shoulders.

"Poppy," he said, his voice low and close to her ear. "You must stay perfectly still."

She almost nodded, but stopped herself. "I understand."

And so she found herself peering around the rock, watching a gang of smugglers as they beached a longboat and began to unload their cargo—stacks of identical crates. They carried them into the cave she'd noticed earlier.

The smugglers worked swiftly, but Poppy felt the growing bite of the cold sea air. Even in high summer, cool, damp breezes blew off the water. Despite Carlos's coat, she began to shiver due to her forced stillness. Then Carlos's arms circled her. Poppy dared to lean back into him, craving the warmth but rather terrified of her boldness.

"There's twelve of them," he said deliberately, as if committing facts to memory. "Four to row, and more to unload. They're confident—no lookout at all."

"Lucky for us," she breathed. Squinting, she now saw a larger ship in the distance. The constant sound of the waves on the shore hid their voices, but Poppy dared not speak above a whisper. "How many trips will they take?" she asked. The smugglers might well be here all night. A full night in a man's company would be extremely awkward to explain.

"Not many, I hope," Carlos whispered back. "Though if all the men on the beach return to the ship, we can chance moving back to the stairs."

As it happened, after only two trips, all the men reboarded the longboat and rowed swiftly back to the ship at anchor. "Can you see the name on the ship?" Carlos asked her.

She squinted into the darkness. There was a name painted on the bow, but it was indistinct. "No, it's too far away. I think those little flags below the highest mast are red and white. Does that mean anything?"

"Not to me, but perhaps they can identify the ship again, should it come into harbor nearby." He gave her shoulders a squeeze. "Well spotted, Poppy."

She smiled at his praise, despite the situation. They watched as the smaller boat rejoined its ship, and the figures scrambled up ropes to the deck. "I think they're leaving."

Carlos heaved a sigh of relief, his body relaxing. "Good. Let's wait just a few moments longer. I'd rather the ship be well away before we move."

The ship turned about and tacked away from the shoreline at last.

Poppy let out a long breath. She hadn't quite appreciated how tense she'd grown over the course of the last
hour, but she now felt the strain in her shoulders and,
worse, the way the cold, damp air had stiffened up her
muscles.

"I don't know if I can make it up the stairs right now,"
she confessed. "My legs feel like they've been replaced
with driftwood. And is it possible for knees to rust?"

He laughed low in his throat. "I'm sure you don't have
a spot of rust on you. But this is not the best weather for
your outfit. The sooner you get back to the house, the
better."

Poppy nodded, and took a step. Unfortunately, her
cramped legs and the soft sand made her stumble almost
immediately.

Carlos circled an arm around her and held her steady.
She looked up and realized her face was inches from his
own, and he was watching her with an inscrutable expression.

"Bella, tienes suerte que no te rapto y te llevo conmi-
go."

"Excuse me?" Poppy squeaked.

"Nothing," he murmured, leaning down.

The outline of his mouth was entrancing, and she
wondered what it would be like to be kissed by such a
mouth, to feel the heat of him when the rest of the world
was so cold.

"Dime que te haga mío y lo haré. Una noche o todas
las noches. He estado soñando contigo."

Poppy's eyes slid closed as she listened to the sound
of his voice rolling over her. As for the words...*well.*
She'd have to come back to that when she had sunlight
and time to think. Truly, the beach was a different world
in the nighttime. A much more dangerous one.

"Um, you mentioned earlier that the tide is coming in," she said, her breath coming quickly.

Carlos gave a little laugh, and released her from his embrace. "We have a while, but yes. You're right as usual, Miss St George."

Poppy began to shrug out of his jacket. "Thank you…" she started to say.

"Keep it for now. The wind is getting colder." He looked up and down the beach, scanning for the return of any smugglers. But it was now silent except for the waves, lapping ever closer to the cliff. "All right, let's go."

"Indeed." Poppy began to move toward the far end of the beach…toward the smugglers' cave.

Chapter 6

CARLOS STARED AFTER HER FOR a moment, too surprised to stop her. "Wait! The stairs are the other way," he said, making a grab for her arm and missing.

"I know that," Poppy replied, casting a disdainful glance over her shoulder. "I want to see what they took into that cave. Aren't you curious?"

"I'm curious, not suicidal." He caught up and matched her pace. "What if someone is guarding it?"

"You counted twelve men on the way in and the way out. So who would be guarding it?"

"We'll see," he said, inwardly admitting that he did want to know what the men had been up to, and if they were connected to the gang that killed Mateo.

At the cave entrance, Carlos took her hand and held it firmly until he was sure there was no one inside. Surprisingly, Poppy didn't object.

He let out a soft breath, not even aware till then that he'd been holding it in. "I think we're the only ones here. I'm going to have a look inside."

"*You* are?" Poppy said, exhaling in a whoosh, revealing that she'd also been worried. "I'm the one who said we should look!"

"You ought to stay out here."

"When a smuggler could come back at any moment?" She arched her eyebrow. "I'm safer with you."

Carlos shook his head. "Fine. We go in. We take one look and we leave. It's probably just liquor."

"One way to find out." Poppy squeezed his hand, and offered him a smile he assumed was meant to be encouraging. (She could have no idea how much he needed encouragement just then. He *hated* caves.)

The narrow passage led into the cliff at an angle, so the darkness quickly became thick. He halted after a few steps. "This is a bad idea. We can't even see anything in the dark." His breath came a little faster just thinking about the close quarters and the weight of rock above them. He turned around to lead them both out.

Poppy evidently didn't want to give up, because she blocked his way. "There must be something they used for light along the way," she insisted, looking beyond him. "There, on the ground. A lantern."

The lantern soon illuminated a dark, damp passage. It was wide enough for four men to walk abreast, but the ceiling was low, and the sand floor might well be covered at high tide.

"Charming," Carlos muttered. He looked around in disgust. "Like a grave."

"Oh, come on. Aren't you excited?"

He shook his head, amazed that she could be happy in such a place. "That is not how I'd describe my state at the moment."

Nevertheless, he kept near her, knowing it would be dangerous if they were separated. Poppy walked onward, and gasped when the passage suddenly opened up into a larger space, albeit one with low headroom and many dark corners. But the purpose of the cavern was obvious.

Stacks of wooden crates occupied the middle of the space. They both hurried forward, peering at the nearest one.

"The crates are marked," Poppy said, lifting the lantern to see better. "They shipped from India. This crate originated in Bengal," she said, tapping on a word printed on the side. "That's quite a distance."

"You read Hindi? Or Bengalese?" he asked skeptically.

"Oh don't be silly. I just learned to recognize the shapes of some words so that I could verify shipments at my stepfather's warehouse. Lots of fabrics are woven or printed in India."

"That makes sense, though I doubt these men were smuggling fabric," he said. Then he noticed an iron bar leaning against one of the crates and seized it.

He pried up the lid of a crate. Inside, under the packing straw, they found smaller mango wood cases. Carlos opened one of these inner boxes and exposed stacks of cake-shaped objects wrapped in dried poppy petals. "I've seen this before," he said. "It's partially processed opium."

Poppy looked around at all the crates, blinking. "But wouldn't that be quite a *lot* of opium?"

He put the cake back and snapped the lid of the mango wood box shut. "You're not wrong."

"So they're smuggling opium into Britain? Is it in such demand here?"

"I have no idea. I can tell you that it's often used by armies." He knew all too well what happened to soldiers who couldn't dull the pain of their wounds during or after surgery. It was excruciating.

Poppy was frowning as she continued to look around. "These crates all look identical. Shouldn't there be a whole range of items? Fabric? Fruit? Liquors? Lace?"

"As you say, it's odd all the crates look the same. This isn't an ordinary smuggling run at all." And Carlos would know.

"We have to get back to the house," she said. "And then we have to tell…well, somebody! A magistrate has to see this."

"I agree." He carefully replaced the lid of the opened crate, hammering the nails back in place to hide the fact that they'd examined it. "Let's go. And I'll go outside first."

"Why?"

"Because if anyone is out there, I'll say I'm alone. That will give you time to hide in the caves."

Poppy's eyes widened, and she suddenly shivered. "Oh. This was a really risky thing to do, wasn't it?"

"Yes, it was," he said, not mincing words. "Now let's go, before the tide traps us in here and drowns us."

"Oh, my God." Poppy practically pushed him along through the passageway. At the entrance, where the cave dark gave way to the vaguely more luminous dark of the night air, he told her to douse the lantern. Then they waited, barely breathing.

He edged closed and looked outside, but saw nothing. "All right, the coast is clear."

"This is not the time for levity."

"But the coast *is* clear," Carlos said. He couldn't keep a laugh out of his voice though, happy that Poppy actually thought he was back to making bad puns, instead of barely containing his panic.

Carlos's mood improved even more as soon as they stepped on the beach, and he took a huge breath of salty sea air. The pair walked quickly to the stone stairs and made their way back up the cliff face. He had never found the lights of a house more comforting than at that moment.

Just then, he saw an odd flashing at the top of the house. He looked up, but it wasn't repeated. Perhaps one of the rooms had been lit—or darkened—abruptly. Or a curtain had been pulled back. But he didn't have leisure to consider that now. He had to help Poppy get back into the house. He didn't want her to get in trouble, no matter how airily she spoke about her reputation.

"I suppose I can't just stroll back into the drawing room," she said, watching the windows along the ground floor.

"Not with the way your outfit looks now," he warned. "Your slippers sound like they're made of mud."

"You're not far off," she admitted. Poppy looked down, then realized she was still wearing his coat. She shrugged out of it and handed it back to him. "My thanks, Señor de la Guerra."

"Carlos," he insisted. "After traversing a smugglers' cave together, it is socially acceptable to use Christian names…when alone."

"You are truly a master of etiquette," she said with a wry smile. Then she looked back at the house. "How should I do this?"

"There's a door on the far side of the house that the servants use to get to the outbuildings. It's the same door tradesmen use. Go along the side yard here, behind that yew hedge. Your gown will practically glow if the moon comes out, so move quickly. When you get inside, be as silent as you can. You'll see the servants' stairs at one end. Take that up to the upper floor and when the hallway is empty, sneak back to your room and stay there for the rest of the night."

Poppy's eyes were wide. "Well. *You're* prepared."

He didn't want to get into why that was. "In the morning, if anyone asks where you went, tell them that after you stormed out of the dining room doors to the terrace, you had a change of heart and you immediately went back in through the foyer doors, which were open, and you pouted in your bedroom all night. You ignored any knocks at the door, and refused to call a maid to help you get ready for bed."

"I already told Mrs. Towers I didn't need any maid assigned to me," she said.

"Good. And I'll tell people that I did go out and look for you, since I was worried about a young lady alone. But I didn't find you, and I just walked around the grounds—if anyone was looking for me, we must have just missed each other in the darkness."

"You have an answer for everything, don't you?" she said.

"It helps to plan ahead. You don't want to have to answer awkward questions about how you've spent the last hour."

"What will you do? Won't people wonder where you've been?"

"Probably," he said. "But I've never particularly cared if people think less of me."

"No, you just leave for another part of the world, don't you?" Poppy noted in an arch tone. Then she put up one hand to stop him from responding. "I'm sorry. That was unfair. It's my first time escaping smugglers and high tide and party guests while trying to preserve my good name."

He gave her a little smile. "Poppy St George is a very good name. Now go. Don't be seen."

After Poppy dashed away into the darkness, Carlos thought he'd never met a cleverer woman. He hoped no one who cared would see her and raise a fuss. And by the state of her gown, there would be a hell of a fuss. The hem soaked in salt water, the skirts snagged on the rough rock, and the smears of mud all over...even the quick-witted Poppy would have a difficult time explaining her way out of that.

Trusting that she'd be able to take care of herself, Carlos turned his attention to the matter of the smugglers. He'd explored the beach shortly after his own arrival a few weeks before, mostly just because it was there. He found the cave entrance, but had no desire to explore further. Dark, narrow spaces made him nervous. And at the time, there was no reason to think smuggling was going on literally beneath his feet.

He walked the opposite direction from the house, and scanned the vast darkness beyond. The sea at night didn't reveal many secrets, and he stared for a long, long time before his eyes picked out a slight shift in the pattern of the abyss. A ship was sailing north to south across the bay, its canvas sails catching the faintest light from the stars and reflecting it back. Most people wouldn't have seen it, but Carlos spent a lot of his life watching for such things —his life and the lives of his crew often depended on it.

Was the operation he and Poppy just stumbled across the one he was seeking? It seemed too easy. Of course, he hadn't done anything to stop the smugglers yet, so perhaps he shouldn't be too confident.

If these were the smugglers who killed Mateo, Carlos would make sure they'd pay for it. Ximena wouldn't have any peace until she knew her brother's killers had been stopped. Plus, the vast amounts of opium in the caves below hinted at something far more serious than the usual tax avoidance.

He returned to the house through the same French doors he'd left by. The drawing room was quiet now. Apparently most of the guests had dispersed or gone off to other amusements. He breathed a sigh of relief.

At that moment, Miss Ainsworth appeared at his elbow. How did the woman manage to move so silently?

"My goodness, it's as if you'd vanished in the night air. I should like your company, sir," Blanche said winsomely.

Carlos reminded himself that Blanche wasn't to blame for either of her parents' rude behavior. "I'm not sure I'll be interesting at the moment."

"Oh, that's no matter," Blanche said soothingly. "Let us plan a diversion for tomorrow. What shall we do?"

"In fact, I need to go to Treversey tomorrow. A personal matter."

Blanche wasn't the slightest bit put off by that. "Perfect! As it happens, I wanted to go to town to see about some new lace. You can drive me after breakfast!"

"I should be glad to," he said, without meaning it. Yesterday, he wouldn't have thought twice about spending half a day with Blanche. And while he had nothing against her, she had never captured his interest, something that Poppy's sudden reappearance made abundantly clear. The truth was, he'd been interested in exactly one woman since meeting Poppy...and her name was Poppy.

"Will you have another drink?" Blanche asked. "Several of the gentlemen went to the Blue Room to indulge in a round of brandy and cards. Or if you prefer," she added in a breathy tone peering at him from beneath lowered lashes, "We could remain here, and get to know each other a little better."

Hell no. He knew a trap when he saw one. And staying in the drawing room with Blanche was ten times more dangerous for him that running headlong into a smuggler's cave with Poppy.

"I regret I must decline," Carlos said. Without a

backward glance, he retreated from the room, hoping that Poppy had also got back into the house, unseen and unheard.

Christ, for what was supposed to be a summer house party, things had gotten very complicated.

Chapter 7

POPPY FOLLOWED CARLOS'S (SUSPICIOUSLY?) precise directions for how to sneak into the side door of the house without being seen. She made it into the house and down the corridor to the servants' stairs before anyone saw her. However, on the flight of stairs between the ground floor and the upper floor, she encountered someone unexpected.

"Elowen?" Poppy asked, too surprised to do the intelligent thing (which would have been to retreat downward to a place she could hide).

Elowen Metcalfe jumped in alarm, her hand flying to her throat. "Oh, my goodness! Miss St George, you frightened me half to death!"

"What are you doing here?" Poppy asked. "This is the servants' stairs."

"Oh, er…I took this way to avoid…Mr. Ainsworth," Elowen said in a rush. She looked everywhere but at Poppy, and her cheeks flushed scarlet.

"Is he roaming the halls?" Poppy asked. "Has he done anything…inappropriate?" She wouldn't put it past the man, mostly because she disliked him so much.

"Oh, um, no. I don't wish to imply that he…I just…

He's a very unpleasant man," Elowen said. "And if I can use this staircase while he uses the main one, then it's much better. But why are *you* using this staircase?"

Poppy expected this question (considering she'd just demanded the same from Elowen). So she said, "It's rather embarrassing, actually. I'd also had an unpleasant exchange with some Ainsworths in the drawing room— Mrs. Ainsworth and her daughter. So I left...but I left through the French doors to the terrace. And I'm afraid I was so upset that I tromped across a flower bed and got my slippers and hem all muddy. Of course I couldn't be seen in such a state, so I snuck around to the servants' entrance and up here. Mrs. Towers would hate to get muddy footprints all over her lovely carpets, don't you think?"

This explanation fired Elowen's sympathy. "How terrible for you! Walking outside at night could be so dangerous, Miss St George."

"Call me Poppy, please."

"Poppy," Elowen said shyly. "Do you want me to summon a maid for you? Surely you'll want to wash and have your things sent down for cleaning."

"No!" Poppy said quickly, remembering Carlos's plan for her to not see anyone for the rest of the evening. "That is, I'd just hate to be thought of as so clumsy, and you know how servants talk. Really, I just want to go up to my room and sort myself out. You won't tell anyone you saw me, will you?"

"Of course not!" Elowen replied. "In fact, let's just pretend we never met here."

"Capital. Good night, Elowen."

"See you tomorrow," the other woman said, watching as Poppy made her soggy way to the upper landing.

When she got to her room and lit a candle, Poppy

stared at the mirror in chagrin. Her hair was a windblown tangle, the blue ribbon gone, the curls destroyed. Further, her slippers were absolutely mud-soaked and the hem of her dress was stained with saltwater. She doubted that any item could be restored to its former state.

"I look like flotsam," she said to herself in despair. "Carlos must have thought I was a fright."

The small figure of Miss Mist sauntered to Poppy, and then stretched up, her front paws against the glass of the mirror. She opened her mouth in a silent yawn, looking very fierce.

"Well, my tiny tigress," Poppy said, picking the cat up and moving to the bed. "What did you do this evening? I encountered criminals on the seashore. I'll wager that you only caught a mouse."

Miss Mist looked quite pleased with herself, so she probably had caught a mouse or two. She purred as Poppy stroked her back and scratched her ears.

Caught. Poppy recalled the startled face of Elowen on the stairs a few moments ago. That young lady definitely looked caught out. What *had* she been doing on the servants' stairs? Poppy would bet her last shilling that it had nothing to do with Ainsworth. The man was rude and snobbish, but it was easy enough to pass by him. Elowen had another reason to be sneaking about the house. A forbidden romance, possibly? Perhaps she'd fallen for one of the footmen, or another man in service here. And they could only meet for a few stolen moments while others were occupied.

But Elowen didn't seem the type of young woman to do that. She was too devoted to her sister, and very shy and retiring to boot.

Of course, she could also be the head of a smuggling gang, signaling to her men from the top of the house in the dark of night. Poppy suppressed a giggle at the image of the sweet, shy Elowen dressed up like a pirate.

But the thought, silly as it was, brought her mind back to the cave she just explored with Carlos. Was it possible that the Towers knew of the illegal activity happening just below their home? Mr. Towers had been a barrister before he retired, so it seemed quite implausible that he'd get mixed up in such activity. Then again, she'd already heard how commonplace smuggling was in Cornwall. And Mr. Towers was very fond of his French brandy.

No. She couldn't believe the Towers were involved in smuggling along their own beach, fine brandy or no. And the oddity of finding opium in the cave made it all the more curious.

As far as she knew, the sort of items smuggled into Cornwall tended to be destined for ordinary people: brandy and wine, fine fabric, lace…items from the Continent that became exorbitantly expensive thanks to the Customs stamp, largely a result of the ongoing war with France that mucked up all shipping trade.

Opium was different. Who could possibly want—*and* afford—so much of the expensive product? Was Carlos correct that it might have been diverted from a war front? She hated to think that someone was profiting off goods meant for soldiers who needed it.

Oh, it was all too much to think about right now. Whenever Poppy's mind was overwhelmed, she had an urge to write things down. It was one of the lessons Mrs. Bloomfield taught them as students: putting your ideas on paper helped you to organize them, examine them, and decide what to do next. Thus, it wasn't surprising that the Wildwood alumnae all tended to be prolific letter-writers.

Leaving the cat lolling on the bed, Poppy moved to her writing desk, instinctively pulling out a few sheets of

POPPY AND THE PIRATE 70

paper, then opened the little jar of ink (which she was alarmed to discover was almost empty).

Dear Heather,

I write to you from Cornwall, where I am spending the summer (along with Miss Mist). I had hoped it would be a peaceful and restorative visit, but it seems that Fate has other plans. I am deeply annoyed to report that Carlos de la Guerra is a guest here as well. He's got some business to attend to in Cornwall, though why he needs to literally live under the same roof as I do is a mystery I cannot fathom. I do not think I can avoid him all summer—indeed, to judge by this first day and evening, we will be constantly stumbling over one another. I'd pack up and return to London immediately, but it would feel like admitting defeat (not to mention that London is truly appalling in July and August). However, if you have a spare room in that drafty castle of yours, do tell me and I will hop aboard the next coach northward. I am running out of ink so I will merely promise to keep you apprised of any developments.

Poppy

She wrote the address on the outside (Lady Heather MacNair, Countess of Carregness, Carregness, Scotland), sealed the letter and placed it to the side of the desk, sighing as she did so. Her school friends seemed to be acquiring husbands and titles, while all Poppy could point to over the past year was a cat and a sense that she had missed something important. Not that Poppy believed a woman needed to be married to have a fulfilling life (indeed, she'd seen several examples where marriage brought misery instead). Girls educated at Wildwood Hall learned self-reliance along with French, mathematics, rhetoric, and geography. But Poppy knew that her friends were all deeply in love, and very happy. Daisy had met and married a duke, who had happened to be her neighbor and then her most ardent admirer. Her own cousin Rose tamed one of the worst rakes in London, turning him into a faithful husband who had already showed that he'd literally fight duels for her honor. And then Heather (wild, unpredictable Heather) ran off to Scotland and somehow landed in the arms of one of the sweetest men Poppy had ever met—although you'd not know it to look at the lumbering giant in his ancient Highland castle. Camellia once made a joke about all the weddings she had to attend…but Poppy didn't seem to be in danger of making Lia dress up for yet another.

In fact, Poppy only managed to lose her head over a too-charming gentleman with his own ship and his own plans to free his homeland from colonial overlords. How could Poppy compete with such a goal? She wasn't rich, she wasn't titled, and she didn't know anything about conducting revolutions.

"I don't want to compete," she reminded her reflection. "He'd make a terrible husband, sailing all over the world all the time. And I don't even like him."

Yes, keep telling yourself that, her reflection seemed to retort. If Poppy didn't like him, why couldn't she get him out of her mind? And why did she still smell the wool-and-musk scent of his jacket that he'd draped around her? And why did she still feel the touch of his hands on her arms? And hear his voice murmuring in Spanish in the darkness of the beach, where no woman ought to be alone with such a sinfully attractive man?

Poppy muttered about her own swooniness—it was humiliating to sit and wonder if he was thinking of her at the same time she was dreaming of him. Standing up, she walked to the nightstand and poured out some water. She'd need every drop to clean herself of the beach sand and dirt from the cave. The gown and shoes were probably doomed.

"To the rag bin with you!" she told her gown sadly. "And I'll need to go to town tomorrow to get more slippers. I doubt my walking shoes will be welcome in the drawing room."

Using the washcloth, she cleaned her face and limbs of the sand that clung to her. The mud was more difficult, and she did indeed squeeze every last drop from the cloth before she felt clean enough to put on her night clothes and climb into bed.

It had been a very long day, and she dropped off to sleep almost immediately. She didn't sleep well, however. Her dreams were filled with long, twisting subterranean passageways where she had to run from shadowy figures. She'd hit a dead end and whirl around, only to find a man reaching out for her. Poppy wanted to scream when the figure pulled her close—but how could she scream when she was being kissed so passionately? Then the kiss would break off, and the figure told her they had to run once more. She woke several times in the night, her heartbeat rapid from fear or arousal or both.

Then Miss Mist awoke from her own dreams, and curled herself on the pillow in the crook of Poppy's shoulder and neck. She rumbled out a steady purr, a soothing sound that chased away all dreams and sent Poppy back to sleep, this time a deep and dreamless one.

Chapter 8

❄ ⚘❄

DEAR POPPY,

I have sent this letter ahead of your visit to Cornwall in the hopes that it will arrive shortly after you do, and that you may have a little companionship through my words, if you are otherwise lonely. I know that you have other reasons for perhaps avoiding London just now, but I must say, you were wise to decamp before the worst of the heat begins. It is ever so much more pleasant here in Gloucestershire in summer, with the pond so near Lyondale. It reminds me of when we went boating near Wildwood Hall so many years ago. You stood up in the bow and declared yourself to be the pirate princess Judith and you made us all your faithful lady crew. Of all the children's stories we reenacted, that may have been my favorite.

Do pet Miss Mist for me, and tell her she is darling and perfect. How are the Cornish cats? Has she conquered all the local specimens yet? I will assume so until you write to me with the answer.

I hope you will not be bored, Poppy! Cornwall seems such a sleepy land, with no excitement to be had compared to the city. If you need anything to divert you, you must let me know.

Your constant friend,

Daisy

When the sun finally rose, filling the room with peachy, golden light, Poppy woke in a more cheerful mood. Her dreams had faded to a tangle of half-remembered images. Today was a new day, and she had a lot to do. Breakfast, then posting the letter, then arranging a trip into town. And perhaps a few well-placed questions about the local smuggling operations…

Just then, she noticed that a letter had been slipped under the door by the maid, so it had probably arrived in the first post. Poppy retrieved it and darted back to the warm bed to read it. On finishing it, she laughed out loud. So Daisy was worried that she'd be bored and lonely? She had two new friends in Elowen and Elisa. She had a mystery to solve. And she had a vexing gentleman to deal with. Miss Mist would have to fend for herself!

Armed with the support of her distant but true friendships, Poppy slid out of bed for real this time—moving carefully so she didn't disturb Miss Mist, who had curled up in the exact center on top of the blankets, and was now lightly snoring as she doubtless dreamed of murder.

Poppy was determined to face the day. She had momentarily forgotten the acute danger of the previous evening, instead reflecting on the excitement. She and Carlos saw an actual smuggling run! Smuggling might be rampant, but to import such a massive quantity of a substance like opium hinted at a much larger scheme.

She dressed quickly, and put her ruined slippers and dress next to the door, where the maid would find them and know that they had to go to the rag bin.

Then she went to the breakfast room. She had never been shy about breakfast, a meal which barely existed for many ladies. Poppy drank some strong Assam tea and shamelessly sampled each of the half-dozen jams on as many little slices of bread.

As she was finishing the last one, Elowen came in. She looked as if she were about to bolt out again, but Poppy called out, "Good morning! The tea in the silver pot is particularly good."

Elowen nodded shyly. She poured a cup at the sideboard and sat across from Poppy.

Remembering something from last night, Poppy leaned forward. She said, "I wanted to apologize for what Mrs. Ainsworth said after dinner in the drawing room. It was quite rude to gossip about you."

Elowen's eyes dropped. "I heard no gossip."

"Yes, you did." Poppy remembered the flash of Elowen's skirt as she ran out of the way.

"It was not gossip," Elowen said then, "because it's true. I have no suitors, and it's no secret why many stay away."

"I refuse to believe that, and anyway *she* had no place to say it."

"Regardless, she was correct."

Poppy was struck by the sorrow in Elowen's tone. "I'm sorry to have brought it up again."

"It isn't important," Elowen said. "All that matters is that Elisa has the family she needs."

Just then, Mrs. Towers entered, joined by Blanche a moment later. Then Mr. Hobbson came in, and the conversation turned very general and safe. After breakfasting, Poppy asked Mrs. Towers about the likelihood of a carriage into town.

"I find myself in need of another pair of slippers," she said, without mentioning why.

"There's an excellent cobbler in town," Blanche said.

"I intend to do some shopping myself today."

"Oh, an excursion into Treversey is always fun," Mrs. Towers replied. "In fact, Mrs. Hobbson wants to go as well."

"And I need to take Elisa to her appointment," Elowen chimed in.

"We'd be delighted to take you girls in the carriage, if you don't mind squeezing in three to your seat. I'm afraid we'll quite fill our side!" Mr. Hobbson chuckled as he patted the girth of his belly.

"Sorry, Blanche," said Mrs. Hobbson, without sounding very sorry. "I'm afraid that the carriage won't fit any more."

"Oh, not to worry," Blanche said, with a little smirk toward Poppy. "Last night, Mr. de la Guerra and I made plans to travel together. We'll use the gig."

Poppy had a vision of Carlos and Blanche cuddled up together in the two-person seat, and had to look down at her tea to hide the scowl. So, he'd cooked up that plan last night, had he? It must have happened after he sent her off to her room like a spoiled child!

"Please excuse me," Poppy said, not wanting to see Blanche's self-satisfied expression just then. "I have a letter to get into the post, and I left it upstairs."

She left the breakfast room, intending to write a letter to Mrs. Bloomfield as well, but didn't get as far as her bedroom, because she was distracted by something outside on the terrace.

As a kitten, Miss Mist had been a tiny ball of fluff, with big innocent eyes that looked out onto the world with the sort of expression that said "I know absolutely nothing and that's fine." But now, as a full-grown cat, she'd become sleek, slinky, and deadly. Still grey, but there was nothing fluffy or innocent about her. She stalked her environs with all the confidence of a tiger, and she inspired fear in all rodents. She was also rather picky about who she chose to associate with.

Thus, Poppy was annoyed to discover the cat was now out on the terrace wall...accepting ear scratches from Carlos.

Beyond the lawn, the water sparkled blue, so unlike the dark water last night. It seemed to be a different place altogether. Poppy failed to appreciate it. She charged out to the terrace and demanded, "What are you doing? Miss Mist doesn't like people."

"She likes me," Carlos countered, looking up at Poppy as if there were nothing odd about him sitting there, sipping coffee, with *her* cat. "And she ought to, considering that *I* rescued her out of a tree last year."

"Your finest hour," Poppy muttered, trying not to picture the scene. It was difficult, because it had been a very fine hour. Carlos, who she'd met only moments prior, had clambered up the tree to retrieve the kitten without hesitation...and also without a shirt, since he'd removed it to avoid getting snagged on a branch. Until that morning, Poppy had never seen a man naked from the waist up.

It was, of course, completely scandalous that he'd done that. But how could she complain when he was handing her a tiny creature he'd just rescued at some personal risk? (Not to mention that Poppy couldn't complain anyway, being struck speechless by the sight of him.)

And now Miss Mist was purring up a storm, delighted with his attention. Traitor!

"I hear you're taking Blanche Ainsworth into Treversey," Poppy said.

"She practically insisted on it," he agreed blandly. "And since I want to go speak to the magistrate anyway, it won't be going out of my way."

Poppy asked, "Does the magistrate have authority to arrest the smugglers?"

"If we knew who they were, yes. But I think the really important issue is to let him know that opium is involved."

"Maybe I can go to the harbor and look for that ship from last night," Poppy offered.

Carlos frowned, pausing in his ministrations to the cat. "I'd prefer for you to not get involved."

"Too late. I've already sacrificed a pair of slippers, a gown, and a hair ribbon to the cause. Looking for a ship won't be too difficult."

"Let's meet somewhere and look together," he suggested. "The thought of you wandering Treversey alone is enough to give me chills. With your luck, you'll stumble upon the gang and take over operations by dinner time."

"Or I could seize a ship and become a lady pirate. Like Princess Judith."

"Who?"

"Oh, it's an old tale. There's this princess who gets jilted on her wedding day, and she ends up on a pirate ship, but then she takes over the ship and builds up a crew of all ladies to sail with her, and they win all sorts of sea battles and they rescue a prince from a pirate attack...it was one of my favorite bedtime stories."

"Yes, I could see that," he muttered. "Poppy the pirate."

Just then, Elisa wandered out of the house. When she saw Poppy and Carlos, she smiled and headed toward them.

"Good morning," she said, sitting down on a chair next to Carlos. Miss Mist promptly abandoned him and strolled over to Elisa, who immediately set the cat in her lap.

"What are you doing today?" Poppy asked, sinking down beside her. (She was not in the least surprised that the cat liked Elisa. Who wouldn't?)

"I have to go visit Dr. Drake again later. But until we leave, I'm going to watch for birds."

"Any particular ones?"

"All of them," said Elisa. "What are you doing?"

"We were, um, watching for ships."

Elisa nodded. "I saw eleven of them yesterday."

"Did you happen to notice if any had a string of small red and white flags between the masts?" Carlos asked, leaning forward.

"No." Elisa shook her head firmly.

Poppy sighed. "I wouldn't expect you to have noticed, of course. It's an odd thing to look for."

"I did notice," Elisa corrected. "None of the ships had flags like that."

Poppy looked at Elisa in real surprise. "You mean to say you can remember seeing the flags on all the ships?"

"I watch things," Elisa said, and then pointed. "See? The big gull with the grey head? That's the gull who took my cucumber sandwich Tuesday last."

Poppy stared upward at the gull. "Did he? How greedy!"

"I wasn't hungry. And I don't care for cucumber all that much."

Before Poppy could reply to that, Blanche emerged. She gave a passing glance to Poppy and Elisa, focusing her smile on Carlos. She said, "Why Mr. de la Guerra, there you are. Whatever caused you to come out here instead of enjoying the conversation in the breakfast room? I do hope you're ready to go. It's such a perfect day, and I can't wait to enjoy the drive there with you."

Carlos stood up, and Poppy couldn't help but notice

how everything he did was graceful. "Please excuse me," he said to Poppy and Elisa.

And then he left, Blanche hanging on his arm.

Poppy glared after them. "Perfect day, my foot."

* * * *

Carlos wished he hadn't agreed to take Blanche into town last night, but he was stuck now. Blanche chattered as they walked to the house. She was dressed for a day out, in a jade green jacket over a lighter green gown. Her dark hair was braided rather than curled, but it was still elaborate enough to make him wonder how early she'd gotten up to make the carriage ride into town.

"You're sure you don't need more to eat?" she asked.

"I only have coffee in the mornings," Carlos explained. Perhaps because he so often woke up on board a ship, he usually wasn't hungry for a few hours. "Are you ready to go?"

"But of course! I would never keep a gentleman waiting. And I gave instructions for the gig to be brought up to the door for us."

She donned a white hat before stepping outside, and when she pulled down a little veil to protect her face from the sun and wind, she looked almost as if she were hiding.

The gig was very open, without even a canopy. The seat accommodated only two people, and it was assumed that those two people got along very well. Blanche was practically sitting in his lap. Two horses pulled the vehicle, ensuring a speedy ride.

"It's quite all right that you're going into town alone?" he asked as he flicked the reins to get the horses moving.

"Why, I'm not alone. I'm with you!"

"Unchaperoned, I meant."

She giggled. "Oh, Mr. de la Guerra. We're practically engaged."

"But not *actually* engaged," he said flatly. Nor would they ever be—though he'd play along for a bit longer if it helped him understand Mr. Ainsworth's role in the local smuggling operations.

She smiled at him. "I know what a proper gentleman you are. Not at all like your roguish friend you mentioned yesterday. Viscount Norbury, was it?"

"Yes."

"And a duel! That does sound rather…transporting. Even if you claim it never happened."

"I make no claims at all."

Blanche let that pass. "What takes you into town?" she asked.

"Business," he said.

"What business do you have that Papa is not involved in?" she asked. "I thought you two had an…understanding." The double meaning wasn't lost on him. Of course Ainsworth liked the idea of marrying his daughter to a business partner to solidify the arrangement.

"Your father is hardly the only person I do business with," he told her, hoping that she'd catch the implication that nothing was set in stone. "In fact, I have to speak to the magistrate."

"Whatever for?"

"I have some questions about the smuggling going on around the area."

She looked surprised, but then laughed. "Well, *anyone* can tell you that. Smuggling is barely smuggling around here! Look in any shop in Treversey and you'll see."

"You think it common?"

"Of course! Anything with a tariff will find its way to a beach in Cornwall sooner or later. Whiskey, wine, silk, lace…"

"Opium?"

She frowned at the unexpected item. "Well…perhaps. Why not? Nearly anything can be put on a ship."

"You have a cosmopolitan view, Miss Ainsworth."

"I am a very cosmopolitan woman, Mr. de la Guerra," she said, with a suggestive smile.

Thank God, they reached Treversey soon after. He drove directly to the Seven Sisters, an inn at the center of town where all incoming coaches stopped. It had stables large enough to accommodate several carriages.

"Well, Mr. de la Guerra. Where shall we go first?"

Carlos shook his head. "I have no idea how long my task will take. You shouldn't waste time on my account. I'll let you take care of your errands, Miss Ainsworth, and I do hope that we'll see each other soon after. Lunch, perhaps." (In truth, Carlos fully intended to disappear from Blanche's sights as quickly as he could. But he was too smart to tell her that.)

"What a lovely idea," Blanche cooed, evidently thinking that she had him well in hand.

He pulled the gig alongside the inn. A young boy was already running out to take hold of the reins, and a footman was there to help Blanche step down. She alighted with perfect grace.

Carlos climbed out himself and surrendered the gig to the boy, offering a coin to him. Then he made a tactical retreat. Despite his hints that their marriage was far from settled, Blanche had not given up. He wondered if he could persuade Poppy to accept a proposal purely out of altruism.

Luckily, Carlos found the home of the magistrate quickly enough, just off the main thoroughfare on a tiny street called Bower Lane. Based on the furnishings he saw, he realized that the ground floor also served as a courtroom (a sign stated that court was in session two mornings every week). The magistrate lived above the space, though he didn't own the building—room and board being part of his remuneration from the town.

He knocked at the door, which was soon opened by a middle aged woman with dark curly hair and a weary look on her face. "Yes, sir?" she asked, in the tone of someone very put out that her dusting had been interrupted.

"Good day, ma'am. I wish to see the magistrate. Mr. Armitage, I believe."

"One moment, sir. I'll see if he's done with his cases."

Carlos waited outside on the step, feeling very conspicuous. But within a few minutes, the woman returned to escort him up to the magistrate's little working room. Several sets of law books were shelved behind him, and the magistrate himself sat at a desk covered in more books. He was a surprisingly vigorous-looking man, on the thin side, with distinctive red hair.

"Mr. Armitage?" Carlos asked. "My name is Carlos de la Guerra."

"How do you do, sir," Armitage said, rising to greet Carlos. He then gestured to a young man seated nearby, who appeared to be taking notes. "And this is my deputy, Rowe. What brings you to see me today? Some trouble? You're not a local, are you?"

"Not at all. I hail from Santo Domingo. But I'm staying at Pencliff Towers for the summer."

"Ah, the Towers do have so many guests," Armitage said. "I trust you are enjoying your time there."

"Certainly. However, speaking of Pencliff Towers, I must report an occurrence of smuggling."

Armitage exchanged a glance with Rowe before saying, "Very conscientious of you, sir. Since taking up this post several months ago, I've found most people around here do no such thing."

"I'm not against a bit of profit," Carlos explained, with perfect honesty. "But this instance goes rather beyond that."

Armitage nodded. "Please go on."

"Last night, around ten in the evening, a ship anchored just offshore of the beach below Pencliff Towers. A longboat rowed to the beach and several crates of opium were unloaded and stored in a cave at the base of the cliff."

The magistrate raised his eyebrows. "Opium? What makes you so sure of the cargo?"

"I was curious. After the smugglers left their goods behind, I went and looked." Carlos shrugged. "I've spent a little time in India, so I knew what the contents were." (He left out Poppy's involvement, naturally.)

Rowe half-raised a hand. "Er, should I be recording this, sir?"

"Not at the moment, Rowe," Armitage said, waving him off. "For the moment, let's say we're having an interesting discussion."

Carlos felt a stirring of unease. Why would the magistrate not want to record a report like this?

Shaking his head, Armitage went on, "That was a foolhardy action, if I may say, Mr...de la Guerra, is it? Since you're not from here, you may not know the reputation of the local smuggling gangs. In short, they're vicious. If you had been seen, you would have been killed without question." His eyes bored into Carlos, and he felt there was a special warning in them. Possibly an outright threat.

"Do you know who the smugglers are?" Carlos asked, not put off.

"Peter Spargo runs the biggest crew," the deputy offered. "Half the men in town have done some owling at least once."

The magistrate sent him a sharp look. "That will do, Rowe!"

The deputy shut up.

"The Towers are friends of mine," Carlos said. "And I should not like them to be harmed by this—I suppose you'd call it an operation—using their property. I am quite sure Mr. Towers would never permit such actions, especially if it was a violent gang. There are a number of ladies at the house right now. Just imagine the problems that could arise if one of those smugglers happened to go a bit afield and encounter one of them. "

The magistrate looked frustrated. He rapped lightly on one of the open books on his desk. "Hmmm, yes. I see your point, Mr. de la Guerra. In truth, I have few resources to do anything about it. I am allotted only two paid deputies, which would put us at a considerable disadvantage against even the smallest gang of smugglers. And Spargo's gang isn't small—assuming that's who's behind it, of course."

"You must be able to do something."

"I could take the issue to the Customs officer in Truro," said Armitage. "But with no hard evidence, it will be a tough case to make. They have problems of their own and are unwilling to waste the manpower on what could be a wild goose chase."

"Wild goose chase? Opium is surely more significant than your average shipment of tax-free silk."

"I cannot prove to anyone that opium was involved," Armitage said, spreading his hands. "Not that I doubt your word, but I need evidence."

"Then I'll bring you evidence. I'll return to the caves and take one of the packages."

Armitage shook his head vehemently. "That you must not do! It's far too dangerous."

Rowe also half-stood in alarm. "Sir, you've no idea when they might come back. Peter Spargo might not be there himself. He tends to haunt the Red Anchor by day. But one of his men could be in the caves, and they'd not think twice about killing you for seeing something that could implicate them."

"Have they killed before?" Carlos asked Rowe.

"Almost certainly," Rowe said. "We find bodies washed up on the beaches sometimes, sir. The coroner calls them drownings, but…that is the safe thing to say."

Exactly what happened to Mateo, Carlos thought.

"Enough, Rowe," Armitage warned in a low voice. "I'm sure our guest understands the gravity of the situation."

"And do you, Mr. Armitage?" Carlos asked. "This isn't a few barrels of whiskey snuck past the Customs officer to avoid paying a duty. The government will take this seriously. That opium was meant to be sent where it's needed. The Peninsula, perhaps?"

"Or even the hospitals around here," Rowe added. "I've heard that there are never enough medicines for the returning soldiers. The East India Company sends more opium to China than to Britain now."

Carlos looked to the deputy, glad that someone was taking this seriously. "So someone may be diverting resources for our soldiers in order to distribute it on the black market."

"Quite likely, sir. Spargo isn't exactly a patriot."

Armitage stood up and said in a cool tone, "That's enough talk for today, gentlemen. Mr. de la Guerra, thank you for bringing this to my attention. Should we have further questions, we will send word to Pencliff Towers. I will see what I can do about the whole matter, but I forbid you getting involved in the investigation."

"Forbid me?" Carlos asked, forgetting for the moment that he wanted to present himself as an ordinary person, rather than a freelance ship captain hellbent on justice for the death of his friend.

Armitage noticed the heat in Carlos's words. "Perhaps forbid is a strong word. But please step aside during our investigation. Civilians can thwart the cause of justice, even when their intentions are good."

"So you *will* investigate?"

Armitage nodded stiffly. "I'll send Rowe to the beach you mentioned to examine the hiding place and the contraband, assuming it's still there."

"I can go as soon as we're finished here, sir!" Rowe volunteered.

The magistrate looked at Carlos. "Will that satisfy you?"

It did not particularly satisfy, but Carlos knew he didn't have much choice. "Very well."

"And you should *forget* about it, sir," Armitage said, again locking eyes with Carlos. "I urge you to place your trust in the law. This is not your affair."

Carlos left, feeling distinctly that the law was not something to trust in this part of the world.

Good thing he had a lot of experience going around the law.

Chapter 9

SOME TIME AFTER CARLOS AND Blanche went off in the gig, the larger coach left Pencliff, loaded down with both Hobbsons, the Metcalfe sisters, and Poppy (who had managed to write her additional letters after all). Despite all being packed like sardines, the group was excited and merry, and there were endless jokes told along the way.

When the carriage rolled to a stop at the Seven Sisters, the main inn in the square, Poppy was impressed by what she saw. For some reason, she expected a sleepy, even rundown fishing village. However, the place was bigger than she thought, and the buildings were well kept, with brightly painted doors and trim.

Elowen and Elisa bid them goodbye, saying that they would head directly to the doctor's practice, and that if they didn't meet up again by two, the sisters would hire a coach for the ride home.

"Not that we'll permit that," Hobbson said after the two walked off. "I don't think Miss Metcalfe has much money to her name, not to mention that it would be very rude to take the girls into town and then leave them there like an old shoe."

"Oh, speaking of shoes," Mrs. Hobbson said. "Let's

find that cobbler Blanche mentioned. Miss Poppy can't go around barefoot, now can she?"

The cobbler was easy to find, and Poppy was even able to purchase a pair of plain, black leather slippers from the shelf. The cobbler's assistant (who also happened to be her daughter) measured Poppy's feet and promised that the slippers would be trimmed to size and finished quickly. "You can pick them up after lunch, miss."

"Thank you," Poppy said, impressed by the service.

With her main task completed, she walked along High Street with the Hobbsons, peering in shop windows and admiring all the goods offered for sale. It was quite as good as nearly any street in London for variety and quality.

Poppy stopped short when she saw Blanche emerge from a shop, dressed in another stunning outfit. It made Poppy painfully aware she was wearing the same traveling coat as yesterday.

Mrs. Hobbson flagged her down. "Miss Ainsworth, you fairly bolted away from Pencliff Towers this morning."

"Well, the early bird gets the worm," Blanche said, her eyes on Poppy. "Mr. de la Guerra and I had a *wonderful* drive into town. He is most skilled…at handling the gig, I mean." She wore a knowing smile on her face.

Poppy wondered if any of the shops on this street sold knives.

"And what are you about, Miss Ainsworth?" Mr. Hobbson was saying. "Shopping yet again?"

Blanche nodded happily. "A shipment of Valenciennes lace arrived. It is finer than what makes it to London, and one fifth the price."

"Well managed, dear!" Mrs. Hobbson cried, with just

a hint of mockery. "You'll dazzle any future husband with your clever marketing."

Blanche pointed out the shop, and then bid them goodbye as quickly as she could. After she left, Mrs. Hobbson grumbled, "Valenciennes lace, my foot. Let's go see what this so-called lace looks like."

But inside, the shopkeeper at first refused to admit he carried any lace at all.

"What!" Mrs. Hobbson said. "What kind of a shop are you running, sir?"

Poppy, who had been silent at first, thought she could guess the man's concern. So she said, "But Miss Ainsworth spoke so highly of your resourcefulness in procuring good lace, sir."

"Oh, Miss Ainsworth sent you! Well, that's all right." He tapped the side of his nose, then reached under the counter and pulled out a bolt of fine lace. "I remember now. Came in just this morning."

Poppy and the Hobbsons looked at the lace, but didn't buy any, despite the fact that it was quite affordable for its quality. Since Poppy's parents depended on the legal trade of imported goods, it felt very odd to be in a shop where the owner all but boasted of selling illegal products. However, she did purchase several yards of white satin ribbon, mostly so the shopkeeper believed her to be a good customer—there might come a time when she'd need to talk to him again.

With the sale concluded, they stepped outside. "All this walking has me famished," Mr. Hobbson declared. "Let's have a bite to eat. The tearoom on Greene Street was recommended."

The ladies were easy to persuade. The tearoom was well-populated by locals—always the best sign of a quality establishment. The woman who came to serve them looked so like the carriage driver Mr. Kellow that Poppy knew immediately they must be related.

When she mentioned the driver's name, the girl's eyes lit up. "My brother Peran, you know! Our mother runs this place, as he no doubt told you."

The level of service grew even more attentive after that, and the little sweet cakes arriving with the hyson tea were unparalleled. Mr. Hobbson praised them with such fervor that nearby guests chuckled. He showed no remorse at stealing the last one from his wife's plate. "I shall buy you another dozen, my dear," he promised.

"Yes, but of that dozen, will I see more than three?" she quipped, evidently quite used to such behavior.

Mrs Hobbson asked what Poppy thought of the town thus far.

"I'm surprised," she said. "I was expecting, well, a backwater."

"Oh, no," said Hobbson. "As you've seen, sometimes fashions come here before they reach London. Such is the trade in these parts."

"Miss Ainsworth's gowns attest to that," his wife added. "For all she talks about her modiste in London, the materials for last night's gown were purchased right here. The finest French linen!"

"She must save a great deal," Poppy noted.

"Well, it's far cheaper to buy such fripperies when the duties don't apply," Mr. Hobbson said with a chuckle.

"Because the ship didn't take the usual route?" Poppy asked, hoping to glean some information about the smuggling trade around here. What if she could find out where that opium was destined to go?

"Precisely, my dear!" Mrs. Hobbson leaned closer. "And that's the same reason why we've been sipping Madeira wine at dinner. I shouldn't tell on the Towers, but at least their housekeeper and butler know how to get goods without the Customs stamp. Such wines would be quite out of *my* price range, I can tell you…unless it's sold by a gentleman, you know."

A gentleman. One of the euphemisms for smugglers, Poppy remembered. *The gentlemen are coming by…* If a person knew what was good for them, they averted their gaze, lest they see too much. Except here in Cornwall, where the law seemed to hold little sway.

The Hobbsons passed on to other subjects, and Poppy let the conversation go where it would (appearing too interested in smuggling would only lead to very awkward questions). In all, it was a delightful hour, and Poppy nearly forgot the events of the previous night as she listened to their chatter.

As soon as they left the tearoom, Poppy caught sight of the harbor between the buildings.

"You know," she said to the Hobbsons. "I really would enjoy walking to the harbor and looking at all the ships."

"Oh, it's a very long way down," Mrs. Hobbson said, looking alarmed at the very idea of climbing down (and up) the hill.

"Well, it's a fine day, and there are many people about. I'll just stroll a little ways and then go back up and fetch my slippers before returning to the Seven Sisters for the ride home. There's absolutely nothing to worry about!"

Before the older couple could object, Poppy strolled away, heading towards the harbor, and all the ships anchored there.

* * * *

After visiting the magistrate, Carlos spent a while pacing the streets, heedless of where he was going. (Well, not completely heedless. He knew enough to avoid the high street shops where he might encounter any of the Pencliff guests, especially Blanche.) Over and over, he replayed the conversation in his mind, and he became convinced that Armitage was hiding something. However, he also remembered Rowe's words. The deputy had rather pointedly mentioned the smuggler Peter Spargo *and* let Carlos know where the man was likely to be found. He might as well find out where this tavern was, and if he could at least take a look at the notorious smuggler.

In his experience, such men tended to stay near the waterfront. That's where the rougher taverns were, the ones populated both by typical sailors and the riff-raff who didn't work honest jobs.

It didn't take long for him to locate the place. The Red Anchor was a long, rambling building very close to the harbor itself. Though the day was young, hard-drinking sailors and watermen would be inside already. And Carlos didn't look anything like the typical patron.

He pulled off his jacket, since it was too fine to be plausible for a regular sailor. Luckily, he'd chosen a very plain shirt today, and his pants were a deep brown. In the dimness of the tavern, no one should notice that they were better quality than the average sailor. He tugged at the shirt to make it looser about his body—sailors not being known to be fastidious dressers, unless a naval officer was forcing the issue. To complete the picture, he pulled out the worn, battered compass that he wore on a chain in place of a watch. It signaled louder than words that he belonged on the water.

Then, whistling a song he learned at his grandfather's knee, he strolled inside.

He got up to the bar, his vision slowly adjusting to the light. He was acutely conscious of being studied by several sets of eyes. This place felt more like a lion's den than a place to enjoy a drink. But before he could even speak to the man standing behind the counter, he was accosted by a skinny man who wore a sleeveless shirt, revealing arms slashed with long scars and a smattering of tattoos.

"Nobody just walks into the Anchor. Who the hell are you?" the man growled.

Carlos didn't answer in words. He reached up and grabbed the man's wrist, wrenching his whole arm down and twisting it until the man cried out.

"That's about enough of that," a voice said.

Carlos looked over to see a burly man with a whisky in hand watching him. The man's dark blue coat blended in with the shadows of his corner booth, making it hard to tell much about him other than that he had dark hair and eyes, and a thick beard that concealed much of his face. He could be smiling or frowning now, it was impossible to tell.

"He started it," Carlos retorted, then dropped the man, who sprang back up, eager to get revenge on Carlos for the perceived insult.

"Have another drink, Howel," the burly man said, clearly putting an end to any fight.

After a second, Carlos's skinny opponent scurried to the bar, casting evil looks over his shoulder toward Carlos as he did so.

"Don't think I know you, friend," the burly man said, indicating that Carlos should join him at the table. It was less of an invitation and more of a threat, considering the several other men standing around, obviously just waiting for a signal to grab Carlos and forcibly seat him in front of their boss.

That was when he really got a look at Spargo's face, in particular the soulessness of his eyes, despite the outward appearance of being a jovial host. *Mateo said he had eyes like a demon.* That was what Ximena had told him, and now Carlos knew exactly what his friend had meant.

"Just passing through," Carlos said, allowing his English to become much more accented. "My ship got in from the West Indies and I have a few days leave while the captain gets his next load of goods. Thought I'd get a drink. Didn't know it was a private club." Now even more wary, he deliberately demoted himself to an ordinary sailor, not yet sure how this conversation was going to go.

"What's your ship?"

"*Agustina.*"

One of the lackeys bent down and whispered to Spargo. He nodded, looking satisfied.

"Aye, we saw it in the harbor. What cargo did she bring in?"

Carlos shrugged. "The usual. Preserved beef. Rum. Saltpeter." All those products were typical of the Caribbean ports, unlikely to cause comment.

"And how did you feel about our good Customs agents?" Spargo asked slyly.

Carlos turned his head and spat on the floor.

Spargo laughed. "Malcolm, get this man a drink!" he ordered.

"Rum," Carlos added. One of the lackeys hurried off to the bar to retrieve said drink, and Carlos took a cautious breath. It seemed he'd passed muster.

"Peter Spargo, at your service," his host said, offering a huge hand across the table.

He shook it. "Carlos, señor. Is this your tavern?"

Spargo grinned. "Aye, 'tis my tavern, and my harbor, and my town, truth be known. The docks are my kingdom, and I know everything that passes through here, coming and going.

A glass of rum appeared in front of Carlos. He picked up the glass and inhaled, surprised by the quality.

His host chuckled. "On the house, friend. Consider it a welcome to Cornwall."

Carlos took a drink, and made a show of enjoying every drop.

"Who's the captain of the *Augustina*?" Spurge asked, clearly moving onto the next phase of his informal interrogation.

"*Agustina*," Carlos corrected the pronunciation, annoyed whenever someone couldn't be bothered to say a name right. "Captain de la Guerra. Though you'll want to talk to the first mate. The captain is…how do you say? Not all there."

"Odd duck, is he?" Spargo sounded interested. "Hard man to work for?"

"Oh, no, señor. He's fair and he pays. But he's always going on about war and independence. Wants to arm his countrymen and drive out the oppressors." Carlos shrugged, as if he didn't care in the least. "What does it matter what flag flies over the head? I keep myself out of trouble. Can't spend your money if you're dead."

"Amen to that," Spargo said. "I think I should look up your captain. As it happens, I have some very useful cargo to move. Think he'd listen to an offer?"

Again, Carlos shrugged, finished the rum, and stood up. "Por que no? He'll listen."

"Excellent. I'll send word to the ship. Oh, and the first mate's name?"

"Valentin."

"Well, I won't keep you, friend. Enjoy Treversey. Just watch your back."

Carlos nodded and turned to leave.

As he was heading toward the door, he felt the skinny

man's approach, and inwardly rolled his eyes. So predictable.

But it would be good for Spargo and his gang to think they ruled here, so he was willing to be taken by "surprise." He allowed the skinny man to get the first hit in (which legitimately hurt, even though Carlos dodged subtly to avoid the worst of the blow). He whirled and managed to ward off the next few blows, making it look like he was working harder than he really was.

The laughter of the crowd was raucous, and reinforced everything Carlos guessed about Spargo and his gang.

"Get him, Howel. Show him how we fight in Cornwall!"

"Aye, give that koeg a proper welcome."

Carlos made a show of ducking and stepping away, telling Howel in Spanish that he was a pathetic excuse for a sailor and that a Dominican boy of five could fight better than he could. Hell, a girl of five could take him on, and Howel would still lose.

But these gentlemen didn't speak Spanish, and they all assumed Carlos was scared, or apologetic, or both. The merriment continued as Carlos permitted Howel to push him toward the door.

"Get on your way, you scum. You only walk out of here because Spargo let you."

Propelled by the helpful shove from his new pal, Carlos hurtled out the door into the bright daylight, blinding after the darkness of the waterfront dive. He stumbled a few steps and nearly fell, except that a random passerby reached out to steady him.

No, not just a random passerby. Poppy.

Chapter 10

POPPY FROWNED AT THE MAN Fate just threw in her path...*again*. She caught the jacket that had come flying out after Carlos, hurled by some unknown man in the tavern.

"And stay out if ye know what's good for you!" someone shouted.

She helped Carlos to his feet and then handed him his jacket. "Why are you forever taking off your clothing in public?" she queried. "You did that the very first time I met you, and now you're doing it again."

"You're just lucky," he said. He took her by the arm. "Let's get out of here. I don't want you making the acquaintance of anyone inside of that place."

"Why were *you* in there? Ugh, you smell like rum. It seems early for a drink." Not to mention that there were far better places in town to get said drink. Poppy would prefer a dank back alley compared to the building Carlos just left.

"I was investigating," he muttered, shrugging into his jacket once more. Thankfully, the harbor was busy, and no one seemed to take any special note of either of them. Poppy was dressed much like any woman in the town, and though Carlos was striking, he wasn't terribly out of place (especially with his clothing now somewhat rumpled and marked up like all the laborers around them). He ran his hand through his hair, which somehow, magically fell into a style that looked carelessly windswept but also extremely attractive. Somewhat resentful, Poppy remembered her own "windswept" hair of the previous night, which had looked like a bird's nest.

"We seem to ruin our outfits every time we get involved with smugglers," Poppy said, walking briskly along the quay. "A warning if I ever saw one."

"Speaking of that, what were you doing down at the waterfront without an escort?"

"I wanted to see the ships, but I didn't want the Hobbsons to have to walk down and up again."

He grunted. "You shouldn't be alone."

"Well, now I'm not. I've got you to protect me. Though I'd prefer it if you didn't get into more fights today. What could possibly have motivated you to wander into that rat-infested shack?"

"That's where the leader of Treversey's most notorious smuggling gang spends his days."

Poppy stopped short. "Really? What's he like?"

"Not like anyone I'd introduce to you, *querida*. Also I lied quite a bit so I didn't alarm him. If any strangers happen to ask you about the *Agustina* or her captain, plead ignorance."

"Where is the *Agustina*? Can I see her?"

"You can get a glimpse. But I think I ought to tell the crew to sail her away for a few days. I don't like Spargo keeping eyes on her while she's in the harbor."

He led her down a particular pier and at the end, he pointed to a ship at anchor. Its sails were all furled, of course, and it wasn't a very large ship. But Poppy liked it.

"She's very elegant, isn't she? Not showy, I mean. But you get the sense that she can glide through the roughest seas and still be whole. And I assume she's dear to you."

"Very."

"It must be wonderful to be aboard and go wherever you please. Just knowing that you have all that power in your control."

"It's not so much control as understanding."

"You mean you know how she'll behave when the wind acts up?"

"Exactly."

"I wish I could step onto the deck," Poppy said wistfully. "I've never been sailing."

"Well, I happen to know the captain," Carlos teased. "I imagine you could get an invitation…if you ask nicely."

Poppy laughed. "Someday, maybe. But it would have to be a whole party of people to make it permissible for a lady to be aboard. And that would spoil things."

"Would it?"

"I wish that I could experience sailing for the first time without a lot of people watching and asking how I feel about it. I'd rather just…feel it." She sighed. "Never mind. I'm not making any sense."

"No, I understood. Some of my most peaceful moments are when I'm at the helm, alone at night, steering by the stars. The world becomes very simple at times like those."

Poppy turned to him, smiling. When she was caught his gaze, she forgot exactly what she meant to say.

There was a beat of silence—only them, standing at the edge of the world.

Then Poppy heard a shout from a nearby ship, and the whinny of horses on the quay, and the screech of seagulls overhead. The moment was broken.

"I suppose I should be heading back to the inn," she said. "And I've one more errand to do."

"Fine day," Carlos remarked, with a side glance at Poppy. "Let's walk slowly."

Carlos offered his arm, and Poppy took it. The couple walked down the pier to solid ground. The wind was brisk, and even though it was high summer, Poppy was glad for her wrap.

It was a short enough journey to the top of the hill, and Poppy was delighted when she looked back over the harbor and saw the bustle along the beach and the docks. The waters of the Channel sparkled in the distance.

"There are so many ships!" she commented. "I would not have guessed it could be so busy."

"Most of the fishing boats are coming in now. The fishermen leave before dawn to get to the best spots. Their nets ought to be full."

"Of course you would know about the schedule of all the boats," she said. "It's just part of life on the water."

"I've fished for my own supper more than once," he said. "I've learned a few things."

"And have you learned if a sloop with red and white flags has been spotted nearby?"

He shot her an approving look. "I haven't…though not ‑ for lack of trying."

"Is that why you came to town? To find that smuggler and look over all the ships?"

"Well, I also met the local magistrate today."

"Indeed! And what did he say?" asked Poppy. "Had he heard of the operation before?"

"Despite the news I brought him about the opium, he doesn't seem especially inclined to aid my inquiry."

"You mean the magistrate wouldn't offer men to retrieve the crates? Or even to help keep watch?"

Carlos grimaced. "From his behavior, I'd guess the magistrate is in the employ of the smugglers themselves. At the very least, he's paid to look the other way."

"That's appalling."

"It's not unusual." He looked resigned. "He all but warned me to stay away completely, lest the smugglers teach me a lesson."

"What would they dare do to you?"

"The smugglers? At worst, kill me and let the fish eat my corpse."

"You don't sound nearly as perturbed by that notion as I am myself."

He smiled at her. "Don't worry. I have no intention of letting it go so far."

"But you do intend to pursue it?"

"I have to." Carlos briefly explained his theory that the opium was diverted from its intended use for soldiers. "I think someone at the house is part of the scheme. A signal must have been sent to alert the smugglers, and Pencliff House is the best place to send it from."

"What sort of signal?"

"I'm not sure. Maybe a flag flown at a certain time of day, or…I don't know…"

"Or a light in a certain room?"

"What makes you say that?"

Poppy thought back. "When we reached the top of the stairs, I noticed a bright flash in one of the upper windows."

"So did I, but getting you back into the house unseen took precedence." He wasn't surprised that Poppy had registered the light, or that she was now wondering if it could be a signal. She had the sort of mind that put pieces together very quickly…usually so she could make a sharp remark.

"I was rather distracted at the time, so I didn't say anything," she admitted. "And of course, it may be a co-incidence..."

"No. The timing is too perfect," he said. "I could watch the house from the outside myself over the coming nights."

"Sleepless work," Poppy noted.

He nodded. "And it's difficult to watch for a signal when one has no idea when the signal will occur or what it might be."

"Why not ask Miss Ainsworth?" Poppy said suddenly.

Carlos was surprised. "Her father's definitely involved in the smuggling trade, but why would *she* know anything?"

"Oh, she's quite aware of who in town sells goods that came in free of duties. She all but rubbed my nose in her superior knowledge this morning. And you'll notice she wears outfits made in Paris, which should be impossible to purchase legally."

"She may purchase contraband goods, but that doesn't make her complicit in this particular scheme," said Carlos. "It's a long way from lace to opium."

"Why do you defend her?"

"Why are you so keen to condemn her?"

Poppy shut her mouth, too embarrassed to admit the reason she disliked Blanche. "I only point out whoever it is must have a reason. It's not random."

"For now, let's focus on the method. Last night, it was cloudy. The moon was hidden," he said. "The weather must factor in."

"Isn't there such a thing as a smugglers' moon?" Poppy asked hesitantly.

He nodded. "Of course. It's a bright, full moon...so

the smugglers can work without lights to give them away."

"I should have thought the opposite. A dark night, so no one can see them."

"Not here. They have little to fear in this part of the country."

"They ought to," she said, heat in her voice. "I hate the idea of diverting supplies needed for soldiers! It's selfish, and it's petty."

He smiled at her. "I always remembered how fierce you are."

"I thought that's what drove you halfway around the world. I'm sure if you knew I was coming to Cornwall, you'd have stayed on Hispaniola."

Carlos paused, then took a breath. "Look, I didn't want to tell you this...but I'm not in Cornwall by coincidence. And it isn't exactly the family's business that brought me here."

"Oh, you're not also shipping some items that perhaps you're not informing Customs about?" she asked archly.

"True, the de la Guerra family has a liberal attitude toward taxes and duties. If goods can be bought or sold without the oversight of the Customs agents...well, that saves everyone a bit of money, doesn't it? But no, that's not what brings me here."

"Then what?" Poppy sensed the seriousness in his tone.

Before he could answer, they heard their names called out.

"Why, we meet again, Miss St George, and now you have Mr. de la Guerra to escort you. What luck!" Hobbson said, walking up to them. "Did you both meet down at the harbor?"

"Yes, just now," Carlos said easily.

"I'm so glad we ran into you. As it turns out, Miss Ainsworth turned her ankle on a cobblestone, and can't walk. She's at the Seven Sisters now. She was adamant that she'd wait for you to take her back in the gig, but I think we should take her right now. I say, Mr. de La Guerra, should you mind awfully if we asked you to see Miss St George and the Metcalfe sisters safely back in the coach we used this morning?"

"But what about the gig? Surely all three of you can't fit."

"Certainly not! We're hiring that young Mr. Kellow to drive us back. The gig can stay in town until one of the servants picks it up."

"If you're sure…" Poppy said.

"Oh, don't you worry about us, Miss Poppy. Just enjoy the day."

"I will certainly see that everyone returns safely," Carlos said, with a little bow.

"Capital! We'll see you back at the house for dinner." Smiling, the Hobbsons strolled off. They looked quite content with Carlos's shepherding of Poppy, so she supposed it was all right for him to escort her about town.

"Well, that solves a problem," Carlos said softly.

"I'm guessing Blanche would prefer your company to the Hobbsons," she observed, secretly elated.

"We don't always get what we want. A fine lesson for a young lady to learn."

They walked from one end of town to the other (it wasn't exactly a metropolis). Poppy picked up her new slippers at the cobbler, vowing that this pair would remain clean and wearable for more than a day. When they passed Bower Lane, Carlos pointed to a particular house. "That's where the magistrate…magistrates. I'm actually quite annoyed by how that went." He certainly sounded annoyed, and coming from a man who usually acted as though nothing fazed him at all, Poppy guessed that he was understating his frustration.

"You could simply leave it," she said hesitantly. "I know you're curious—I certainly am—but if you were warned away, there must be a reason."

"I didn't come all this way to give up," he almost growled.

Poppy recalled his earlier, interrupted statement—that he hadn't come to Cornwall by chance. It was none of her business, but she took a deep breath and asked in a quiet tone, "Why *are* you here?"

He glanced at her, his expression suddenly shifting to blank. "I can't tell you."

"Can't? Who set that rule?"

"I did."

"You can trust me."

"It's not a question of trust. I don't want you involved."

Poppy bit back a snappish reply. She felt thoroughly reprimanded, and not a little hurt.

"Let's talk about other things," he said. "How is your cousin?"

"Rose is doing wonderfully. Marriage suits her, and she's been able to hold all sorts of musical events in town. Not now, of course…she and Lord Norbury left for the country at the start of summer. I've never been to his family estate, but I assume it's lovely."

"It's very grand," Carlos agreed. "I've spent some time there myself. I'm glad it all worked out…with your cousin and Adrian, I mean. They both deserve to be happy."

He sounded a little wistful.

"Everyone deserves to be happy," Poppy said. "Even

you."

Carlos actually laughed at that, and she was glad to have pulled him out of the mood he'd fallen into.

Poppy and Carlos had just reached the Seven Sisters and requested for the carriage to be brought from the stables when they saw Elowen and Elisa approaching from the other end of the street. Poppy waved to them, and Carlos dutifully came to a halt.

"Ready to return to Pencliff?" he said. "The Hobbsons took Miss Ainsworth back already."

"Good," Elowen muttered under her breath, obviously delighted they wouldn't have to share the carriage with her. "I bought a few items and had them delivered to the inn. Just let me gather them."

Elowen had just turned to pick up the package when a man emerged from the inn's front door. He was talking over his shoulder to someone still inside. That meant he wasn't looking where he was going, and he collided head-long into Elowen, who fell to the ground in a heap.

"Elly!" Elisa cried out in alarm.

The man had barely managed to not fall himself, and he looked deeply embarrassed. "Oh, my word, I am so sorry, miss. My fault entirely! Let me help you up. I wasn't…looking…" His flow of words stopped short as he reached out to help Elowen up, and he finally saw the person he'd knocked over.

Evidently, it was his first time ever seeing a young woman, because he stared at her like she was some rare creature from afar. His jaw dropped open, and he went completely still.

In turn, Elowen's eyes were wide as her hand remained in his, waiting for the offered assistance that didn't come. Her dark, lustrous hair had come a bit loose, curls falling winsomely about her face and slipping out from under her hat. Two spots of pink bloomed on her cheeks, and she let out a breathy little sigh.

The tableau held for another instant (though it seemed like a century). Then Carlos stepped in, tapped the man on the shoulder, and very discreetly suggested that it might be better to get the girl on her feet.

To his credit, the other man snapped to attention then, and quickly helped Elowen up. The two ended up face to face, their eyes still locked.

"My sincere apologies, miss," he said again.

"Oh, it was of no moment," she replied, unaware of the fact that her gown was now stained with dust and dirt all along the back side. "I was just about to return home with my sister, anyway." Unconsciously, she reached for Elisa's hand.

"No, I must beg your forgiveness after I was so clumsy. What must you think of Treversey, miss, if I were to be rude as well as clumsy."

"I think Treversey is a very wonderful town, sir," Elowen said, rather shyly.

"Oh! Where is my mind! Riding Officer Oliver Lowry at your service!" he responded eagerly, bowing over her hand.

The two stared at each other, smiling.

Poppy finally could stand it no longer. "Mr. Lowry, may I introduce you to my good friend, *Miss* Elowen Metcalfe." No sense in being subtle at this point.

"How do you do, Miss Metcalfe," he said.

"How do you do, Mr. Lowry," she whispered back.

More staring.

"And her sister Miss Elisa," Poppy continued.

Lowry turned to Elisa and bowed politely over her hand as well. "Such a pleasure, Miss Elisa." He smiled at her, and Elisa beamed back at him with that sweet expression she often wore.

"It's nice to meet nice people," she said. "No matter how it happens."

Lowry's smile widened further and he said, sounding delighted, "*Very* well stated, Miss Elisa!"

"Well," Poppy said. "I fear we must return to Pencliff Towers, where we are all staying for the summer. Perhaps we will have the good fortune to run into you again, Mr. Lowry."

"I do hope so," he said.

The driver wheeled the carriage up then, and Officer Lowry jumped into action. "Oh, allow me!" The young officer immediately offered a hand to help first Elisa, then Elowen into the coach.

"Thank you, sir," Elowen said once everyone had boarded (Carlos helped Poppy in, which was good, since she'd grow old waiting for Lowry to tear his worshipful gaze away from Elowen).

"Thank *you*," he echoed, as the coach drove away.

On the ride back, Elowen had a dreamy expression on her face, until Elisa asked, "Are you going to marry him?"

Elowen sat bolt upright. "Elisa! I don't even know him!"

"I think you should marry him," Elisa reiterated.

"There's usually more to the process," Poppy said. "Though I do have to say he seemed…"

"Struck," Carlos supplied, with a sly grin. He and Poppy shared the backward facing seat, since she didn't want to crowd the sisters (and she wanted to see Elowen's face).

"I was trying to avoid a pun."

"No avoiding that one. One couldn't have asked for a more direct meeting."

"Just think," Poppy told Elowen. "If we'd talked a

little less, we'd have been in that carriage before he ever came out of the inn, and you'd never have met him at all."

"Oh, *no*," Elowen breathed in dismay.

"But since you have, I suppose we can come up with reasons to return to town. You think he was with the navy? I didn't recognize the uniform he wore."

"He's a Customs agent," Carlos informed them. "Riding officers patrol a section of the coastline. He must be rather a new one, judging by the crispness of his uniform."

"Hmmm." Poppy wondered if the young, impressionable Lowry was representative of the agents in Cornwall—he didn't seem like the sort to intimidate a smuggler.

They reached Pencliff Towers and Elowen floated off toward the house, her sister in tow.

"Damn," Carlos murmured after Elowen was out of earshot. "I don't think I've ever before witnessed two people falling in love so instantly. Do you think they have a chance?"

"There's a lot more to love than gazing into each other's eyes," Poppy said. "Though they do seem to have *that* part sorted."

"It's never simple," he agreed.

"He'll have a family to convince. And she and her sister don't live here. And there's a dowry to be thought of…"

"You are the opposite of a romantic, Miss St George."

"Someone has to keep their feet on the ground."

But as they approached the house, his mood became serious again. Carlos said, "I'm going back down to the beach. I intend to retrieve some of the opium as evidence. That deputy seemed willing enough, but for all I know the magistrate told him not to go the instant I left."

"Is it wise for you to go?" she asked, worried.

"It's still daylight. If I see anyone, I'll make myself scarce."

"What should I do if you don't come back?"

Carlos smiled wryly. "If I'm not back in an hour, send a note to Norbury."

"Why? So he can avenge your death?"

He got an odd expression on his face for a moment, but then said, "Norbury's not that honor-bound. However, as a viscount, he'll be able to get you back to London and protect you if any of the gang discovers who you are."

She shuddered. "Oh, don't say that."

"Fear not, querida. I have no intention of dying."

"If only it were so simple. Please be careful."

He gave her a mocking salute. "I'll report back as soon as possible, General St George."

After Carlos went down the steps to the beach, Poppy sat on the low stone wall and waited for him to return. She shouldn't be so concerned about him. It was full daylight, and there was no reason to think that he was in danger. But she worried anyway.

"Because I'm an idiot," she muttered. *And perhaps slightly enamored.*

Carlos trudged up the steps about twenty minutes later.

She rose from the wall and walked with him.

"Did you get some?" she asked eagerly. "Will you be able to press the magistrate now?"

"All the crates are gone," he said in a low voice.

"What? All of them? Who could have...?"

"I almost thought I dreamed seeing them, except you saw them too."

"Of course I did! But what does it mean?"

"This is a clever operation. The sailors unloaded the

cargo at midnight last night, and the goods were removed from the caves within half a day."

"Another ship?" she guessed hesitantly.

"Maybe. Though that doesn't make much sense. Why have one ship unload simply so another can take the cargo right away? Wouldn't you simply have the first ship deliver the goods to the final destination?"

"The first ship might not be able to go all the way to wherever the goods are destined," said Poppy.

"That's possible," Carlos said cautiously. "Don't mention anything to anyone, Poppy. And don't ask questions."

"But we could help uncover a crime."

"Let me worry about crime," he told her. "I didn't sail all the way over here just to let you take charge."

Chapter 11

❀ ঞ❀

"EXCUSE ME?" POPPY ASKED COLDLY, her previous worry for him evaporating into irritation at his high-handed words. "I don't recall you being in charge of anything, let alone me. I thought you'd accepted that we were equals in this. Honestly, if I hadn't gone into that cave first, you'd never have seen that contraband at all!"

He seemed to realize that he'd hit a nerve, because he stepped back and put his hands up to quell her. "All I meant was that I want you to be circumspect. We don't know who or what we're dealing with—though I have a few guesses—and it's better to be safe than sorry."

"Says the occasional pirate," she retorted, not at all quelled.

"I'm not a pirate. Pirates take ships. I just handle cargo in enterprising ways. Will you promise me not to do anything rash?"

She glared at him. "I should return to the house. Dinner is in a few hours, and there's so much loafing and lounging to accomplish before then." She turned and started to walk across the lawn.

"You didn't promise," he called to her back.

"Excellent observation!" she snapped over her shoulder at him. The wind caught his hair, and she looked away quickly. Ugh, why did he have to look so good while he was being so overly patronizing?

The house was relatively quiet, as most of the guests were indeed involved in lounging. Poppy avoided the rooms where she might have to converse with anyone and went directly upstairs.

Once in her bedroom, Poppy stared in puzzlement at a gown hanging from the clothes press. It looked very like the gown she'd consigned to the rag bin that morning. But this gown was clean, and it was *red*.

"What is going on?" she murmured.

"Oh, miss, you're back!" a voice spoke behind her.

Poppy whirled to see the maid standing there, jaunty with her uniform and starched white cap. "Millie?"

"Yes, miss, that's right," the maid acknowledged.

"Did you salvage this gown?" Poppy asked, pointing to the item.

"I did my best, miss. Oh, it was too pretty and well made to cut up into rags. I washed it, but couldn't get all the stains out from the hem. But then it happened that Mrs. Biddle was dying a lot of curtains from the parlor— Mrs. Towers wants the whole room to be red—and I asked if I could add the gown to the vat."

"It's *very* red," Poppy declared. "What dye did she use?"

"Beetroot, miss. With alum for mordant. I don't care for the taste of beets myself, but I must say they make a vivid dye. We did all the curtains and they turned out wonderfully. The gown too, though it may smell a bit… beety for a while."

Poppy sniffed. Yes, there was an unmistakable vegetal aroma to the dress. But it looked like new, with the deep, rich color saturating the fabric. "I should have bought some of that Valenciennes lace when I was in town," she murmured. "It would have been perfect against this red."

Then she remembered the white satin ribbon she'd

bought from the slightly shady shopkeeper—had that all been the same day? Amazing.

Poppy knew exactly how to add the ribbon to the newly-red gown. She actually laughed. It would be fun to wear exactly the same gown twice in two evenings, especially because no one would dream that they were the same!

Poppy whipped out her sewing kit and got to work. She looped and tucked and trimmed like a madwoman. Finally, she attached lengths of the ribbon at intervals around the waistline, so the strips fell vertically toward the floor. They'd hide in the folds of the skirt most of the time, but if Poppy walked or turned suddenly, the loose ends would flare out, creating little flashes of white amid the scarlet fabric. Together with her new leather evening slippers, she felt armed for battle...so to speak.

When she left her room, she saw Elowen at the other end of the hall and waited at the stairs so they could walk down together.

"Is Elisa not joining us for dinner?" Poppy asked.

"She's tired and wants to lie down. The maid has already brought her dinner up, so no need to worry about her starving."

"Did the tray include dessert? If not, I shall have to smuggle some up to Elisa's room."

Elowen's eyes went wide for a second, but then she smiled. "How thoughtful of you! But as it happens, the tray included a very tasty lemon pudding."

That evening, dinner went off without any fireworks. Possibly because over half the guests had spent a day in town, the mood was sedate.

"Well, after Treversey today, what are everyone's plans for tomorrow?" Mrs. Towers asked the group.

"I thought I might go walking along St. Mark's Head,"

Poppy volunteered, "if the weather holds."

"Be very alert if you do, Miss Poppy," Mr. Towers said. "It can go from blue sky to storms within an hour."

Poppy appreciated that the Towers didn't try to discourage her from going at all.

Elowen was distracted during the meal, needing most people to repeat what they said, and offering answers that didn't quite make sense. Poppy hid her smile, thinking that Elowen must have been hit by not one of Cupid's arrows, but half a dozen.

After the meal, the ladies proceeded to the drawing room, as usual. The gentlemen followed after a short while. Tonight, Mrs. Towers insisted on some entertainment, so Blanche played the pianoforte with tolerable skill. Or perhaps more than tolerable—Poppy was used to listening to her cousin Rosalind play, and Rose was an incredibly gifted musician. Still, she couldn't help glancing at Carlos, who sat in a chair on the other side of the audience. Was he impressed by the perhaps more than tolerable Blanche?

He seemed attentive, but then he caught her eye and gave her a tiny, secret smile that sent heat up her spine.

After Blanche curtseyed and took her seat, the Hobbsons stood up. To Poppy's surprise, they performed a scene from Shakespeare, a rousing dialogue between Oberon and Titania in *A Midsummer Night's Dream*. They gave it their all, and the effect was unexpectedly moving. Poppy applauded enthusiastically at the conclusion.

"Thank you, thank you," Mr. Hobbson said. "A little hobby of ours."

"Sometimes," his wife added, "I envy those women who have made a career on the stage."

Mrs. Ainsworth gasped, looking scandalized. "Don't mention actresses when proper ladies are present!"

"Oh, I'm not advocating any of our young friends choose that path," Mrs. Hobbson said, not at all put out. "I'm just saying that there must be a certain thrill to performing for an adoring audience."

"Well, I adored your performance," Poppy declared, not looking at Mrs. Ainsworth.

Then Mrs. Towers recited a poem—which could have been deadly, but she was a consummate orator and knew how to bring forth the humor in the piece.

After the performances all concluded, Carlos approached Poppy.

"Truce?" he asked softly.

"Were we at war?"

"I don't think we left things in a particularly peaceful place." He sighed. "I'm sorry if I came across as demanding before. I'm just concerned about the whole situation."

Poppy nodded. "I know. So let's agree that we'll both be careful then."

"Fair. Since I've got you talking to me again, I was wondering," Carlos said, "about Mr. Towers. How did he buy this place? If he's just a retired barrister, as you say."

"Oh, *he's* just a barrister," Poppy told him, "but Mrs. Towers was born the only daughter of an earl...an earl who happened to have tin mines on his lands."

"Really."

"Yes, she was born Lady Candice Morse, and she was an heiress of the first order, expected to make the match of the century. However, apparently she turned down dozens of proposals from men who personally knew the king, only to turn around and marry a lawyer, gaining the humble title of Mrs. Towers."

"Lucky man."

"I'd say lucky woman...to have made her own choice."

Chapter 12

❀❧❀

IT WAS LATE, BUT CARLOS couldn't sleep. The evening entertainment was over and the guests all drifted off to bed. He'd already taken two evening strolls around the grounds as an excuse to watch for ships, though he hadn't seen anything of note (just a frigate off in the distance, clearly aiming to make the harbor at Treversey).

He could go out again. Sneaking around a house in the small hours wasn't exactly model behavior, but he was a man and no one would blink at it. They'd probably assume he was heading to find some female companionship, which actually suited him just fine. As long as no one realized how interested he was in the local smuggling operations, they were free to assume whatever they liked. Restless, he shrugged into his darkest-colored jacket and opened his door, ready to patrol the outside of the house once more.

Just then, a shadow moved in the far corner of the hallway. He jumped, reaching for the knife he kept hidden beneath his jacket.

But before he could draw it, the shadow moved again, and he saw the sleek shape of Poppy's cat emerge, a dead mouse in her jaws.

"Ah. You've been hunting," he said to the cat.

Miss Mist stared at him, unimpressed. *Just like her*

owner, he thought. Then she walked right past him and into his room, where she deposited the dead mouse on the floor near the bed.

"Why, thank you for the gift," he told the cat. "But isn't that something you ought to save for your mistress?"

The cat mewed, then apparently decided she was hungry. Carlos was glad—he didn't really want to handle mouse disposal on top of everything else.

"You can stay here if you like," he said, bending down to pet the now-fed cat, who began to purr delightedly. "But I've got some smugglers to stalk."

He heard something else, and he stilled, listening.

"Miss Mist," a voice called softly. "Mistress Mist, where are you?"

Poppy. What the hell. Carlos jerked the door open and glared at the figure, no longer in her red gown from dinner, but in a much filmier concoction that he didn't think was meant for him to see. Which didn't mean he wasn't looking.

"What are you doing here?" he demanded.

Poppy jumped in surprise. "Why are you awake?"

"Why are you wandering the halls at two in the morning? You're going to get into trouble, Poppy."

"Miss Mist is missing."

Just then, Miss Mist appeared, meowing loudly at her owner as she sashayed into the hallway.

"She's a cat," Carlos pointed out. "Cats are nocturnal. She's supposed to be out on the prowl. You, however, are not."

Then there was a creak of floorboards, and fast footsteps. One of the other guests heard the noises and was coming to investigate. Carlos reached out and pulled Poppy inside his room, shutting the door silently. He kept one hand on the door and the other on the wall, with Poppy between them, her back flat to the wall, fury on her face.

"Who's out there?" a voice called, sounding grumpy and sleepy.

Carlos glared at her, warning her to silence. But Poppy was no fool, and she knew very well what would happen if she were caught in a man's room in the middle of the night.

"Someone's out there," the voice continued. Carlos recognized it now as Ainsworth. "Come out, or I'll set all the servants on you!"

Poppy's eyes were wide, the fury replaced with fear.

"Don't worry," Carlos breathed. "He won't dare open any doors."

"If the house is roused, everyone will know I'm not in my bedroom!" she murmured back.

Damn. That was a good point, he thought.

Ainsworth stepped into the hall with heavy treads. A yowl followed.

"Ugh. That cat! Get away, filthy thing!" Ainsworth must have stepped toward Miss Mist, who let out a hiss and another yowl before dashing away. He grunted, and a moment later the door closed again.

Poppy exhaled. "That was nearly a scandal. I should go."

"Wait a few minutes. He's still awake and he might hear you walk by. Let him fall asleep again."

He drew her away from the door so their voices wouldn't carry into the hall.

Poppy frowned at him. "I appreciate that you let me hide in here, but don't think this means anything has changed. I'm still very put out with you for that whole year of silence."

And here he'd thought he'd made a lot of progress when they were together in town that day. "Do you despise me?"

"Yes! No. A little."

"Well, we have a few moments. Perhaps you can let me explain."

"Explain why you vanished for a year?"

"I didn't vanish, I just had to leave London. Believe me, it wasn't planned. I really did want to see you again."

"Would it have killed you to send some message? Dear Poppy, gone to sail the seven seas. Back next year."

"*Dear Poppy* would have been much too familiar," he objected, despite the fact that the woman in question was currently in his own bedroom in her nightclothes.

"At least I would have known! I honestly thought you might have been dead."

"You did?"

"Yes! Until Lord Norbury mentioned that he'd heard from you. When was that? November? Who knows. The point is that you decided I wasn't worth your attention."

"I did not decide anything like that. Events…happened."

"Oh, *events happened*, did they? Now there's an explanation any woman would wait a year for."

"Poppy, it's complicated."

"And I'm too simple to understand it?"

"That's not what I meant."

"What do you mean, then? I don't understand you. At all."

"My time and my life isn't my own. Not fully."

She crossed her arms. "Well, I do understand *that*. Women's lives are entirely given over to others. First parents, and then husbands. But you're a man."

Thank God she'd noticed. "I still owe a lot to my family. They depend on me for a good amount of work with shipping goods. That keeps me busy enough. On top of that, I do what I can for Santo Domingo."

"Again, any woman would grasp the desire for self-rule instantly."

"Don't do that."

"Do what?"

"Compare my entire island's struggles to your annoyance that women aren't free to visit coffeehouses alone."

"Oh, please. As if the two are different."

"They are!"

"In scale. Not in essence. Everyone should have the right and power to make their own decisions about their lives, so long as they hurt no one else. You want your society in Santo Domingo to be fair. I wish the same for mine in England. In fact, I bet I'm more revolutionary than you are."

"Excuse me?"

"Well, let's imagine that your effort succeeds. Santo Domingo gains its own authority, like the United States did before. Other nations recognize your flag and offer it the same respect as any other."

"Yes, that's the goal."

"And what of the women? Will their lives become any freer when the French and British leave? Will the laws change to give them rights to inheritance? Property? To stand up for themselves in a court of law? Or is your great revolution just a way to keep everyone's taxes and tariffs on your side of the Atlantic?"

Carlos could not believe Poppy just told him he was only half a revolutionary. "You think I'm doing all this for money? That I fought battles and lost friends and took a bullet just to send the family's taxes to a local office?"

Her eyes widened. "You took a bullet?"

"Yes. In my side. Two years ago. I'm fully recovered, by the way. Thank you for asking."

"How many friends?"

"What?"

"How many friends have you lost?"

"Too many. And I'll lose more before this is over. My brother Mateo…"

"Oh, my God, your brother?" she asked, horror in her tone.

"Not by blood, but Mateo and I grew up together, and we were as close as any family. He was killed less than two months ago."

"I'm so sorry, Carlos." Poppy's expression softened. "I'd be a wreck if I lost Rose."

"He wasn't just a casualty in a battle. He was murdered. And not back in Santo Domingo. It happened here in Cornwall."

She paused, taking that in. "That's why you're here! You refused to tell me before, but that's it, isn't it? You're here to find out what happened."

"Exactly. I know a little, but I need to find his killer. His sister asked me to, and I promised her I would."

"What will you do if you find him?"

"See that he's punished for it."

"Not through the law," she guessed.

"We'll see."

"You don't live quietly, do you," she said, with a sad smile.

"I live the life I was given." God, what was happening? He had Poppy alone in his room in the middle of the night, and they were arguing about war and philosophy?

"Well, tell me how I can help," she said then.

"What?"

"I'm here all summer because I was lonely and miserable in London. Here I can help you do something important."

"Poppy, I'm looking for a murderer. This isn't a game."

"I'm not asking you to arm me with a gun," she objected. "I meant that I can keep my eyes open."

He wanted to wrap her up and put her on the next coach back to London. "You need to stay out of this. Smugglers won't treat you like a lady. They'll kill you without a second thought."

"He was killed by smugglers," she said, enlightened. "So that's what you were so interested in those caves down below, and the opium shipment! Do you think the smugglers from last night are connected to your friend's death?"

"I don't know," he told her. "Based on the nature of the men I met today, I wouldn't be surprised. But you need to stay out of it. Tell me you won't go down there again, and that you'll keep your mouth shut."

"I'll keep my mouth shut about what you're up to, but I won't promise not to go to the beach. You're not my minder."

"You need a minder," he grumbled. "Or shackles."

She raised an eyebrow. "So you won't be supporting the emancipation of women, then."

"I'm supporting the cause of you not getting hurt or killed because you got bored on a summer's night."

"I'm not bored now."

Neither was he. Sparring with Poppy would keep him awake for hours. Though he could think of a few other things to do with her as well...also not boring.

"Poppy," he said then. "I do apologize for disappearing on you for a year."

"Te perdono."

She forgave him? He blinked. "How do you know how to say that?"

"I studied."

"You learned Spanish? When?"

"This past year. It's not that difficult, especially since I had French and some Latin when I was at Wildwood. The accent is the hardest part for me. My first instructor was a lady from Madrid, but then she left and I hired someone else who had grown up in Caracas. And it sounded completely different."

"Why?"

"Well, I'd imagine because the accent and mode of speech developed in isolation."

"No, why learn Spanish!" Was she trying to be maddening? (No, she didn't have to try.)

"Oh. At first, it was because I wanted to talk to you. I thought it would be nice to be able to greet you in Spanish when I saw you again. But then I didn't see you again. Or hear from you. Or hear *of* you. So I decided to learn several additional words and phrases to tell you what I thought of your behavior."

"Don't think I want to know what those are."

"I had to pay the lady from Caracas extra to teach them to me. She was quite shocked I wanted to know."

Then something occurred to him. "Wait. You understood what I was saying on the beach last night!" When he said some things he definitely would *not* have said if he thought she'd actually know what he was feeling.

"I got the gist."

"Poppy, you…*deceived* me."

"You underestimated me."

"So I did." He wouldn't make that mistake again. He pulled her close and kissed her.

Poppy let out one tiny indignant squeak, which nearly made him laugh out loud, except then she was kissing him back, and he had no time to be amused, because he was too busy being aroused.

She had a sharp tongue when in public, but she had very soft lips when in private. He grazed one thumb along her lower lip, just to make sure, and got a soft, startled *Carlos* for his trouble. And it turned out that he loved to hear his name from her mouth like that. He deepened the kiss, exploring how she reacted to his tongue.

She moaned and wrapped her hands around his shoulders, which he took to mean she liked it. Then she slipped her own tongue over his, and he forgot how to breathe for a second. He couldn't remember ever being so aroused by a simple kiss.

What would happen when they actually slept together? The possibilities excited him beyond reason.

When he broke off the kiss (mostly to get his breath back), her eyes were still closed, and she had a soft, dreamy, decidedly un-Poppyish expression on her face. She looked almost...gentle.

"Why'd you do that?" she asked.

"I decided a year was long enough to wait, and what would people say if they knew I had this enchanting woman in my room and I didn't even try to seduce her?"

"Ah, so you're protecting your reputation by ruining mine." (Now that phrasing was more Poppyish. But also, she didn't sound *that* upset).

"I'm not ruining it," he promised. "No one will know you were here. You've got a gift for sneaking about in the dark."

"Thank you."

"You're welcome." His hand found the tie that fastened the outer layer of her dressing gown, and he pulled at it until it came loose. Underneath she wore a chemise that barely covered her up. The fabric was so thin he could see enough of her figure to raise his own temperature.

"You could have asked first," she noted, not trying to pull the top layer back over her body.

"Fine. Can I undress you?" he asked.

"No, of course not. But you can kiss me again."

He didn't have to be told twice.

Poppy responded with enough heat that he wanted to keep her there till dawn. He didn't exactly plan to pin her against the wall and kiss her senseless, but that's what was happening a few moments later. He felt her lips on his throat and heard her saying something about what a very bad idea this was, and how she didn't even like him, but how she was doing it anyway.

It would be very easy to see just how far her curiosity would take them.

But, dogged by a very annoying sense of responsibility, he told her, "I should make you leave now."

"Or what?"

"Or I *will* ruin you. And I'm fairly sure you'd hate me afterward."

"Would I hate you during?"

Christ. Was she trying to get thrown across the bed?

"No," he said. "But that also isn't going to happen. Not tonight, anyway."

"Really." Poppy looked intrigued.

"I'll see you tomorrow, Poppy. And can I suggest that you finally wear a different dress to dinner?"

"What?"

"You wore the same gown you had on the first night, when I followed you to the beach. Dying it red was a very good way to hide the damage. And all those ribbony things to make it look different."

"It was the maid's idea to dye it red," she said faintly. "I can't believe you noticed that it was the same outfit."

"It's the neckline. I was staring at you for hours both evenings, Poppy. Believe when I say I know exactly how much of you I can see, and how much that stupid dress hides."

"You do?"

"Sálvame. I do, and it's distracting." He opened the door, checking the hallway for people before saying in a low voice, "Please get out of here, Poppy."

She gave him a look of profound exasperation, and slid past him to the hall.

After she left, it took him a very long time to calm down from their too-short encounter. A century ago, when Carlos would have been classified as a pure pirate, he'd have just scooped her up and taken her directly to his ship to keep her as his mistress. (Pirates had an enviable lack of morals that seemed especially attractive just now.) Alas, the world had changed and he had been raised with a strict sense of honor. Stealing women just wasn't acceptable.

And even if he stole Poppy, within a week she'd probably stir up a mutiny and seize his ship for herself.

Christ, he could fall in love with her if he wasn't careful.

Chapter 13

CARLOS —

Well, have you solved your Poppy problem yet? Rose knows she's there (her cousin wrote to her as fast as you wrote to me—the letters arrived in the same post). She is pestering me for details, and I have none to give. I don't know what you're planning, but as a friend, I'd counsel you to give up on vengeance and simply try to win the lady back. Trust me, it's better to have a future you can look forward to than a past you just want to forget. I'd know.

But why do I waste ink on this advice? You won't stop till you get justice—woe to anyone who hurts someone that de la Guerra calls friend. Just don't be an idiot. I'd hate to have to write to your family with the news that you're coming home in a box.

Write when you can, for Rose's sake if not mine.

—Adrian

Though it had arrived yesterday evening, Carlos read over the letter once again in the early hours of the morning, thinking of all that had happened since he first received it. No one could say that his life was dull at the moment.

He'd have to think before responding to that letter, mostly because he was going to ignore Adrian's advice completely today. He intended to dig deeper into the world of smugglers and murders, instead of pursuing Poppy.

It's better to leave her alone, he told himself. Especially after last night, when he learned that having Poppy close led to him making very impulsive decisions and looking for excuses to see her again.

No. He had one reason to be in Cornwall, and it wasn't (sadly) the fiery Poppy St George.

The sun hadn't even crested the horizon when Carlos rode one of the horses out of the stable towards town. On his own, he made the journey in half the time it took for a carriage laden with people. As he approached Treversey, only a few people were moving about the streets, and nearly all the stores were shuttered. He rode to Seven Sisters and left the horse there, then walked away from the high street to a place where the road ended abruptly at a promontory overlooking the Channel, one of countless vistas in the area.

Carlos had arranged to meet his first mate Valentin there, to get the full report on Spargo and anything else he gathered.

Valentin was waiting, looking somewhat nervous until he saw Carlos approach.

"Thank God," he said in Spanish. "I was worried something had happened to you."

"I'm all in one piece, for now," Carlos replied, keeping to Spanish, just in case anyone was close enough to be curious about their conversation. "Did you meet with Spargo?"

"Yes. What an ass. He runs smugglers in one tiny

town and he thinks he's king of the world."

"That was my impression too," Carlos agreed. "But he does seem to be the man to go to when it comes to smuggling. So what did you find out?"

"He wants to sell you arms. He claims he's got good rifles bought from some German sellers, for one of their endless little skirmishes."

"Mateo bought rifles from his contact," Carlos mused.

Valentin went on, "Of course he had a story for why they ended up in Cornwall for a cheap price, but I let him know that I didn't care."

Valentin was a gentle soul who regretted it every time he had to kill a wasp. However, he was also one of those people who just happened to look like the typical newspaper depictions of a murderer. He'd lost an eye in a fight years ago, and a few fingers to mistimed cannonfire, and he was an expert when it came to scowling. Carlos had every confidence that Valentin convinced Spargo that he was a bloodthirsty bastard happy to buy guns off dead men if the price was right.

"Did you get a look at the guns?"

"He showed a sample," Valentin said. "Assuming the others are in as good a condition, it's a legitimate offer."

"How much?"

"Why? Are you really going to buy them?"

"I can think of a good place to use them," Carlos replied, thinking of the continually undersupplied revolutionaries back home.

"It's up to you, captain, but I'd definitely insist on looking at every last one before committing. Spargo has the soul of a swindler."

Carlos nodded. "Still, let's continue to negotiate—or pretend to—so we can learn more about his operation. Did he mention the caves on the Pencliff Towers beach?"

"Not in specific, but he hinted that he's got several spots that are well away from any Customs oversight. Oh, and by the way, I asked about opium."

"What? I told you to be subtle."

Valentin rolled his one good eye. "I *was* subtle. I told him that my captain was always willing to discuss the shipment of alcohol, tobacco, khat, or any drug that users get desperate for. Coming or going. Spargo did get interested when I mentioned that we can pick up tobacco from the Carolinas to bring to England."

"And what did he say about selling drugs to us?"

"Said he'd ask around. I wouldn't be surprised if some portion of that opium got resold to you, at a steep price." Valentin paused. "For what it's worth, I'd believe he killed your friend. He's the type. He hinted that he's eliminated what he called 'bad business partners' to keep the law off his back."

Carlos grunted, thinking. He needed more evidence of Spargo's guilt for killing Mateo before he could take revenge. But he agreed with Valentin. All the signs pointed that way.

"Good work," he said at last, standing up. "Keep the *Agustina* out of sight for the next few days, but stay in the area. I'll get word to you if I need help."

"You'd better," Valentin said. "Oh, one more thing."

He handed Carlos a folded sheet of paper. "The crew has been asking around—carefully—about Mateo. Ramon ran into a drunkard who does occasional owling for Spargo. He didn't know anything about Mateo in particular since he hasn't worked for a few months. But he told Ramon about a place where Spargo takes bodies and other inconvenient items to hide before he gets rid of them completely. Not sure if the man was just spinning a story, but he drew a map for it."

Carlos looked over the crude drawing of the shoreline rendered in charcoal. He put a finger where he knew Pencliff Towers to be, then traced along the line, around the great mass of the headland that stood between the house and the town of Treversey. On the other side of the headland, the creator had marked a location with a star.

"He said there's a small sand beach there, and a sort of grotto with a very high ceiling, so high that a fishing boat or small sloop could shelter there in a storm. But he says that if you find the spot, there's an entrance to the cave network below the headland, and it's in one of those caves that Spargo keeps the nastier of his souvenirs."

"I'll go now and see what I can find," Carlos said. "Better to do it in daylight."

"Hope you find something. The sooner we finish this business, the sooner we can get the hell out of English waters. Good luck...and watch your back."

After giving Valentin some final instructions, Carlos returned to the inn for his horse and rode back toward Pencliff Towers at a leisurely pace, keeping to the paths closest to the water. As he rode, he kept one eye out to sea to watch for ships, and in particular, the ship that unloaded the opium the other night.

He slowly, methodically made his way toward the cove marked on the map. Along the way, he wondered if his quest for vengeance was turning him a little mad. Not that he'd give up—giving up wasn't in his nature. But one man against a whole smuggling gang, plus the ineffectual and probably corrupt officials of the British Empire...

"Just buy the guns and sail back to Santo Domingo," he muttered. "At least some good will come of this."

After all, would Ximena truly feel better if she was told that the man who killed her brother was dead? Mateo wasn't coming back, no matter what. Ximena would have to face the rest of her life regardless.

Then he touched the cross at his neck, exhaling slowly. Of course it mattered. He gave his word to Ximena, and he kept his word. He'd fight the whole world alone if he had to.

You're not alone.

The thought came to him all at once, and it did not feel like his own voice.

He tapped the cross once more, murmuring a thank you to Mateo's spirit for bolstering him.

Of course he was not alone. He had his crew, the finest crew anyone could ask for. He had friends in England and Hispaniola, if he needed help. And of course, he had the entirely unnecessary and thoroughly irritating assistance from Poppy St George, who had absolutely no reason to take up any pursuit against smugglers or pirates or murderers or any other kind of criminal…yet there she was, insisting on joining him to figure out the secret of the opium shipment and the identity of that mysterious ship with the red and white flags.

He should tell her to mind her own business (well, he had told her that, and it had done no good at all). He should write to Adrian and tell him to somehow pluck Poppy out of Cornwall and keep her safe at his estate with Rosalind. Then Carlos wouldn't have to worry about her all the time.

Why the hell hadn't he done that the first day?

Oh, right. Because he liked having Poppy around. He liked how she sparred with him, and pretended to hate him, and how she threw herself headlong into causes that weren't hers just because she had that innate sense of justice some people were born with.

He saw it in her immediately, during the whole fiasco with Adrian and Rose. Poppy defended her cousin and fought for her like a knight because it was the right thing to do.

Damn. He really did need to send her away. He'd take care of the matter as soon as he returned to Pencliff Towers.

While he was thinking on the matter of Poppy, he noticed sails in the corner of his eye. Turning, he saw a ship approaching the shoreline. Squinting, he counted the masts—three, and scanned the shape of the hull. Once the little red and white flags became visible, he didn't even need to see them to know it was the same ship.

And now it was sailing for the very same cove a man had just drawn a map for. Carlos didn't believe in coincidences. It might be divine intervention, or it might be a trap. But he was going to find out what this ship was doing in the cove.

But then he noticed a figure in the far distance, up on the headland looking out to sea.

He knew that figure, and he'd have known it even if it was both foggy and midnight.

Poppy stood on the very edge of the St. Mark's Head cliff, staring through a spyglass at a shipful of criminals who could definitely see her too.

Criminals with a record of killing people who knew too much.

* * * *

Earlier in the morning, Poppy had again announced her intention to explore St. Mark's Head. The other guests around the breakfast table approved of the notion. A few hours of rambling along the beautiful, rugged promontory was just the sort of healthy thing a young lady like Poppy ought to do.

One person *not* at breakfast was Carlos, and Poppy was grateful, because she had no idea how to act around a man after she'd ended up in his bedroom the previous night. She was quite certain that the moment she saw him again, all she'd be able to think about was how it felt to be in his arms.

The cook packed her a picnic lunch and bottle of cider, and Poppy struck out toward the headland, wearing her sturdy walking shoes, a green wool gown, and a short cloak to protect her against any inclement weather.

But from the moment she set off, the sky was summer perfection—cerulean blue, with streamers of white clouds marching west to east. The sun beamed over the whole world, and it would have been hot, except that the brisk sea breeze swept the heat away.

She hiked for a couple of miles, invigorated by the weather and the starkly gorgeous surroundings. From time to time, she saw a boat or ship in the sea. But they were either small fishing boats, or sloops or frigates plying the Channel on ordinary routes. She had to admit that a bright sunny day wasn't exactly ideal for pursuing smugglers.

Just at the edge of the cliff, she stopped, seeing a ship in the distance. Red and white flags…yes, it was the same ship that had dropped off the cargo of opium!

"Now you're back, hmmm?" Poppy whispered. What caused the crew to sail in the daytime?

She took a spyglass she'd borrowed from Mr. Towers out of the leather pack and lifted it up to get a better look. The ship really wasn't so far off, and once Poppy got the spyglass into focus, she could see the figures on deck with startling detail. Crewmen moved from one end to the other on their specific tasks, and a young sailor clambered up a rope ladder with the agility of a monkey. She moved to the bow of the ship and read the name painted there:

Seadragon. Next, she trained her sight on the man at the helm. He was a burly man with black hair and beard, and he called out orders with confidence that he'd be obeyed instantly.

"Mr. Spargo, I presume," she mused out loud. Spargo's face turned into profile, and she realized he was talking to somebody. Eagerly, she shifted her gaze to the other figure. It was a man, about the same age as Spargo, and he also had black hair, though he was clean-shaven and much trimmer. His jacket was a dark cloth—probably linen, Poppy guessed, and quite well made. He did not look like a pirate or a smuggler, though. The contrast between him and Spargo was plain as day.

"Who are you?" Poppy asked out loud, leaning forward and stepping further toward the edge of the land as she attempted to keep the man in her sights. Why would this person be aboard a ship filled with murderous smugglers in the middle of the day?

A slight cracking sound was the only warning Poppy received. She felt the ground beneath her feet shift just a bit...and then she was falling.

Chapter 14

❀⳾ᴥ⳾❀

AS THE GROUND GAVE WAY under her feet, Poppy didn't even have time to scream. She slid down the muddy surface, clods of dirt, pebbles, and bits of grass tumbling along with her. When she reached the bottom of the slope a hundred feet below, she was momentarily stunned.

She didn't know how long she lay there. Eventually, she heard her name…but who would know her out here?

A figure loomed over her, all details obscured by the sun, leaving just a shape. "Poppy! Are you hurt?"

Once she identified the person as Carlos, she smiled. "Oh, hello."

He didn't smile back. "Poppy, listen to me. Are you injured? You must be. You just fell off a cliff."

"It was more of a slide down a slope."

"Jesus. We have to get you away from here." While he spoke, he was gently prodding at her limbs and checking for obvious wounds. He seemed both relieved and confused when nothing appeared to be broken. "Can you stand up, querida?"

"I think so." She took his offered hands and shakily got to her feet. "How'd you get here in the first place?"

"Look me in the eyes," he ordered, staring hard at her. "I was riding back from town when I saw you on the headland. Then you slipped. I had to come after you on foot, since the horse refused to go anywhere near the cliff. All right, your eyes are reacting to the sun just as they should. I don't think you hit your head. Now come on."

"Not yet," she said, remembering why she'd slipped. "Just before I fell, I saw a ship! I think it's the same one that we saw on the beach two nights ago. It's got the red and white flags. It's called *Seadragon*."

"Sálvame. I *know* there's a ship, Poppy. That's why we have to leave." He glanced over his shoulder, and alarm covered his features. "It's coming closer. The men aboard must have seen us. Come on."

"Where are we going?"

"To that grotto." He pointed to a dark, cavernous space at one end of the beach.

"Why not go back up to the headland and your horse?"

"Because it would take too long and we'd be in plain sight the whole way. If someone wanted to shoot us, they'd have a clear shot."

Poppy took a few steps but found herself stumbling a bit. Carlos took one look, and scooped her up.

"Excuse me, I can walk!"

"Then why didn't you?" he muttered. "This is faster, anyway."

"I'm too heavy for you to carry!"

"Not true, because I am carrying you. Holy Mother, why couldn't you have been knocked unconscious?"

"Now that's just rude." Poppy would have continued to argue, but by then they had passed under the huge stone shell of the grotto's ceiling.

Waves lapped at the shoreline, and Carlos set her down gently. "There should be entrances to caves in here. We need to find one deep enough that the crew won't find us when they come looking."

"Will they bother?"

"Considering they just saw two strangers enter their favorite hiding spot for illegal goods...yes, they'll bother."

"Very well then." Poppy blinked several times, finally feeling more like herself and less like a spinning top. She put her hand on the rough walls of the grotto, which were pockmarked and pitted from eons of saltwater and wind.

"Wind..." she murmured. "We need to find one of those openings where we can feel a breeze!"

"Why?" he asked.

"Because that means the space beyond is deep enough to hold air of its own, and the wind comes in and out. Come on, follow me!"

Propelled by a growing sense of urgency, Poppy moved along the wall, peering into each opening and stopping to feel if there was any movement of air across her face. Most of the openings were just shallow pockets where the rock had crumbled away over the years. But some went a little deeper. When Poppy encountered several candle stubs attached to the walls with wax, she broke one off and dropped it in her pocket. "Candles suggest that they do go deeper into the caves," she said, pleased that her theory was working.

Carlos kept looking over his shoulder, reporting on the progress of the ship, which he could just see through the overhang formed by the rocks. Soon Poppy heard the clatter and clang of approaching men.

At that moment, she passed a narrow opening in the wall. She would have disregarded it, except that a strong, cold breeze hit her the moment she stepped up to it.

She grabbed Carlos by the arm and yanked him in after her.

"What the..."

The space was dim, and the narrow passage continued, so Poppy pressed on into the darkness.

"Hell no," Carlos said, stopping, his weight impossible for her to drag. "I am not plunging into some dark pit just to get lost and die." He pulled a flint out of his pocket and managed to light the candle. The flame flickered alarmingly in the breeze.

"Excuse me but you told me we're looking for a cave entrance. And you said if they find us, we die," Poppy responded, cupping her hand around the flame to protect it.

"At least we'll die in the light."

"Come on. A little further. Let's make them work for their victory, shall we?"

"Well, I can't say no after that. I'd sound like a coward."

"Then let's go."

"I wish you weren't here at all."

Poppy felt wounded. "Well, I am and there's nothing you can do about it at this point. We found supplies destined for wounded soldiers, after all. Do you expect me to sit idly and think about all the poor souls who might be in pain—or die—because I did nothing?"

"Poppy, that's not..." he began.

But she was warming to her subject. "If I hadn't insisted on following after those smugglers the other night, you would never have discovered these caves at all. I am not going to return meekly to my room and embroider while you take all the risks."

He took a deep breath. "What I meant, Poppy, was that I wish you weren't here because I'm worried you'll be hurt. Or worse."

"Oh," she said. "Well, too late. And anyway, this may be my very last interesting adventure before I am boxed away with all the other spinsters."

"You talk as if you're on the shelf."

"In case you hadn't noticed, Mr. de la Guerra," she said, intent on moving through the rough passageway, "I am not exactly in demand."

"That depends on who you ask." He was a few steps behind her as they walked, so she didn't have to worry that he'd see her sudden blush.

Luckily, the task of navigating the cave passage was challenging enough that she didn't have to respond. Not long after, they reached a much larger cavern, and Poppy's foot struck a box that turned out to contain more candles and lanterns. "Oh, good," she said happily, working to light one lantern with her guttering candle. "This won't blow out so easily."

"Not good. It means they use this space regularly. We have to keep moving...assuming it's not a dead end."

"It can't be. I still feel air moving." Poppy looked around in the dim light from the lantern. "We must examine the walls and find out if there's another way out."

"Yes, General St George." They agreed to work around the perimeter of the cavern in opposite directions. Poppy lit another lantern she found.

The walls were damp, and as Poppy trailed her fingers along the surface, she shivered at the idea of being stuck down there.

"Anything?" she whispered to Carlos.

"Not yet." His voice sounded further away than it really was, and Poppy turned to make sure he was visible, even as a silhouette in the dark space.

At that moment, she nearly lost her balance as her hand on the wall suddenly encountered a space.

"Oh!" she gasped.

"What's wrong? Are you hurt?" Carlos asked. The

light from his lantern immediately bobbed toward her.

"I think I've found it!" Poppy said. "Yes! This passage keeps going…and there are candle stubs on the walls. This must be the way."

Carlos joined her, looking with trepidation down the dark, narrow passage. "Are you sure?"

"As sure as I can be without knowing what's on the other side. Come on!" She took a few steps into the passage. When she heard nothing behind her, she turned. "What is the matter?"

"Nothing," Carlos said, still peering into the passage, his face more serious than usual. He walked forward a few paces. "I just don't care for tight spaces."

"Well, if this is the route the smugglers use, it can't be that tight. They carry boxes and barrels and such."

"True." He exhaled and began to walk again, holding the lantern higher up. "Let me know if you see anything unusual. A branch tunnel, or a door, or something. I'd hate to lose the path." He seemed uncharacteristically nervous.

"Of course." Poppy went on ahead, keeping a steady pace. She was so excited she didn't want to wait. But she kept getting ahead of Carlos, and had to pause. She assumed Carlos was slowed by the low ceiling. But when the tunnel took an abrupt turn to the right, he stopped short.

"I can't go on," he said finally. "This space…"

"What's wrong?" Poppy walked back to him. "I'm sure this is the right path."

"It's not that." The lantern's light shone on him, revealing wide eyes.

"You don't like the dark?" she guessed.

"I'm fine with the dark. It's the closeness. The walls…" He stopped. His chest heaved as though he'd just run a mile. "I hate it."

"Then let me go on alone—"

"No. You absolutely can't do that." He sounded a bit more like himself then.

"I'll be perfectly safe."

"According to what logic?"

"None, I suppose," she admitted. "But I don't want you to suffer."

He shook his head. "I'm not *suffering*."

"Yes, you are." Poppy watched Carlos carefully, at last understanding his distress. "You've got a fear of being shut in small spaces. Why?"

"I don't want to talk about it. I don't want to be here."

"Carlos. Listen to me." Poppy put her free hand on his shoulder, compelling him to focus on her. "We are going to get out of here one way or another. We are not trapped. We are not alone. We are not in danger. Now, take a few deep breaths, and close your eyes. Think about being on your ship, with the horizon all around you, fresh air, the sky above..."

After a few minutes of Poppy describing a very different setting, Carlos's breathing slowed to normal, and the lines in his face relaxed slightly.

Then he said, "When I was seven years old, my older brother locked me in a linen closet once during a game of hide and seek that we were playing with some other children. He thought it was so clever."

"He knew you didn't like tight spaces and he did it anyway?" she asked, dismayed.

"I wasn't afraid when he did it. I thought it was a good hiding place, too. But then he left and didn't come back. I shouted and pounded on the door for a long time. It was dark and tight, and I couldn't do *anything*. No one came back. I got hungry and scared and I couldn't fall asleep."

"How long were you in there?"

"The next morning, a maid opened the closet to get some sheets, and she found me, unconscious at last. The previous day, everyone thought that someone *else* had found me and I'd simply wandered off. I did that a lot. Then he and Mamá went for an overnight visit to a friend's home. Our grandmother thought I was on the visit as well, and Mamá thought I was at home with my abuela. If the maid hadn't come to find new linens…" He trailed off. "I didn't speak to my brother for two weeks after. And for years, I wouldn't set foot in any room without at least two doors or a window. I still look for ways out…I know it's irrational."

"Not at all." Poppy squeezed his hand in her own. "Listen, I have an idea for how to get through this place."

"Make the tunnel five times wider?"

"Not exactly," she said. "But what if you didn't know how wide it was?"

"Too late. I already know."

"If you close your eyes and let me *tell* you how wide the tunnel is getting, you'll feel better."

"You want me to be blind?" he asked, puzzled.

"Yes! Remember, I guided my cousin Rosalind for years. I'm good at it. I'll tell you where to step and whether to stoop down, and before you know it, we'll be at the end."

"I can't keep my eyes shut. Sorry. I just can't. Not in a place like this. I'll have to look, and that will destroy the illusion."

Poppy only thought a moment. "Then you'll need a blindfold." She put her lantern down and untied the wide ribbon at the high waist of her dress. "Here," she said, holding it out. "It's the only thing I've got."

Carlos looked at it like it was a snake. "I can't do that."

"You'd better, or I'll have started to undress for nothing." Poppy tried to sound nonchalant, but she was suddenly aware they were alone. Utterly alone. And he had already asked her to undress once before.

He didn't seem to notice. He was still focused on the idea of playing blind. "I'll do this if you promise me you'll never breathe a *word*. I'll never live it down."

"I promise," Poppy swore.

He reluctantly wrapped the ribbon twice around his head, tied it off, then took a deep breath.

"Green suits you," she said.

"Shut up."

Poppy just chuckled, taking hold of the lantern again. She took Carlos's hand, feeling how tightly he gripped her own.

"Just don't let me run into any walls," he muttered.

"I promise. Listen to my instructions, and don't think of where you are."

"In fact, I am already thinking of something else entirely."

"Good," she said, feeling that she didn't dare ask what that might be. "Now walk forward."

Poppy moved slowly ahead, keeping the remaining lantern in front. Though it had been almost a year since she'd been a companion to Rosalind, Poppy discovered the old patterns came back to her immediately. She watched for obstacles. She called out when he should step to the side, or duck his head, and she never laughed at the odd shuffling gait they both adopted.

When the width of the tunnel expanded suddenly, she told Carlos so.

"Oh, actually it's a whole big cavern. Huge!" she added, when she realized that the lantern light didn't illuminate any walls for several paces. "Let me see. There are a lot of openings in the walls here. It's almost like the hub of a wheel. I wonder if one of these tunnels goes to the beach below Pencliff. I bet it must! St. Marks Head is really just a gigantic piece of Swiss cheese, when you think about it."

He didn't seem overjoyed at the comparison. "Just keep moving," he said, his voice almost pleading. When Poppy saw a few rats scamper by at the edge of the light's circle, she shuddered, eager to oblige.

She chose a tunnel on the opposite side, where a steady (if faint) breeze teased her hair. At last, the tunnel started to slope upwards. "I think we're close to the end. It's interesting. The walls here are very smooth. Like someone carved them out more."

"Fascinating," he responded, his breathing still rather uneven.

"Keep straight ahead," she said, "and don't worry."

"I'm not worried. I'm humiliated."

"Oh, don't be dramatic. You had a small problem and I helped you. What are friends for?"

Before he could respond to that, she saw something new. It was a door, right at the top of a set of rough cut steps at the end of the passage. "Ah, we're done!"

Carlos dropped her hand and reached up to rip the blindfold off. "Thank God." His relief was palpable.

"Well, *done* might be optimistic," Poppy admitted. "We don't know what's on the other side of that door."

"No matter. Anything is better than the cave. A dragon is better than the cave." He smiled at her. "Good thing I had a St George." He offered the blindfold back, saying, "You got us to an exit. I'm going to kiss you."

Before she could say a word, he did. Poppy felt his mouth on hers and nearly swooned with the sudden wash of emotions, compounded by the sheer mental strain of the last hour. His arms were tight around her, supporting her, keeping her from losing her footing. And he was wonderfully warm, like a cocoon against the cold, dark world of the caves.

Poppy opened her mouth to deepen the kiss, her whole body sparking into life in reaction to him. Yes, this was worth all the waiting and questioning from before. If he was holding her like this now, he must feel something for her.

"Carlos," she whispered, "This is all very nice, but maybe if you want to keep kissing me, we should go somewhere warmer? And possibly less cavernous?"

His lips curved into a smile. When the kiss ended, she held the ghost of his laugh in her throat.

"It's a mark of your allure, querida, that my desire for you is overriding my fear of this place." After a moment, he tied the ribbon around her waist again, his hands nearly burning a hole in the dress as they lingered on her. "I have more to say on that subject, but now's not the time. Let's get out of this little hell."

Heading up the rough steps, he leaned on the door and let it open a bit. All was quiet, so he opened it all the way and stepped out.

He took a huge breath, and then another. "God, it's wonderful to be out of there!"

Poppy looked around the dim space curiously, seeing only barrels and crates and sacks. It smelled of malt and bread. "This is wonderful? Where are we?"

"A storeroom of some sort?"

"A basement, to judge by the damp." Then Poppy pointed. "Over there! There's a door, and a crack of light underneath. Maybe it leads somewhere better than this."

They moved toward the door, and Carlos opened it carefully. Poppy peeked out from behind him, startled to see a figure she recognized cross the hall some distance away.

Carlos shut the door quickly.

"I know that man!" Poppy whispered. "That's Daveth, one of the footmen!"

"Holy Mother," he muttered. "We're in the basement of Pencliff Towers."

Poppy shook her head, as though that could change the truth. And after a moment, the shock faded a bit. Was it really so odd that a pathway went from the house to the caves? After all, there'd been a residence here for hundreds of years, and Cornwall had a long, long history of using the vast cave networks that were part of the landscape.

But still, it was very alarming to think that someone could sneak into the house itself using this secret door. Worse, it didn't look as if there was any way to bolt it. A person would have to slide a heavy object across the trapdoor to block access.

"Do you think the Towers know about this passageway?" she asked.

He snorted. "You'd have to be in a coma not to. This storeroom is holding food that's destined for the kitchen upstairs. This place gets used."

"But Mr. Towers would never permit this."

"Maybe *he* doesn't know," Carlos admitted. "But someone does."

Then he looked sharply at a stack of crates in the far corner. "Poppy, look. The writing on those boxes."

Poppy hurried over. "It looks the same as the ones we saw the other night. These are the same crates."

Carlos joined her, and worked fast to lift the lid off one box. Inside, nestled in the straw just as before, was the opium.

Chapter 15

"WHAT ARE WE GOING TO do?" Poppy whispered, her eyes wide.

"About the opium? Well, this to start." He pocketed one round disc. "I'll use this as evidence that I'm not imagining the whole thing. I'm going to talk to someone who can do something about it. But before I do, we need to figure out how to get out of this place unseen. If anyone suspects that you or I know about that door…"

"Oh, say it. Secret tunnel!" Poppy said, excitement overriding her fear. "We're in a gothic novel! How marvelous is that?"

"Are you feeling well? It's not marvelous. There are people who would kill us over this. I can name some of them."

She was instantly contrite. "I'm sorry. Of course it's nothing to be happy about. Do you think that's what happened to your friend Mateo? That during the course of a transaction, he found out something he shouldn't?"

"That's the core of what I want to know. But that's not the concern now. You need to leave here, unseen. And definitely we need to establish that we haven't just spent the last couple of hours together—alone in the dark."

She almost laughed. "Well, when you say it like

that..."

He scanned her again. "Lord, look at you. They'll put me in chains."

Poppy looked down at her ensemble. Her shoes were muddy. Her hem was torn, and the ribbon at her waist barely tied. She could only assume her hair and face were as ravaged. "I'm a fright. There's no other word for it. But none of it was your fault."

"Are you joking? All of it was my fault. How will I explain what actually happened?"

"You'll explain nothing," Poppy said firmly. "We'll make sure no one knows *anything* happened."

"How will you manage that?"

"I'll go first, and you wait. If anyone sees me, I'll say I was looking for Miss Mist. She wanders the whole house, so it would be plausible. And the mud and dirt on my dress can be blamed on the cat as well."

"Who would believe that?"

"Servants are trained to accept the unbelievable, so long as it doesn't threaten their livelihood. All right, I'm going. I do hope to see you at dinner, Mr. de la Guerra," she added formally.

He caught her hand and brought it to his lips. "Likewise, Miss St George."

She wished he didn't make her heart so fluttery. It was *very* distracting.

By some miracle, Poppy was able to get through the lower part of the house unnoticed, and via the servants' stairway she got to the upper floor and dashed to the safety of her room.

In the mirror, she contemplated the wreck of yet another gown. Despite being a sturdy wool, there were rips and marks along the hem due to wandering around underground. And her slide down the rocky cliff face hadn't helped.

Well, this would not be solved without assistance. She rang for the maid.

When Millie arrived, she looked askance at Poppy. "Miss! What have you been doing?"

"While I was out hiking along the headland, some of the ground gave way, and I fell."

"Heavens, miss! You're lucky you didn't get hurt."

"Well, I may have turned an ankle, and I do ache all over...now that I think about it."

"You need a hot bath," Millie declared.

A short while later, with the aid of hot, soapy water and the fussing of the sympathetic housemaid, Poppy felt much better. Her hair had been washed with lavender soap, and she reveled in the delight of being free of dirt.

The dress would require more effort. Millie took it away, saying she'd do her best to clean it, though she looked doubtful. Poppy shared her skepticism. Honestly, if she was going to keep running into Carlos, her wardrobe was in serious danger.

"What will you wear for dinner tonight, miss?" Millie asked, looking over the options. She pulled a dark green gown out of the clothes press. "This one is very pretty. With white gloves and that lace wrap, and your pearls? Yes, and let's fix your hair up properly."

"Oh, Millie, you're not my lady's maid. I can't ask you to ignore your other duties to tend to me."

"Nonsense. Mrs. Towers would want me to. Why did you not bring your own maid, if I may ask?"

"The answer is simple—I haven't got one. My family's not wealthy, and anyway, I don't really need one day-to-day. I'm not calling on friends or attending teas. I work in my stepfather's business."

"That accounts for it," Millie said.

"Accounts for what?"

"Most of the Towers's guests can't do a thing for themselves. Especially those Ains—er, never mind me, miss. Shouldn't be gossiping like that."

"I understand your point, Millie," Poppy said with a smile.

"But just to think!" Millie went on, apparently not quite ready to follow her own advice. "If *he'd* bought the place, we'd all be working for him and his wife and daughter!" Millie shuddered at the notion.

"That's right," Poppy said. "I remember Mr. Towers saying that Mr. Ainsworth also wanted to buy the place."

"Much better than Mr. Towers did…even if they did insist on the silly name for the house. No real harm in that, I suppose."

While Millie styled Poppy's hair, she sat quietly, musing about what the maid had said. Was it just a coincidence that Ainsworth wanted Pencliff Towers? Or did the network of caves have something to do with his interest?

At dinner that evening, she did her best to sit idly and not attract any undue attention.

"How was your ramble today, Poppy?" Mr. Towers asked.

"Oh, quite lovely," she said. "The view along the headland was well worth it."

"It seems so lonely, with just the rock and sky," Blanche commented. "But then, I suppose you must get used to being alone, Miss St George."

Poppy's eyes narrowed. "Because no one cares to hike on St. Mark's Head?" she asked innocently, refusing to acknowledge Blanche's hint.

"Because…" Blanche began. Then she looked to the door and smiled. "Why, dear Carlos! We wondered where you had been all day!"

"Just gone to town on a small matter," Carlos said carelessly. "That young coachman, Peran Kellow, drove me back."

Naturally, he was pressed, clean, and handsome—a far cry from his appearance when they left the caves. Carlos took the empty seat next to Blanche. He gave a quick, secret smile to Poppy, but otherwise behaved as if nothing happened between them. "I have to say, I am so

glad I'm in Cornwall this summer, after all."

Blanche smiled triumphantly, assuming she was the reason for the statement.

After dinner ended, Poppy quickly abandoned the others in the drawing room, where most guests gathered to while away the rest of the evening. She didn't have the strength to put up with the Ainsworths's stares. Blanche had gone up early, complaining of a headache. Then Elowen had left to give her sister her nightly dose of tonic, leaving Poppy bereft of a steady female companion to talk to.

She drifted down the hall, and then, without knowing why, left through the side door to the lawn again. The moon had risen, less than half-full but still bright on the water.

"Poppy?" a low voice asked.

She turned to see Carlos standing close by. "Is it wise to follow me out here, considering the lengths we both went to to pretend we didn't spend hours together earlier?"

"I wanted to talk to you without being overheard," he said.

"Are you going to berate me for getting involved again?"

"No," he said, taking a step toward her. "I truly am sorry."

"For what? I *chose* to get involved. Perhaps it wasn't the most intelligent choice, but I am so sick of sitting to the side of the room, watching everything and waiting for the next chapter of my life to begin."

"You don't seem as if you wait for anything."

"Does it look like that to you?" she asked. "Then you really don't know how little choice I have. Will another lady want me for a companion the way Rose did? Doubtful. Will I marry some gentleman who will overlook my reduced status and shopgirl habits? Unlikely. What will happen is that I'll work for my living, and with luck take over the management of my stepfather's business…unless he finds a man to do it."

"Is that what you want?"

She shrugged, uncertain of how to answer. She used to know what she wanted…or perhaps she never really thought about it before. In fact, Poppy spent most of her life being helpful to other people. People she loved, to be sure. But years as companion to Rose, and then the shift to helping her mother and stepfather with the business meant that Poppy never got the chance to truly consider what she would want if the chance was offered.

"Poppy," Carlos said, stepping closer. "This might be the first time I've ever seen you at a loss for words."

She looked up into his eyes. All of a sudden, her heart was beating wildly.

He bent his head and kissed her. When her lips parted, she felt the touch of his tongue on her lower lip, making her whole body terribly alert, as if he'd somehow exposed her skin to the night air…in a wonderful way.

He asked her what she wanted, and part of her had an answer. She wanted him.

She put her hands on his shoulders, and then it seemed easy to let them slide down and grab the lapels of his jacket, pulling him closer.

He took the hint, and when their mouths met again, Poppy closed her eyes, giving herself over to the pure pleasure of this closeness. It would be so good to have time to explore this feeling, not just to snatch little bits of bliss when no one was looking.

She broke off to inhale a ragged breath. Every time she got near Carlos, both her gowns and her reputation were threatened with ruin.

"We should stop," she whispered, very much wishing they could keep going. Then Poppy looked up at the house, distracted by something, though she didn't know what.

"Poppy," he was saying. "Please listen…"

A light flashed in a window on the top floor. Poppy blinked. "Carlos," she whispered. "It's happening again."

"What is?" he asked, still quite distracted.

"The light!"

He turned to look, and straightened up when he saw the light flash again. "Someone's up there now." His expression cooled, the sensuality replaced by something else entirely.

"I bet it's Blanche," Poppy said. "Did you notice how fast she left the drawing room after dinner? She had an appointment with a lantern."

"Let's find out."

He took her hand, and the pair moved swiftly back toward the house. Poppy was grateful he didn't even consider telling her to stay behind this time. She was as eager as he was to find out who was aiding the smugglers.

They reached the door of the house when Carlos stopped. "We can't be seen strolling up to the top floor together."

"Just take the servants' stairs. They won't question

you. I'll take the main steps and wait at the door to the final flight to the top."

"I'll see you in a few moments."

Poppy walked to the main stairs, hoping that no one would find her and try to talk. She heard voices in the drawing room and dashed past before anyone could see her. The stairs were vacant, but she ran into Mrs. Hobbson on the next floor.

"Are you still up and about, dear?" she asked. "I thought you'd gone up. Elowen and Elisa already retired."

"I'm just going to my room now," Poppy said. "Good night!"

She hurried on. When she reached the green baize door that marked the stairs to the top floor, Carlos was already waiting for her.

"Do you think they're alone up there?" she asked.

"One way to find out." He reached for the doorknob, then looked back. "Stay behind me. Just in case."

Poppy was suddenly nervous. What if the person was armed with more than a light?

Carlos eased the door open and moved up the stairs with surprising stealthiness for his size. Poppy followed, hoping her feet wouldn't encounter any loose or squeaky floorboards.

They got all the way to the top without alerting the signaler. Carlos pointed to the window, and Poppy saw a black silhouette outlined by the only slightly less dark window. The figure held a lantern in one hand and was slowly moving it across the window in front of her body.

Poppy took a deep breath. She *knew* it. Blanche was involved after all.

She reached out and put one hand on Carlos's arm. He looked back, curious. Poppy tried to convey with her expression that she should confront the signaler first—a woman would be less apt to startle her into doing something dangerous.

Whether he quite understood or not, Carlos nodded and held still. Poppy stepped around him and moved closer to the shadowy figure.

"Put that lantern down," she ordered in a quiet, but she hoped authoritative, voice. "And tell us exactly what you're doing."

With a startled gasp, the other woman whirled around to face them. She didn't put the lantern down, so the light illuminated her frightened face.

Poppy gaped. It wasn't Blanche Ainsworth.

It was Elowen Metcalfe.

Chapter 16

❧ ❧ ❧

CARLOS SAW POPPY'S SHOCK, AND understood exactly how she felt. Miss Metcalfe would have to be the *last* name on anyone's list of suspects. It never even got on to his own list.

"Please don't tell anyone I'm here!" Elowen said. "I can explain!"

"That would be a good start," Carlos said, stepping forward. Elowen's eyes rounded when he loomed over her.

But he merely took the lantern from her hand and lowered it to the floor. "Has your signal been received? Will they think something has gone wrong if you stop now?"

After a moment, Elowen shook her head slowly. "No-o. No. I was just finishing."

"What signal did you give?" Poppy asked curiously. "And to whom?"

Elowen looked at her, as if just noticing she stood there. "My job is to signal that it's all right to come into the shore. If anyone in the house mentions something suspicious, or if Customs officials or the magistrate ride up, I'm to give a different signal—a warning to stay away."

"So you're in the pay of the smugglers," Carlos said.

"No! That is, not exactly." All at once, Elowen burst into tears.

Poppy moved quickly to embrace her. "Don't be scared, dear. Whatever you're involved in, I'm sure you can make things right. Think of your sister...she needs you."

"It's for Elisa's sake that I got into this!" Elowen sobbed.

"I think you had better explain from the beginning," said Carlos, feeling rather out of his depth at the sight of Elowen crying. "Unfortunately, we can't move to a more comfortable location—not without getting some uncomfortable questions."

"We can talk here," Poppy said, keeping Elowen in a half embrace. He was struck by how instantly Poppy offered her help to literally anyone in need. It was inspiring (and also a little alarming).

He looked around and noticed a few large trunks and what appeared to be a wingback chair draped with a cloth. "Let's sit down."

He pulled the cloth off the chair and used it to dust off the trunks. Poppy sat Elowen down in the slightly musty and ripped chair, then sat on the trunk opposite.

Carlos remained standing. "You do understand, Miss Elowen, you're involved in something quite illegal," he said.

"Of course I do! It was not by choice..."

"What if I ask the questions?" Poppy told Carlos, rather pointedly. Then in a more gentle tone, she asked Elowen, "Dear, when did this all start?"

Elowen's eyes were still wet with crying. "Early this year. February. I had been in London to meet yet another doctor for Elisa. I was having no luck, and the trip was expensive. I worried I would run out of funds and have nothing to show for it, and nothing to tell Elisa that might help. I mentioned this frustration to a few of the doctors. They were not concerned…except one, who seemed sympathetic. He told me he would help Elisa, and it would cost nothing, but we had to come to Cornwall, and I had to do a few little tasks for him."

"And the name of this gentleman?"

"Dr. Burton Drake."

Carlos frowned. "That's not a name I've heard."

"He is a real doctor," Elowen said. "He has an office in London, and here in Cornwall. He's from here, you see."

"How did you know to send the signals?" Poppy asked, again taking over the questioning.

"Dr. Drake let me know what to do. I'd receive instructions while I saw him during Elisa's visits."

"And did he tell you what was being smuggled?"

"Oh, no. And I didn't ask. I assumed it must be the same sort of thing always taken across the Channel."

"It wasn't," Poppy said quietly. "Should we tell her?"

Carlos took a deep breath, considering, then said, "Among other things, this Dr. Drake seems to be in the opium business."

"Opium?" Elowen asked, surprised.

"Specifically, opium marked with the East India Company's name. And since he doesn't sound like an agent of the company, it's safe to assume the shipments consist of stolen cargo…diverted from where they're originally intended to go."

"A doctor would likely know where the need for such medicine was highest," Poppy added.

"And therefore he'd know where to charge the highest prices on the product," Carlos said. "Considering the quantity we saw in that single shipment, this is a very profitable operation."

"I had no idea!" said Elowen. "He just said he wanted to avoid complications from Customs…"

"I expect so," Carlos said dryly. "Does the name Peter Spargo mean anything to you?"

Elowen shook her head. "Who is that?"

"The leader of the largest smuggling operation around here." Carlos paused, thinking it over. "Drake was clever. He broke up the communication chain so no one could point a finger at more than one other person. And there was almost no way to prove a connection." He focused on Elowen again. "So the doctor would tell you to signal on a certain night whether it was safe to land a shipment…"

"Yes. He couldn't trust a servant, he said. He wanted someone with a mind. If the household would be alert, or outside…if the law was mentioned, or any reason at all, I could signal no. Dr Drake is a very cautious man."

"Evidently. But not cautious enough. We found you."

She dropped her eyes. Even in the poor light, her shame was evident. "I knew it was wrong, but Elisa needed me. I was told that I'd never get into trouble for what I'd done."

Carlos said, "You were lied to. The smuggling being done by this particular set is quite dangerous. If you were ever connected with the gang, you could suffer grave consequences."

"And so you've connected me now," she said in a defeated tone. "Will you take me to the magistrate?"

His impulse was to tell her that of course he wouldn't. But her fear of exposure provided the leverage he needed. "I won't…if you help me get them arrested."

"And you'll be able to continue caring for Elisa," Poppy added.

Elowen's eyes cleared again, and she nodded. "What must I do?" Her voice was much more decisive than before.

Poppy glanced at Carlos. It was up to him to tell Elowen what her role was.

He said, "The next night you're to signal to land a shipment on the beach below Pencliff, you must notify me as soon as possible." After a moment, Carlos added, "Or you may tell Poppy, if that's easier. I'll take it from there."

How he would do that, he wasn't sure. But Carlos felt that he was finally doing something worthwhile. And seeing Poppy smile at him made it seem even more so.

"Very well," Poppy said to Elowen. "You said no more signaling is required tonight. Get to bed with you. We'll talk tomorrow, but don't worry. I won't let any harm come to Elisa over this. You have my word."

Elowen smiled at Poppy through her tears and left.

There was a beat of silence, then Poppy looked to Carlos. "Well? Shall we go?"

"Go where?" he asked, puzzled. It was a bit late to head to the magistrate's office.

"To the beach! Elowen told us she signaled that it was safe for the smugglers to come ashore. That means we have another chance to identify them for certain…and maybe even stop them tonight."

"We?"

She tilted her chin up. "You're either with me or against me, Carlos de la Guerra. I'm going down there. And if you're very nice, I'll let you come along. Deal?"

He'd have agreed to anything she said at that point. "Deal."

Once he agreed, Carlos insisted that she had to obey every instruction he gave, and Poppy (rather surprisingly) conceded.

"Should we leave a note or something?" she asked. "Just in case we…run into trouble?"

"A note that says what? Gone after smugglers. Hold breakfast.?"

She made a face. "I see your point. Very well, let's go."

It was fortunate that both of them wore dark colors tonight. Carlos usually preferred darker shades, but Poppy seemed to favor white or brilliantly dyed gowns, which looked beautiful but tended to act like a beacon in the darkness. The deep green of tonight's dress was helpful.

Outside, the night air had turned downright cold, with a stiff wind coming out of the west. The swells would be high tonight. Carlos could hear the breakers even up here at the top of the cliff.

He put a hand out to stop Poppy from walking further, and looked out toward the sea. The moon was higher in the sky and pure white now, creating a marble path along the water to the eastern horizon where it hovered in the sky, blotting out the nearby stars. In the gloaming, faint shapes could be seen. He sighted the smugglers' ship first, for it was anchored not far out, and he even saw the row-boats heading into shore.

Then, further away, he saw another ship with a silhouette as familiar as a family member.

"Gracias a dios," he muttered. He'd given instructions to Valentin to follow the unknown ship, and the *Agustina* was doing just that.

"What is it?"

"Reinforcements," he said. "Hopefully we won't need to signal them. Come on. Remember, we have to be invisible."

"I'm twenty-one years old and still unmarried," Poppy retorted. "I'm invisible by definition."

When they began to descend the stairs to the beach, he looked over his shoulder. Poppy's expression was tight with worry, and he almost asked if she wanted to go back to the house. He bit his tongue—he knew what her answer would be.

They reached the bottom of the staircase just before the smugglers' boats hit the shallows, and they both moved to the huge boulder they'd hidden behind the first night.

Poppy peeked out, staring at the ship in the distance. "It looks like the one from earlier. The *Seadragon*. But I'm not positive."

"Don't worry. It's more important to identify the men. If they're who I think they are, I'll know what to do next."

"You're not going to kill someone right here, are you?"

"Poppy! As if I'd execute a murderer with a lady present."

"Well, remember that you did invite me to a duel, and Adrian's opponent could have died."

"That was different," he muttered. "Anyway, I intend to turn him over to the proper authorities, assuming the proper authorities will listen."

"And if they don't?"

"There's always the more direct option." Then he put up his hand, signaling her to silence. The smugglers were coming.

Carlos and Poppy watched the proceedings as best they could from their hiding spot. Carlos studied each man and committed the details of their physical appearance to memory.

A few times, one of the smugglers would give a command to the crew, and he heard Poppy repeat the names that were shouted in a whisper.

The gang unloaded several boxes that appeared to be very heavy for their size, judging by the grunts and curses of the men who moved them.

Just then, a dog leapt out of one of the rowboats and jumped onto the shore, running and yapping excitedly.

"Ay, rayos," Carlos muttered.

Sure enough, the dog suddenly went still, and then sniffed the air excitedly. It barked and began to trot toward the big boulder.

"What you got there, Wulf?" one smuggler said, following the dog's path.

"If it's a fucking Customs agent, shoot him in the head," another man called, the words carrying all too clearly to Carlos and Poppy.

"They're going to find us in a few seconds," Carlos said. He pulled out a knife and handed it to her. "Here."

"Are you mad?" she hissed, even as she took it. "What am I going to do with this, offer to slice up some beef for dinner?"

"They won't expect a woman to be armed," he explained. "God, I wish we had a distraction. If I could just get a few seconds' head start…"

"Well, there's one thing that might throw them off for a moment. How's this?"

Carlos looked back and the sight hit him in the gut. Poppy had hitched up the skirts of her gown to reveal possibly the most glorious pair of legs he'd ever seen.

"More women should hike," he muttered, his gaze captured by the vision.

Poppy reached out and dragged him to her. "Hurry up. If you look like you're kissing me, they won't think you're ready to pounce on them."

He was ready to pounce on something, all right. He pushed Poppy back against the rock, partly to protect her from possible stray bullets, but mostly to hitch one leg up around his thigh—an arresting sight for any man with a pulse.

With his mouth over hers, he breathed, "If things get bad, you need to get behind me."

"I can run for the cliff stairs."

"No, you can't. They're blocking the way. Same for the caves. Just trust me."

Then he kissed her, hard.

That was how the vanguard of the smugglers found them.

"Who the hell are—" a voice shouted, but then laughter broke out all around Carlos and Poppy.

"It's just a lad and his girl!" another voice called. "What should we do with them?"

"Hey, you both. Stop all that!"

Hearing the threat behind the words, Carlos did stop, and turned so that Poppy was partially concealed by his body.

Four men stood in a semi-circle, watching them. In the middle was a big bear of a man who Carlos recognized as one of Spargo's lieutenants. What had Spargo called him in the tavern? Malcolm.

"Little ragged, but she's a beauty," another man said, peering at Poppy.

"She's my beauty," Carlos snapped, looking back at them. His voice acquired a drunken edge. "So why are you lot looking at her?"

Malcolm didn't appear to recognize Carlos, not yet. Unsurprisingly, his gaze kept traveling to Poppy, who was blushing scarlet at his perusal. She yanked her skirts back down.

"You've picked a bad place for your little dalliance," Malcolm said.

"Have I?" Carlos asked. "Seemed good enough."

"Seems ain't the same as is, friend. We're using it. So move along," Malcolm said, not raising his voice. He put his hand on the pistol at his belt. "Let's have no violence about it."

"Please, darling," Poppy said, her obvious embarrassment at being seen like this completely believable. "Let's go."

"Listen to your lady friend," the man went on. "This is not worth a fight."

"Oh, very well," Carlos grumbled. "Keep your eyes off her," he warned as he pulled Poppy toward the stairs. Was it possible they could get out of this unscathed?

"Hey, I've seen you before," one man said. It was the skinny man who picked the fight with Carlos in the bar. "You're that Spanish sailor. What the hell are you doing here, dressed like a swell?"

Malcolm's attention snapped back to Carlos. "So it is. Something's not right here. Both of you, walk forward. Slowly, hands out."

Carlos made a show of keeping his hands well away from his body, which also helped shield Poppy's actions from their view.

"Poppy. Cuando te lo diga, corre hacia la orilla. Entendido?"

"Si," she whispered. "Cuando?"

"Hey, what are you two jabbering on about?" Malcolm growled.

Carlos took a breath. "Ahora."

He grabbed her hand and they ran for the waterline. That was the opposite of what the gang expected, and it gave Carlos and Poppy a few precious seconds to reach one of the rowboats pulled up on the beach.

"Jump in the boat," he told her.

"*What?*"

"Poppy, now!" He didn't wait for her to follow his order. He simply grabbed her by the waist and swung her over the side. She landed in a heap, her gown soaking up the seawater that had pooled in the bottom.

A gunshot rang out, and Carlos ducked as he shoved the rowboat off the pebble beach. His feet splashed into the water until he jumped in, clambering onto the only bench, where he grabbed the oars and started rowing. He used one arm to circle around with the left oar, but the moment the bow was facing the sea, he heaved hard with both. The little boat shot forward through the surf.

Poppy clung to the wooden edge of the boat as Carlos moved them out beyond the shore. More gunshots rang out, causing them both to duck again.

"Look behind," he ordered. "Are there more men coming out of the cave? Anyone going for the other boat? And keep your head low!"

Poppy twisted around, bracing herself with a hand on each side of the bow. Keeping her head slightly above the wooden edge, she surveyed the beach with narrowed eyes.

"Seven…no, eight men. Only three with guns. I don't recognize them…not that that means much. The bald one, and the one they called Malcolm. And the next man's shooting arm is all blue!"

"Tattoos," Carlos grunted. "Good. Keep watching."

"They're reloading! Duck!" she said, just as the bald man raised his arm to aim and shoot once more.

Carlos hunched over, giving one strong stroke at the left oar to change the boat's direction.

Poppy gasped as something whipped past them. Wood splintered behind her. She looked at Carlos, who merely raised an eyebrow.

"He missed. Sorry."

"Just row," she muttered.

He rounded the curve of land, and knew the instant Poppy saw the ship anchored there. "Oh, no. Is that another smugglers' ship?"

"Not exactly. It's the *Agustina*."

"Your ship? What's it doing here? I thought it was in the harbor at Treversey."

"I told my first mate to follow Spargo's gang if he could. I'll explain later," he said, slightly out of breath.

The swells had grown higher the moment the boat left the relatively sheltered bay, and Carlos had to strain to keep rowing at the right angle to meet the ship. Water had splashed up, soaking his right side. The fabric of his shirt now clung to his shoulders and arms.

He caught Poppy looking at him, and suddenly forgot all the discomfort he was going through. "Enjoying yourself?" he asked.

She quickly looked away, and he bit back a smile.

When they reached the ship, one of the sailors leaned over, and called down, "¿Quién anda ahí?"

Carlos sighed. Did the man really not recognize his own captain? He yelled up, "De tal palo, tal astilla." The code phrase was known to all the men on the ship.

The sailor on deck top called back a welcome, and a rope ladder tumbled down the hull of the ship.

"Up the ladder," Carlos said, grabbing the bottom rung and holding it steady. "Quickly, before we die of exposure."

"Hold a moment." Poppy bent down and grabbed the hem of her skirts, tying a knot in the middle, turning the skirt into impromptu trousers. She seized a rung and clambered up the ladder as if she'd done it a hundred times before.

At the top, a startled crewman helped her aboard, and

Carlos followed her a moment later. Valentin strode up, a question in his eye.

"Who came aboard just now?" Carlos asked in Spanish.

"Just you, sir," Valentin replied instantly.

"No one else?"

"Absolutely not. Definitely no women." Valentin bowed to Poppy, saying in English, "A pleasure to not meet you, señorita."

"Thank you for not seeing me," Poppy replied.

It was an absurd exchange, especially considering that Poppy's dress was clinging to her like a second skin, hinting at every beautiful curve underneath. Who could pretend she wasn't the most alluring thing on the ship right now?

"Can you sail for Treversey?" Carlos asked. "After we lose the smugglers' ship, that is?"

Valentin replied, "There's a fog bank coming in on a warm current. It'll help us hide from pursuit, but I'd hate to be sailing close to the shore. This Cornish coast is all reefs and shoals. Not to mention that the tides aren't right. We could run aground before we knew it."

"All right, sail for deeper waters. I'm taking her to my cabin," Carlos explained. "I'll be back in a moment."

"Why?" Valentin murmured, still in Spanish. "I know how to outrun some idiot pirates as well as you. And it seems a shame to waste the opportunity. A beautiful woman for company all night? I know what I'd choose."

"Let's not make assumptions about my character," Poppy spoke in English but her words let Valentin know that she understood him. The first mate regarded her in surprise.

"I should have mentioned that the lady has been learning Spanish," Carlos muttered.

"Uff." Valentin extracted himself from the conversation very quickly, and Carlos led Poppy toward his quarters.

Her eyes were wide with interest on being led into the captain's cabin, which was all heavy, dark wood, and huge beams across the ceiling—which was in fact the flooring of the actual deck above. Carlos lit a hanging lantern, which swung lazily in the constant toss of the ship on the waves.

"What if I get seasick?" she asked. "I'd hate to ruin your room."

"It's called a cabin. And this is the only cabin. *Agustina* is not a large ship. The other sailors sleep in the common area, or on the deck if the weather allows. So you'll be staying in here while you're aboard."

"I…didn't pack for a sea voyage when you threw me in the boat," she said, lifting her sodden skirt a few inches.

"You mean when I was saving your life from pirates about to shoot you?" He stepped up to her, surveying her damp hair, now curling into little ringlets of dark gold, and noticing how soft she looked in the candlelight. He ached to touch her. "Feel free to thank me, by the way."

"Thank you so much for taking me to a ship where I can't escape, and I'll be completely and utterly ruined the moment I step ashore…no matter what your faithful crewman says about not seeing me."

"You won't be ruined. Unless you want to be," he added, the devil in him not wishing to miss an opportunity.

Poppy looked up, catching his gaze. She refused to look away as she said, "Yes, please. If it's not too much trouble."

"You mean it?" Carlos asked, not sure he heard that

correctly.

"Of course I mean it," she said, very decisively, as if she were choosing the right bolt of cloth to order. "I'm not an idiot. There will be consequences after tonight, no matter what. So I may as well get the complete experience if I'm going to be treated that way anyway."

"So...I'm just convenient?"

"You've never been convenient, Carlos de la Guerra."

And with that, his soaked and seductive Poppy leaned in to kiss him.

Chapter 17

POPPY'S MIND REELED FROM THE kiss, and she sighed as all the tension of their escape from the smugglers turned into simple need for release. She reveled in just how marvelous it was to touch him, though the sad reality of their wet outfits did hamper her enjoyment a bit.

"Your shirt is soaked," she observed, with a little laugh.

"As you're aware, I'm happy to take it off." And he did, pulling the wet shirt over his head, leaving his upper body naked.

Poppy had seen it before, but never so close. She reached out, running her hands over his skin, encountering a few scars and marks along the way.

"Was this from the bullet?" she asked, coming to one round spot that was lighter in color than the rest of him.

He nodded. "There's a matching scar on my back."

"I'm glad you lived," she said, feeling suddenly very shy.

"Me too. Otherwise I wouldn't be here with you."

The next kiss had Poppy dizzy with longing. He ran his hands through her hair and pushed her gently against the desk, which was bolted to the floor.

"Have a seat," he told her, lifting her so she could

perch on top of the desk. "I need to get the rest of my clothes off."

"Oh, I'm generally clever enough to figure things out," she replied, reaching out to unbutton his falls.

"I assure you I know how to dress and undress myself."

"Shut up," she said, and to her surprise, he did.

Soon, she'd discarded every damp, sea-salt-soaked, chill-inducing article of clothing and dropped it in a heap. The result was a magnificently nude man standing in front of her as if he did this every day. Poppy felt her cheeks flaming as she took in the sight of him.

"Now you," he said. "I'd hate for you to get sick and die because I couldn't get your clothing off."

"Ah, a true gentleman," she noted. "But let me do it. That way I won't have to get cross at you if something tears."

Standing up, she peeled the gown off gently, knowing that she had no replacement.

He watched, intensely interested in every move. Stays and shift and stockings all followed, until Poppy was wearing nothing at all.

"No scars," he said, with a smile.

"Well, there's this one." Poppy pointed to a tiny ridge on the top of her ankle. "During a game of hide and seek at Wildwood Hall, I tripped and fell on some loose paving stones."

"And you lived to tell the tale."

Poppy didn't know why she was smiling like an idiot, so she glanced quickly around the room.

"That bed looks…small," she noted. In fact, it was more like a nook in the wall, designed to keep one person from falling out—not to help two fall in.

"I've typically used the floor for this sort of thing," he

admitted. "Or the wall. Or the desk."

Poppy considered the options, wondering exactly how each differed when it came to lovemaking. "Let's start with the floor."

He swallowed. "Start with. Yes."

A moment later he had yanked the mattress and blankets out and arranged them on the floor.

"You've got the procedure down," she said.

"Not really. I don't do this very often," he said. "Not here, anyway. Actually, not at all the past year, I don't think—"

"Carlos, you don't have to explain your life to me," Poppy told him softly. "It's not as if I expect you to be some blushing virgin."

"Good, because in that case I'd disappoint you."

"I doubt you'll disappoint me at all." She kissed him. "Now, let's get to all this ruination, shall we? I'm very curious about it."

He laid her back on the mattress, and sat back on his heels, surveying her with pleasure in his eyes. "You're everything I've been imagining. More."

She smiled, feeling shy. "You've been imagining me?"

"That's what men do," he told her bluntly. "As soon as there's a woman we want, she invades every spare moment in our minds."

"How distracting."

"It's a curse."

"And what did you imagine doing with me?"

"I'll show you."

He bent down, running his hands along her waist and hips while he kissed her stomach. Poppy gasped at the feeling, her muscles contracting in response to his attentions. She had read of such things in books she was absolutely not permitted to read...but that was very different from actually doing them.

He moved lower along her body, his hand sweeping her thighs, very gently encouraging her to part her legs. Poppy inhaled, uncertain. "What are you going to do?" she asked.

"I'm going to make you come undone with just my mouth," he told her, smiling in a way that made her stomach flip over and her breath stop. "Now lay back and put your hands on my head. Tell me when to go faster or slower, or harder or softer. I'm listening. And feel free to beg me for things, or just scream my name."

"You have a high opinion of your skills, don't you," she said, trying to hold onto a semblance of her usual wit while also reeling from the notion that this beautiful man intended to touch her in ways no one else had touched her in her entire life.

"When I'm done, Poppy, you'll have a high opinion of my skills, too."

He was arrogant. But also correct.

Poppy learned that bliss took all sorts of forms, but one of the nicest was when a person devoted themselves to pleasuring another completely, postponing any and all attention for themselves. Under his tongue, Poppy moaned and sighed and spoke absolute nonsense as her body vibrated in reaction. She did find out that she enjoyed both slow and fast, and that she was inclined to twist and arch her back when overwhelmed with pleasure. When the sensations grew intense, beads of sweat broke out along her forehead and under her arms and between her breasts and along her spine.

He ran his fingers over her skin, turning that moisture into something sublime for her nerves. Poppy whimpered, needing release. Since he requested it, she did beg Carlos to give her that release, earning a low laugh from him that she felt in her core. A moment later, Poppy cried out as the moment came, leaving her shaken from the waves of pleasure breaking over her.

Carlos moved to lay next to her, gathering her in his arms. She curled up onto him, nuzzling her head where his shoulder met his neck. He seemed to have an endless supply of internal heat, and his skin was delightfully warm. She sighed as she stretched one hand across his chest. Under her fingertips, she felt the thud of his heartbeat—he looked calm, but he wasn't. She realized that all this time, he'd been holding back his own urges to give her more attention.

"I don't have anything to compare it to," she said at last. "But I suspect that I'll remember that forever."

"Or until the next time," he said.

She smiled at that. "Oh, you think you've conquered me, do you? That I'm just going to lie about pining for you, unable to look at any other man?"

"Will you? I like that idea," he said, tipping her head up to lay a kiss on her mouth.

The kiss quickly deepened, and he ran his hand along her leg, pressing it against his erection. Poppy wanted to move right along with the ruination, so she moved her leg away and slid her hand down instead, curious to touch him and learn all about this bit of anatomy that caused half of society to get locked in their rooms for safety.

Carlos swore under his breath in Spanish, and she had definitely not learned those phrases in her lessons.

"Should I stop?" she asked.

"No, you should do that for the rest of the night. Every night. Possibly forever. Christ, Poppy, that feels so good."

"I'm glad," she whispered. "You made me feel good."

"I will again. I'm going to make you need me."

She bit her lip, excited yet scared by his words. Poppy

didn't like to need people. Especially not men.

He must have noticed her expression, because he suddenly moved, managing to roll her onto her back while he stretched over her, all within the space of a breath.

"It's not that kind of need," he told her, his voice low in her ear. "You'll still be the same gorgeous, maddening, lovely little snapdragon you are now. But you'll know what you want. And you'll want me."

"Show me," Poppy breathed.

"I will. But first, I have to do something."

He reached out to a drawer in his desk (truly, the cabin wasn't that spacious). A second later, he had a small envelope in his hands. He pulled out what looked at first like a strip of parchment, though she realized a second later what it was meant for. (This knowledge was also the result of reading things she was not permitted to read.)

"Is that...typical to use?" she asked, watching as he slid it on.

"It is when you don't want unwelcome consequences," he told her. "Now, where was I? Oh yes."

He used his mouth to kiss her senseless, used his hands to wreak havoc in her body again, bringing her to near-ecstasy, and then teasing her until she begged him to end it. By that point, her legs were wrapped around his waist, and she was feverish with desire for him.

So when he eased into her, all that hardness pushing against her body, Poppy was more than ready. She clutched his shoulders and buried her head in his chest, moaning his name with every thrust.

It took almost no time for her to come undone once more, and she melted under him while the pleasure shot through her. He came a scant moment later, with a guttural shout that sounded totally primitive and utterly right.

* * * *

Poppy didn't know how much time had passed....evidently enough for her to have outgrown any sense of shame, because she lay on the floor of the cabin, her naked body draped over his.

Carlos had found another blanket at some point, and she was quite warm and comfortable, enjoying the rise and fall of his chest beneath her cheek.

"Well?" he asked then, the sound of his voice rumbling in her ear. "How does it feel to be ruined?"

"Wonderful," Poppy replied. "I can understand why everyone makes such a fuss about it. And with your, erm, precautions, I don't have to spend the next month in utter fear that I'll be carrying a child."

"It reduces the chances," he cautioned. "It doesn't eliminate them."

"Hmmm. Well, I've been taking risks ever since I got to Pencliff House...though really ever since I saw *you* again."

"I tried to warn you to stay out of it. I don't want you to get hurt, Poppy."

"So what do you want me to do if I find out I'm pregnant?"

He looked at her in exasperation. "I want you to tell me!"

"Carlos," she said reasonably. "You live on the other side of the ocean."

His arms tightened around her. "I'm here now."

"But will you be here in several weeks? A few months? Who knows when I'll know?"

"I'll live wherever I need to."

"Oh, please. You'd wither away and die if you couldn't be part of your country and your revolution. And honestly, there's only a small chance that this will become an issue. So let's not worry about it." Privately, Poppy was a little annoyed that he'd suggested he'd stay in England for his yet-to-exist child, but he hadn't bothered to do so last year for her. Indeed, once she could confidently say that she wasn't pregnant, he'd probably sail with the next tide.

"You will tell me, yes? Perhaps we should have discussed this before." He looked concerned, and Poppy reminded herself that for all his bravado and pretense of being a rogue, he was ultimately the sort of person who cared deeply about doing the right thing.

"It's very difficult to ponder all possible outcomes when you've got me naked on the floor of your ship cabin. I was a little distracted!"

He frowned. "Only a little?"

"God, you're so arrogant."

Carlos laughed, and reached for her again. Poppy sighed under his touch. It was difficult to maintain an argument with him when he was making her feel so delightful. Before she knew it, her body was responding to his attention, clamoring for a repeat of the ecstasy before.

"No," he said when she urged him to do exactly that.

"No?" But she was getting so impatient with desire again.

"It's too soon. I don't want you to associate sex with pain." He kissed her, then slid his hand between her legs. "But that doesn't mean I'll neglect you."

She was certainly not neglected, not the way he paid minute attention to her every gasp and moan, and answered questions she didn't know how to ask a few hours before. And when the enormity of what they were doing finally broke into her fevered brain and made her shy all over again, he somehow sensed it and turned her so she didn't have to look at him, or anything. Just close her eyes and feel the waves of pleasure rippling through her, without talk or promises or worries about what came after.

That was how she came undone that time, stretching her arms up as her back pressed against his chest, his right hand pleasuring her core while his left teased her breast. He pressed soft open kisses against her neck and ear, telling her that she was a wonder, better than any fantasy he'd had of her.

"Thought about doing this to you for over a year," he murmured, between kisses. "Never thought I'd get the chance."

Poppy took in his words with dazed satisfaction. Her mind was hazy, still overcome with the little aftershocks of pleasure he was creating with his hands. She finally let out a little sigh as he withdrew his hand.

Then, he took her by the hips and slowly pressed her bottom against his groin. She rolled herself into the hard length of him, and got a wave of gratification when she heard him groan in response.

He used her to come that way, and she slid her hands along his sides to his hips, encouraging him. His kisses became rougher, and as he came, he bit her neck to muffle his shout. Poppy felt a wash of heat over her whole body.

He lay next to her, his hands softly skimming her curves. Touching her neck very gently, he murmured, "I didn't mean to bite you so hard."

"I liked it," Poppy confessed, earning a squeeze as he held her tighter.

"Really."

"There might be a lot of things I like," she went on, finally turning to look at him again, "but I've not experienced them yet, so how would I know?"

"Poppy, I've got half a mind to chain you up and keep you here forever."

"I don't see why the chains are necessary. Do you think I'd jump overboard?"

"God I hope not." He kissed her tenderly, and she couldn't imagine wanting to get away from this man. Not if he was going to keep doing such delicious things to her.

There was a sharp double knock at the door. Carlos didn't respond, and no one entered, but he sighed.

"That was Valentin, telling me that it's time."

"Time for what?"

"First, to get you back on shore, and then to some-place where you can be safe from all suggestions of compromise and ruin."

"How will we manage that?" She laughed as she got up, reaching for her still-damp clothing, and finding a completely different gown folded up on the chair.

"You fell asleep for a bit," he explained on seeing her confusion. "I happened to have some spare clothing in a chest in the hold—it's meant to be shipped home, but I don't think my family will mind you taking what you need."

The soft green gown was very pretty, and Poppy got dressed quickly. She continued to think about what he'd said before, and decided, "Anyway, I truly don't think it matters much. If I'm found out for being all wanton or whatnot, that is. I'm not gentry, and no one particularly cares about the state of my virtue."

"Do you want to get married?"

Poppy shrugged. "Someday, perhaps. If a man ever actually offers for me, and it's someone I actually want to spend my life with, I'll consider it."

He moved to block her progress. "I meant did you

want to get married to me?"

"You?"

"Of course me." He frowned at her, his dark eyes locking onto hers. "Why the hell would I ask you to marry another man?"

"Carlos, you're not the marrying kind."

"How do you know? Anyway, it's the right thing to do."

"Ugh, what a terrible reason. Look, darling, you're remarkable in a lot of ways, and I don't regret what we did together."

He smiled. "Say darling again."

"Darling." Poppy couldn't stop her stomach from fluttering. But she pressed on, "I do not want to exchange some vows that will shackle me for life just because you need to satisfy a sense of honor. As you've said before, you've got other commitments. So let's simply remain... friends, I suppose. If there's a child, we'll deal with the matter then. Otherwise, you're free to go."

"It's not just a sense of honor. I care for you. You think I just took you to bed for fun?"

"Well, it was fun," Poppy admitted. "But I can see that you're trying to fit some frame that you simply don't match. And I'm telling you that it's not necessary. I care for you too, and it would be very mean of me to trap you for life just because we decided to....er, have fun for a night."

Carlos stared at her, seemingly nonplussed by the argument. Finally, he said, "What if I told you I love you?"

Chapter 18

❀ ⚘ ❀

"I WOULDN'T BELIEVE YOU," POPPY responded after far too long a pause. Her eyes were wide, and she looked alarmed by the very prospect of being loved by him.

Carlos felt the dismissal in his gut. "Why not?"

"Oh, I don't know. Because the last time I thought you might stay around long enough for me to get to know you, you disappeared over the horizon and I didn't see you again for over a year."

"I explained that. It was unavoidable. Family business. I didn't want to go."

"That's not the issue, Carlos," Poppy said, sounding maddeningly reasonable. "My point is that I have to go by my experience. And in my experience, you leave."

"Once!"

"So far. I'm not angry at you. You have a life to live."

"And I want you in it."

Poppy bit her lip, and looked away. "Perhaps we should talk about this another time. When we're not so… post-coital. Or half-dressed. Or alone."

"We will definitely talk about this," he warned.

He dressed and went up on deck to discover what the hell had happened while Poppy was losing her virginity and he was losing his mind.

Valentin stood at the helm. He must not have slept all night, though it was now past three in the morning. Within an hour, the first hints of dawn would color the sky. They needed to make some decisions.

"Where are we?" Carlos asked.

"Cruising the Channel. The *Seadragon* never even got close to pursuing us. It took them too long to hoist anchor and turn about."

"Amateurs."

"They're smugglers at heart, not pirates. They don't run down other ships—they run from them. They weren't prepared for this situation."

"A good crew is ready for any situation."

"Speaking of that, how would you like to deal with your current pretty little situation? Are you keeping her aboard?"

"God, no. We need to get her off the ship as soon as possible. How big is this fog bank?"

"As far as I can tell, it's eternal. It's been a gift, since no one can possibly see us. And only the insane or the desperate would sail in this if they didn't have to."

Carlos accepted the implied criticism. "Couldn't be helped. Let's get our bearings. I want to sail back to St. Mark's Head. The west side."

"That's close to Treversey. Spargo's crew could spot us if the fog thins."

"Then we'll pray that it doesn't."

The *Agustina* was a ghost, sailing through the fog with her sails barely rippling. The reduced speed helped, because the crew had to navigate unfamiliar waters. Poppy, having refused to remain below like cargo (as she put it), had walked to the bow and stood looking out over nothing but pearl grey oblivion.

Carlos hated it. He hated that she thought he wasn't

serious about her, or that he'd be content to give her up after last night.

A half hour later, the *Agustina* approached the point on the shoreline that Carlos wanted. The ship's pace slowed even more, and a longboat was readied on the port side.

"This is as close as we can get, captain," Valentin said, keeping his voice low.

Carlos nodded, and went to find Poppy.

"Where are we?" she asked when he joined her at the bow.

"Remember when you fell off the cliff? This is the same beach. I'll row you to shore and take you to the grotto, just to make sure none of Spargo's gang are there. Then you go alone through the same tunnel to the basement of Pencliff Towers."

She looked over at him, surprise on her features. "You're not coming with me?"

"The point of this exercise is to get you back to a safe place without anyone knowing where you've been…or with who."

"And I'll see you back at the house tomorrow? That is, later today?"

Carlos nodded curtly. "Of course. Unless I decide to disappear over the horizon again."

Poppy's jaw tightened, but she didn't reply. Too bad. He felt much better when she argued with him.

He rowed to shore, and helped her out so her clothing didn't get soaked again.

The grotto was deserted, although Carlos had a creeping feeling that they weren't alone. He shook his head. That was the fog. It warped shapes and sounds and light and distance. It was all too easy to imagine things in the fog.

He and Poppy walked, unspeaking, to the narrow gap

in the rock where she'd first grabbed him and pulled him into concealment.

He handed her a lantern from the *Agustina*. "Here. You know the way?"

"Claro." She gave a little toss of her head, and added in English, "I could find my way blindfolded."

"There's not much time before dawn. Be careful, Poppy." *I'll die if anything happens to you.*

Her eyes widened, almost as if she heard him speak the words aloud. But then she turned, and vanished into the darkness of the cave. He swallowed painfully. Just thinking about her all alone, wandering those twisted, oppressive passages... Of course, Poppy had already proven herself to be far more capable than he was in such situations, which only made him feel even more annoyed at his own fears.

When Carlos returned to the *Agustina*, he was in a foul mood. "Let's get away from here."

"Where to?"

"Who the hell cares? Out of this fog bank, to start. I hate the fog. I feel like a thousand eyes are watching me."

Valentin nodded. "I'll head to Truro. You'll want to speak to Customs. Now that we've confirmed that the *Seadragon* brought in that opium, and we know Spargo's crew sails the *Seadragon*, you can get those agents to do something about it."

"If they listen."

At Truro later that morning, Carlos waited impatiently until the clerk opened the Customs house doors.

He was able to show the opium cake as evidence, which got him ushered into the office of the head of His Majesty's Customs operations in Truro, referred to as the Collector. Mr. Snell was an older man with sagging features but glittering ice-blue eyes, and he wore an old-fashioned white wig.

Carlos explained all that had happened in the past several days, while the official listened closely.

"Why not bring the matter up with the local magistrate?" Snell asked at the end.

"I did," Carlos said. "Armitage seems uninterested in pursuing the matter. Of course, Spargo is just down the street."

Collector Snell raised an eyebrow, catching the implication. "I see. Well, you're correct that the presence of opium raises the stakes. As it happens, the army has been noticing a sharp drop in the supply level for many items shipped to the Continent for the war effort. I wouldn't be surprised if the crates you saw were diverted. I'll contact the relevant parties and we'll up the patrols in the area."

"Are you intending to raid Pencliff Towers?"

"Raid a great house?" The official looked alarmed. "My good man, that would be…I can't even imagine how the local gentry would react if they heard we stormed our way into one of their homes. We'd never hear the end of it!"

"Then what will you do?"

"Well, I'm not about to let Spargo and Ainsworth and Dr. Drake and whoever else is part of this mess sell it out from under our noses. Give me time. I may need to contact you at Pencliff."

"I'll be there," Carlos said with a nod. "Anything else I can do to catch Spargo?"

The official fiddled with the pencil on his desk. "I shouldn't involve a private citizen. You're not even British."

"I might be. Santo Domingo is periodically under British rule, and I've haven't heard word from my home in over a week. So who knows?"

"A fragile argument, but we're undermanned, so I'll take it. What would help is if you can continue to act as if you're interested in buying illegal goods off Spargo. Play to his greed, and if you can set up an exchange for a certain night, we can be ready, and arrest everyone and seize the *Seadragon* all at once."

"Now who's a pirate? What good is the *Seadragon* to you, other than the fact that it's one less ship to watch?"

Snell chuckled. "As a matter of fact, we turn seized ships into our fleet. It will be repaired, refitted, and re-named. It will sail again…under His Majesty's flag."

Chapter 19

❧⁓☙⁓❧

POPPY ONCE AGAIN MANAGED TO get through the cave
network to the basement doorway, and then up into the
house to her room all unseen—she was getting quite good
at this particular skill. True, there were servants moving
about in the early morning, but all the other inhabitants
were sound asleep at that hour.

When she reached the bedroom, Miss Mist was curled
up on the bed. She looked up when Poppy crept in, and
mewed in what could only be described as a disapproving
tone.

"Oh, what are you looking at? *You* stay out all night."

The cat did not deign to reply to that.

Poppy quickly removed her clothes and pulled on her
nightrail, then washed her face and arms in the now-chilly
water left for her the previous evening.

She had just pulled the cover away on the bed, intending to climb in, when the door swung open.

"Oh, my God!" Poppy gasped, her heart jumping out
of her chest.

Millie squeaked in alarm, nearly dropping the bucket
of wood she was carrying. "It's only me, miss! I'm setting
up the fireplace…why aren't you abed?"

"I, er…had a restless night." As if that could explain

things!

"So I see, miss," Millie said, picking up Poppy's scuffed slippers and the new green gown from the floor. "I remember this being a much darker shade. Funny how things look different in the light."

"Er, yes. I'm just going to have breakfast in my room today. I've a powerful need to pull the covers over my head and hope that the world stops existing for a bit." Poppy needed to regain her equilibrium so she could decide how to get out of the increasingly tangled web she was weaving for herself.

"As you wish, miss. Oh, and this came in the late post." Millie put an envelope on the dresser and left discreetly.

Poppy wanted to open the letter, but it seemed awfully far from the bed. In fact, Poppy fell asleep almost as soon as her head hit the pillow, and she didn't wake up again until noon.

When she woke, she noticed a breakfast tray on the table, and the *original* dark green gown hanging from the back of a chair, freshly pressed and perfect. Her slippers had also been cleaned and re-blacked. It was as if the previous night hadn't happened.

Poppy got up and examined the green gown. How had it returned to her, and in such a pristine state? How many people were now involved in the subterfuge?

She drank down the cold tea as if it were the nectar of the gods. Cold dry toast was similarly devoured. Then she remembered the letter Millie had left on the dresser. Reaching over, she saw it was from Heather. However, it had been written before Poppy's most recent missive reached her, so it didn't answer any questions she'd had (including a carefully phrased question about when Heather first knew she loved the man she was to marry).

Instead, she read about the escapades of the MacNair family, who seemed to number in the dozens and all had strong opinions about everything from politics to the proper way to make toast. Heather sounded like she was having the time of her life, and Poppy felt both delight for her friend and a little sadness that she was doing things all wrong.

Partly as a result of the letter, Poppy did her best to behave as properly as possible all afternoon. No one mentioned any sighting of a certain couple near Pencliff, or reported her returning alone at a scandalous hour, so Poppy believed that storm blew over. Carlos was also careful to not treat Poppy differently than before. He did tend to hold her gaze whenever he caught her glance, and that—combined with the memory of their single night on board the ship—made Poppy's insides burn each time.

In the afternoon, Elowen pressed her into service as a chaperone (ha!) when Riding Officer Lowry came to call. Thus, Poppy had a front row seat to a courtship that was so completely opposite to her own experience that it was hard to keep from laughing.

"More tea, Mr. Lowry?" Elowen asked politely, for perhaps the tenth time.

"If you would be so kind, Miss Metcalfe."

The conversation between the two would-be lovers was remarkable only for how many times it stopped completely, as the pair fell silent and either gazed into each other's eyes...or looked shyly away at virtually anything else.

Every biscuit offered was praised, and relevant bits of information got parceled out over the course of a half-hour or so.

Mr. Lowry was unmarried, had a very good position, and he was an only son. His parents lived in Cornwall. He liked dogs.

Elowen was unmarried, possessed a small dowry, and was an orphan, along with her younger sister. She came from Yorkshire but had no particular ties there now. She also liked dogs.

"It is both a duty and a privilege to care for my sister," she said at one point (in what was one of the few statements she made that could possibly seem combative).

Lowry didn't take it that way. "She is fortunate to have you, though I could not imagine anyone shirking that responsibility, for Miss Elisa seems to have an angelic nature."

If it was possible for a woman to melt, Elowen would have. Poppy carefully hid a smile—not that the couple even glanced her way.

With great reluctance, Lowry set down his empty teacup. "I regret that I must excuse myself now, Miss Metcalfe. Unfortunately, I have another task to attend to today."

"Oh?" Poppy asked, mostly to remind them that she was there.

"Customs business," Lowry explained. "We are pursuing a gang of smugglers and they seem to be operating very near this house...I say, Miss Metcalfe! You look quite pale!"

Elowen was in fact nearly in a swoon. "Smugglers? Here at Pencliff?" she squeaked out. Poppy could tell that the other girl was terrified that she was about to be clapped in irons.

"Do not trouble yourself, my dear Miss Metcalfe," Lowry said. "I assure you that we are on the case and will soon arrest every last person involved."

"Oh, my." Elowen put her hand to her chest.

Poppy stood up. "Miss Metcalfe ought to rest now.

The sea air does so affect a lady's constitution, and she is of a very delicate nature. Will you see yourself out, Mr. Lowry? I am sure you understand."

He'd leapt to his feet at the same moment Poppy had risen, and now he bowed to them both. "I do hope my mention of the unpleasant subject was not the cause of your distress, Miss Metcalfe. How thoughtless of me."

"Oh, Mr. Lowry," was all that Elowen said. "On the contrary!"

Oh, dear Lord, now I think he *might swoon*, Poppy thought. "Good day, Mr. Lowry. We do hope you call again," she added. It was the customary signal that future visits would be approved—not that Poppy was exactly an authority here.

Just as Poppy was returning downstairs after helping Elowen to her room, she ran into Carlos in the foyer.

"Hello," she said, at a loss for how to greet the man who took her virginity.

"Afternoon. You look...well," he responded, apparently also not sure how to deal with this situation.

After a horribly awkward pause, he said, "I spoke with Officer Lowry on the drive outside the house. I didn't think Customs was going to be quite so prompt."

"Oh, it was a personal call. I had the joy of chaperoning."

"How did it go? Did he propose immediately, or did he wait for tea to be served?"

"Marriage was not mentioned. But it was deduced that everyone very much likes dogs."

Carlos frowned. "Is that a code of some kind? Who doesn't like dogs?"

"No one worth knowing. But as it happens, the visit had to end because poor Elowen practically fainted when Lowry mentioned that he was working on catching some local smugglers."

"She's not really cut out for the criminal life, is she?"

"That's putting it mildly. Where were you today?"

"Truro. Also chatting with Customs, actually. Didn't get a proposal from that one either."

She covered a laugh. "Have you a plan?"

"Working on it." He shot her a look. "You won't have a role in it."

Poppy was about to retort, then considered what happened the last few times she got involved. "That is probably for the best."

The surprise on his face was almost worth it.

"Whatever you end up doing, Carlos," she added, "do be careful."

Chapter 20

DEAR POPPY,

I have your letter. In response to your purely hypothetical query regarding true love, I can only offer this exercise in thought. Imagine yourself as an elderly woman in the last part of your life. You live in a comfortable home with some distant descendants of Miss Mist, and you do not lack for food or funds to provide for your needs. Your friends have proven to be life-long, so you are not a lonely person by any means.

Now, pretend that you hear a knock upon this hypothetical door. Who is on the other side? If it is the person who has professed to love you when you were twenty, can you envision that face changed by the passing of years, and yet be able to fill your heart with joy? Or do you merely think it a stranger come to call upon a lady who has lived her life according to her own terms? Either path has merit, but you must choose which one you will travel. And your heart will tell you who is at the door.

Sincerely,

Florence Bloomfield

The next few days passed quietly, at least as far as

Poppy could tell. The beach below Pencliff House remained empty, and the ships in the Channel traveled only the regular routes. The *Seadragon* hadn't been seen since that fateful night.

She more or less avoided being alone with Carlos, which wasn't difficult because he was often away from the house now. She assumed he was working with his crew or the law to capture Spargo, but she would rather die than ask.

At one point, when Poppy was sitting outside on the terrace with a bit of sewing in her lap, the too-observant Elisa asked, "Did you have a quarrel with Mr. de la Guerra?"

"No, no," Poppy said quickly. "Indeed, I've scarcely spoken to him over the past days."

"That's what made me think you had a quarrel. That, and you're sad."

"Sad? Me?"

"Sad might not be the right word. Before, you always talked and laughed a lot. Now you stare into the distance."

"I do?" Poppy hadn't even realized. Granted, she had a lot on her mind, but she didn't think it was so obvious.

"Yes. When you're outside, you pretend you're looking for ships. But you stare inside too. I think you should talk with Mr. de la Guerra. He's sad too."

"He *is*?" Elisa was a font of knowledge.

The girl nodded. "He looks at you when you're not paying attention. Miss Ainsworth doesn't like it."

Oh, Lord. Ever since Poppy had arrived at Pencliff Towers, Blanche hung on Carlos, flirted outrageously, and generally behaved as if all were well. As far as Poppy knew, Blanche still intended to marry Carlos and fuse their families's business interests. What would the other women do if Poppy casually mentioned that Carlos had already semi-proposed to *her?*

"Well, perhaps I'll chat with Mr. de la Guerra later today. But now I really ought to finish my sewing. It's almost done!"

"It's very beautiful," Elisa said, reaching out to touch the gown.

Poppy had spent the last day and a half stitching seed pearl beads onto her red gown. She had bought them on a whim during another trip into Treversey, because the price was absurdly low for the quality. Poppy had an idea for how to use them, and honestly there was something cathartic about stabbing the deep-red fabric with her needle over and over.

Not that she was feeling any sort of frustration, of course.

However, the result was a very striking gown, with a thick band of seed pearls clustered just above the high waistband, which thinned out slowly over the bodice to the neckline until the pearls were spaced out like scattered raindrops.

She decided that she was having great fun altering a single dress in so many ways, and she'd recommend that her stepfather start importing more ribbons and adornments along with fabric.

Then Elisa made a little sound of surprise, and Poppy looked up to see Carlos walking toward them.

"Oh, bother," she muttered, ignoring the way her heart leapt at the sight of him.

"Ladies," he said on reaching them. "What are you both up to?"

"I'm watching for ships," Elisa said. "Poppy is pretending to sew, but she's also watching for ships."

"And?"

"None of the ships are of interest to me," Poppy said,

with a slight nod toward Elisa to indicate that discussing the *Seadragon* just now might not be the best idea.

Elisa stood up and excused herself. "You two will want to talk anyway. It's time," she announced as she walked away. Poppy decided that for such a sweet person, Elisa could be a bit of a bully.

"Time for what?" he asked, puzzled.

"Never mind," Poppy said, shaking her head. "Elisa is a little romantic, that's all."

Thankfully, Carlos didn't press the matter. He slid into the seat Elisa just vacated, staring moodily out over the water.

"You've been busy," Poppy noted after the silence stretched too long.

He nodded. "Trying to coordinate the navy, Customs, and the local law to catch this man is more work than I ever could have imagined. It's actually a strong argument for the more old-fashioned approach."

"What? You'll kidnap him and make him walk the plank the way the pirates used to do?"

"It has a certain direct charm. But I do so want to do this the proper way if I can."

"Why?"

"I can't very well try to build a country if I refuse to follow basic laws. If Santo Domingo is ever independent and recognized by other nations, it will be because it's a nation of laws. Not just the result of the latest skirmish between colonial powers, which is what's happening now. Men willing to ignore the rules in one situation tend to ignore the rules in the next situation too."

Suddenly, he pointed to her dress. "Isn't that the third dramatic change you've done to that gown?"

"I'm experimenting. Since I seem destined to destroy my dresses, it's good to have ways to refresh them."

"If you continue to do that, you could wear the same dress for decades."

She chuckled. "Sadly, it won't work for long."

"Why not?"

"Because the basic shape of a dress never remains the same. Styles change. Already the waistlines of dresses are dropping lower from just a few years ago, and the sleeves and bodices are changing too. The sort of frothy Continental look from the turn of the century seems passé now. Ladies want fabrics with more weight to them. A robe a la greque wasn't much more than a nightgown. The newer styles are much more structured."

"I prefer the nightgown look."

She sniffed. "This is why men shouldn't be in charge of fashion. They're either swaddling women in miles of fabric to hide them, or declaring one layer of gauze sufficient for an evening gown."

"And yet the ladies all follow the whims," he pointed out. "So who's at fault?"

"If this devolves into blaming women for everything because Eve ate an apple, I'm going to return to the house."

"Please don't. Have you thought about what I asked you?"

"About the dress?"

He rolled his eyes. "About the marriage."

"Oh! No, I haven't."

"What." It wasn't a question.

"Didn't we agree to not discuss it until such time that it becomes, er, necessary?"

"*You* said that," he countered. "My offer stands whether it's necessary or not."

Poppy blushed. "Is this part of your insistence on following the rules? You slept with me, so now you have to make the offer?"

"I made the offer because I love you."

Poppy stared at him. It was one thing to hear the words in the darkness of a cabin after a passionate exchange. It was quite another hearing them in the full sunlight of a summer's day.

"You don't know me that well."

"Everything I do know about you I like."

"Carlos. We lead very different lives. You sail, and I… sew."

"So?"

She stifled a laugh. "Was that a joke?"

"Might be. Are you laughing?"

"A little."

"Then let's say it's a joke." Carlos leaned forward. "What are you afraid of?"

"I'm not *afraid*," she retorted. "I'm just being circumspect. Not letting my heart rule my head."

"How can I convince you?"

Her heart started to race, going far faster than her head. "I think you've done quite enough convincing already."

The smile on his lips was enough to make her skin flush with warmth. "What if I keep asking you every day until you accept?"

"I can't do that. I have obligations, Carlos. My mother, and my stepfather, and their business…"

"So write to them and tell them what's happened."

"My God, you want me to write to my mother to tell her I might be pregnant?"

"No. I want you to write to her and tell her that you received a proposal from a charming, handsome—*incredibly* handsome—and well-to-do gentleman who can absolutely provide for you."

"And I should just not mention that it would mean leaving England forever?"

"Why would it mean that?"

"Don't you want to live in Santo Domingo?" she demanded.

"Well, yes, but that doesn't mean we'd be there always. I've got my own ship, in case you hadn't noticed. We can return here whenever you like, for as long as you like."

Poppy blinked. "Really?"

"Of course. I'm offering to marry you, not take you as a prisoner."

"Sometimes it's hard to tell the difference," Poppy muttered, thinking of the typical expectations for wives. "I suppose you're annoyed that I'm not throwing myself at your feet."

"Not a very Poppy-ish thing to do," he said. "Anyway, I like a challenge."

"You're certainly not short of them this summer. How are things progressing with…the other thing?" She knew he was working hard to arrange matters so Spargo and his smuggling gang could be captured, but she didn't know details.

"Almost ready," Carlos replied, looking out over the Channel, as if the *Seadragon* might appear. "In fact, we are ready. Just waiting for the right opportunity to strike. I don't suppose you've heard anything from Miss Metcalfe?"

"Not yet, but she assured me that she'd pass on any instructions from Dr. Drake as soon as she receives it."

"I hope it's soon. The longer we wait, the more chance that something can go wrong."

"Are you talking about the smugglers or the marriage proposal?" She couldn't help but tease.

"Both are causing me a little concern," he admitted. "But I'm also confident that both will end up exactly how I want them to."

Chapter 21

Dear Poppy,

First, you needn't worry that Adrian has any role in this letter. I asked Camellia to write my thoughts for me while ~~I was visiting~~ while she was visiting (Sorry, I've never been a secretary! — C). Second, since hearing your news, I have been desperate to know all. How could such a thing occur, placing you both in the same house at the same time? It is both marvelous and wonderful and I am beside myself wondering what you did on seeing him. Did you make a scene, darling Poppy? Please tell me you did not, though I should not blame you in the least if you did. And how did he react when he saw you? If he did anything less than beg your forgiveness in the most abject manner, he is a fool. I suspect he is a fool — he must be, to have left you in the first place. Adrian has told me to tell you that Mr. de la Guerra deserves another chance. Of course he would say that about his friend, but in this case I agree. The few times I met him, he seemed intelligent, kind, and sincere, which is a trio of qualities rare in a gentleman. Oh, I pray that this encounter heralds another opportunity for you, and I pray equally that you do not have such a battle with him that you send all of Corn-

wall sliding into the sea like a second Atlantis. In short, my most precious cousin, take a deep breath before you unleash your wit at him. Your wit can be cutting.

I hope for the best, and insist on ~~steady~~ daily reports. I know you had feelings for him before. Do not toss aside a chance for happiness simply because you're clinging to your stubbornness.

With love and nerves,

Rose

P.S. All that which Rose has said is true, and all I can say is that I WISH I were there with you, dearest Poppy. A great house with a handsome rogue and secrets galore? It's a dream come true. You must write us both and tell us every last detail of the developments, or else we shall come to Cornwall ourselves and tell that man just what we think of him!

Camellia

One afternoon a couple of days later, Poppy was reading a letter that arrived from Rose, and musing about how odd it was that so many things had happened to her within the span of mere days, but until her friends read about it, they lived in the past. She wrote a reply, assuring Rose that the peninsula still remained above sea level, and that she and Carlos were still talking with each other. (She didn't say what *else* they had been doing with each other, not trusting such intimacies to paper.)

That afternoon, the Metcalfes returned from Eloisa's appointment with Dr. Drake. Elowen found Poppy where she was reading a book in the shade of the house.

Elowen said in a voice so quiet she could scarcely be heard, "The doctor told me that the next shipment is expected. I'm to signal the ship tonight."

"At what time?" Poppy asked anxiously.

"Ten. What should I do?"

"Stay right there. Let me talk to Mr. de la Guerra." Poppy got up and walked back into the house.

She found Carlos in the parlor, but he wasn't alone. Blanche was there as well, sitting on the other side of the divan, chattering away with him while Mrs. Ainsworth looked on with a benign smile. (She had some embroidery on her lap, but it was clear that the only thing she cared about stitching was Blanche to Carlos.)

"Excuse me," Poppy said from the doorway. Three sets of eyes looked at her, two sets with outright malice. Thankfully, Carlos smiled.

"There you are, Miss St George," he said. "Haven't seen you most of the day."

"I've been reading outside," Poppy explained a bit breathlessly. "Mr. de la Guerra, we need to talk."

"Then talk here, by all means," Mrs. Ainsworth said, with false friendliness. "We shall not interrupt."

"It's a private matter."

Blanche raised an eyebrow, and Poppy blushed. It sounded absurd put like that—a young lady like Poppy shouldn't have *any* private matters with a gentleman she wasn't married to.

"My word, that does sound dire," Mrs. Ainsworth said. "What can possibly require Mr. de la Guerra's attention that could not be solved as readily by the Towers, or even the Hobbsons?"

"None of them speak Spanish," Carlos improvised smoothly as he stood up. "That's what Miss St George requires. The book she is reading has some Spanish in it."

"There are books written in Spanish?" Blanche asked, in what had to be the most English way possible.

"I'm reading *Don Quixote*," Poppy snapped, grabbing

at the first title that came to mind.

Carlos walked to the door, and rather forcefully guided Poppy away. Then he murmured, "One might think that you and Miss Ainsworth don't like each other."

"*You* seem to like her. She was practically sitting in your lap."

He bit his lip. "If only I were married."

"Hush. I just spoke to Elowen." Poppy related the specifics, and Carlos immediately grew serious.

"Very well. Then tonight we've got to put everything in motion. I'll send word to the Customs men working on it. And Mr. Armitage."

"Why alert him?" Poppy said. "Isn't he corrupt?"

"I have no evidence of that, and meanwhile, I will behave as if he isn't," Carlos said.

Poppy hoped he would not regret the decision.

"And what should Elowen do? She's very nervous."

"She needs to signal that the shipment should happen as planned. That's the only way."

When Poppy returned to where Elowen was sitting, she said, "All right. It's arranged. Everything hinges on you signaling just as expected. If all goes well, Customs and the local law will round up the smugglers tonight, and all of this will be done with!"

Elowen twisted the fabric of her skirt in her hands, leaving a wrinkled mess. "Oh, Poppy, I just can't! I have a vision of Mr. Lowry catching me with a lantern in hand, and realizing what I've done. I'd be devastated to lose his good opinions of me."

Poppy made the decision instantly. "Then tell me how to give the signal. *I'll* go up to the attic window and send it."

"Oh, my goodness," the other lady gasped. "I could never ask you to do such a thing!"

"Why not? The act of signaling isn't dangerous in itself. I'll do it and be well away by the time the action starts. Besides, it may help muddy the waters should Dr. Drake choose to expose you. If you are seen among the other guests at ten, when you couldn't possibly be signaling, then no one will believe Dr. Drake's potential accusation, will they?"

Elowen put her hand to her heart. "I hadn't even thought of that. Oh, Poppy, would you do that for me?"

"Of course. It's only for tonight, and then this will all be behind us."

* * * *

Just after Poppy gave him the news that Spargo was making a smuggling run that night, Carlos wrote a message in Spanish to Valentin.

V —

S on run tonight after ten. Make arrangement to pick up goods we spoke of: 60 for 550. Be there at my beach tonight. Lions hunting. Be ready.

—C

It was a very constrained message, meant to make it impossible for anyone who wasn't Valentin to understand the details. Spargo was going on a smuggling run tonight anyway, so Valentin should push him to complete the sale of the arms he'd shown Valentin before. He had sixty pieces for a total price of five hundred and fifty pounds. And the sale was to happen tonight, on "his" beach, below Pencliff Towers. Spargo might be wary, but he wouldn't turn down the money, and if all went well, the *Agustina* and the naval ship would pin the *Seadragon* in the cove below Pencliff Towers. The smugglers would all be rounded up, and Spargo would face criminal prosecution for all the murders he'd committed, but most especially Mateo Vega's.

In his note, Carlos even managed to give the reason for the hasty transaction. The guns had to be moved because the "lions" (a code word for agents of the British crown, whether Customs, or the navy or the local law) were expected to make a raid soon. Valentin would pass that on. Any smuggler with half a brain would want to clear out their supply as fast as possible.

Carlos shook out his hands, feeling the strain in his nerves. He touched the cross at his neck again. "Almost there," he promised Mateo. By the end of the night, it would all be over.

By dawn, the murderer would pay for his crime.

Chapter 22

DEAR POPPY,

 While I cannot know with precision what you have been up to, I am nevertheless certain that you are in deeper than any former teacher would like. Your vague hints about a matter of a romantic nature would send any mother into a tizzy (and while I am not a mother in fact, I certainly feel that way about all my Wildwood girls). Luckily, you were always a sensible and mature young lady, and I trust that you are fully in command of yourself. More than most women, you are aware that few things in life are certain, and that opportunities come when least expected. Seize the ones that call to your heart, my darling, but do not neglect to listen to your own good sense. If there is a gentleman involved, I must assume he is worthy of you (or else you would not consider him). And if he is worthy of you, he is rare.

 Write to me as soon as you may, for I am filled with curiosity...along with a little concern.

 Fondly,

 Florence Bloomfield

Poppy tucked away the letter from her former headmistress, thinking that she'd have so much to tell her in the next letter that it might require a whole ream of paper to do it. With luck, all the parts of Poppy's summer that would cause Mrs. Bloomfield a "little concern" would be done with by morning. She'd simply have to trust that she was fully in command of herself to carry out the last small task tonight.

There were a dozen or so clocks in the common rooms of Pencliff Towers, and Poppy felt like she was staring at one or more of them the whole evening, watching the hands on each face spin around, creeping toward ten. The hourly chimes mocked her, ringing out again and again, but never with the right number of bells.

She wore her red gown (with all the seed pearls now stitched on), and got several compliments on her appearance. Even Mrs. Ainsworth couldn't help but say, "That is a striking outfit, Miss St George." Then she had to spoil it with, "Of course, a spinster does have a great deal of time on her hands to do such fine beadwork."

Well, Poppy *did* have time on her hands tonight, because as soon as the clock struck ten, she would go upstairs to give the message to the smugglers, while Elowen remained in full view of the houseguests. Poppy could barely wait for Carlos to leave, knowing that if he realized she'd volunteered as signaler, he'd be furious about it.

After dinner, when the gentlemen were just rejoining the ladies in the parlor, a servant gave Carlos a message. Carlos took the folded paper and read it. With only the barest side glance to Poppy, he casually headed back to the door. She silently wished him good luck, then decided that silently wasn't good enough.

She got up and followed him into the foyer.

He looked back. "What are you doing?"

"You didn't expect me to not see you off, did you? I

know you're going to change your evening wear for your pirating wear, and then go chase smugglers."

"You can't come, Poppy. You know it's far too dangerous."

"I understand that!" she said. "I only wanted to tell you to be careful."

"And you have."

"And to tell you yes," she added impulsively.

"Yes what?"

"Yes to the marriage proposal. If it still stands."

Carlos stood still for a moment, and then he swept her into his arms.

Poppy was lost in his kiss and his embrace and all they promised. She barely caught her breath when he kissed her again.

"You have a unique sense of timing, *vida mía*," he murmured. "We'll talk about this when I get back."

"Yes, dear," she said sweetly.

He looked at her with narrowed eyes, then laughed. "Soon," he said. And he was gone.

Poppy took a few deep breaths, and then noticed a figure on the other side of the foyer. The maid Millie stood there, looking shocked.

"I accepted his proposal," Poppy explained.

"Oh, *miss*." Millie sighed at the news. "How romantic!"

"But please don't tell anyone. We'll announce it to everyone tomorrow."

Millie nodded eagerly as she crossed her heart.

Poppy glanced at the grandfather clock in the foyer, and saw that it was about to strike ten. "Oh, no! I've got to get to the attic. Bye, Millie!"

She dashed up the staircase, leaving a very bewildered maid behind her.

In the attic, Poppy found everything in readiness. The lantern was there, along with a flint. It was very dark in the attic before she lit the lantern. The moon hadn't yet risen, and when it did, it would be little more than a sliver—a thin, sly smile only criminals would welcome. In Poppy's mind, this was the true smugglers' moon, not the round fat one of two weeks ago. The sky was clear of clouds, and the stars twinkled madly in the hazy air above the sea.

The window didn't have a curtain, so all Poppy had to do was stand in front of the glass and slowly move the lantern in the prescribed pattern. She lifted it up, then let it down, and repeated it several times with a minute between signals. That way, a watcher at sea had more than one chance to notice the message.

Finally, she stopped signaling and set the lantern on the floor. Her arm ached a bit, but she also felt an overwhelming sense of relief. Her part was done. She'd lured the smugglers out with her false message that it was safe. The rest was up to the force of men who'd gathered to capture Spargo and his gang.

She just hoped that Carlos wouldn't do anything foolish and hurt himself in the process. After all, a lady should worry about her fiancé when he ran off to fight criminals.

Poppy smiled to herself, thinking that love did some silly things to a person. Here she was, in the dark attic of a home that wasn't hers, and she was helping catch smugglers as a favor to a woman she'd only just got to know… and all she could think about was Carlos.

"All right, enough of this," she told herself out loud. "Time to get downstairs."

"Couldn't have put it better myself," said a voice out of the darkness.

Poppy spun around, trying to see who snuck up behind

her. She grabbed the lantern, and lifted it to see a man in the uniform of a magistrate.

"Mr. Armitage?" she asked, puzzled. He seemed far too young to be a magistrate!

"The name is Rowe," the man clarified. "I'm a deputy to Mr. Armitage."

Poppy took a cautious breath. It was Mr. Armitage who had concerned Carlos when he went to make his report. He hadn't even mentioned anyone else.

"Look," she said. "This isn't what it seems."

He raised an eyebrow. "You mean signaling to the ship out there that everything is clear so they can come in and offload a cargo of very valuable opium?"

"Well...I can explain."

He smiled and shook his head. "You don't have to explain. I know what's happening. Do you think I found my way up here to your window by chance?" He stepped closer to her. "Glad I did come though. Drake said you were pretty."

"Dr. Drake?" Poppy asked, confused all over again. If he was the ringleader they assumed him to be, why would *he* be talking to the law about tonight's operation?

"Yes," Rowe confirmed. "He's very grateful to you for signaling. We all are—business has been profitable. But the fact is that young ladies make poor conspirators. All that tendency to talk, you know."

Oh, my God. Poppy thought. *He thinks I'm Elowen!*

But she also wasn't about to correct him. Poppy said, in a surprisingly level voice, "Ah. So not all the magistrate's men are actually working for the magistrate."

"Good eye," the deputy said, with a short laugh.

"What exactly are you here for?" Poppy asked bluntly.

Rowe smiled. "I'm here to tie up loose ends...so to speak." He produced a length of rope and a strip of cloth designed to be a gag. "You'll be brought to the *Seadragon* and loaded up with all the other cargo."

"Cargo?"

"Yes, indeed, my dear. Surely you didn't think we were going to kill you. What a waste. Beautiful young virgins are worth a lot of money."

"I'm not a virgin," Poppy blurted out.

He laughed as he grabbed her and swiftly tied her hands behind her back. "Nice try. Don't say that among any of the men tonight—it's the only thing that will prevent them from enjoying you on the ship before they off-load you on the Continent. Now walk."

Using his gun to ensure her good behavior, Rowe marshaled her through the house via the servants' stairs (he wasn't such a fool that he'd go into the main living space). On the ground floor, he pushed her down the hallway to the basement...passing the kitchens and servants' workrooms along the way...where a set of wide eyes happened to see their progress from a cracked-open door.

Poppy made as much of a fuss as she could while being directed at gunpoint, twisting and turning as if to seek escape. Therefore, Rowe didn't notice that several of the seed pearl beads got torn from her bodice and dropped on the floor along the way, like breadcrumbs to mark the path leading to danger.

* * * *

Carlos had just changed into what Poppy had so casually referred to as his "pirating wear," which consisted of a black wool jacket over a plain linen shirt, plus loose black trousers that would get a sidelong glance at any social function, but that knew he could run or climb in, if needed. He tucked his gun underneath his jacket and walked quickly downstairs and out the French doors, intending to go down the cliff steps to join Valentin and his crew.

Stealth was the order of the evening, and thus he was rather upset to hear his name shouted behind him.

"Mr. dee lee Guerra! Mr. dee lee Guerra!"

Carlos whirled around, wondering who the hell was chasing after him in the darkness. He was puzzled to see a housemaid running his way. She skidded to a halt in front of him.

"He took your fiancée, sir!" she blurted out.

The words took a moment to register, but then his heart dropped. "You mean Poppy? Who did what to her?"

"Sir, I just saw a man making her go down into the basement. He had a gun at her back!"

"Show me."

The maid (Millie—he remembered her name once his brain started working again) led him to the part of the ground floor where the servants worked. He heard the clatter of dishes as the cook and her underlings cleaned up from supper.

Looking down, Carlos saw the scattered seed pearl beads, and instantly knew they were from Poppy's gown. "This way," he said, pointing to where the tiny white objects continued to appear. He didn't need the hint at this point. He knew where the man had taken Poppy.

"He's bringing her through the caves," he muttered, when he and Millie reached the heavy door that marked the entrance to the tunnels below.

"You know about the tunnels, sir?" Millie asked, surprised.

"Yes, by luck." He paused. "And you know too."

"It's common knowledge downstairs, sir. First day I

came to work here, the housekeeper told me to avoid ever going there. Said they were haunted, but I think the only spirits haunting the tunnels are the kind you drink."

"I agree with that," he muttered. "But have you been in the tunnels?"

"Me, sir? Lord, no! I'd sooner die." Millie said, then added, in a more chipper tone, "I'll fetch you a lantern. You're going to have to go after them."

The idea of walking into that dank, dark, airless underworld nearly made him pass out. He'd rather die than go in there.

Except that Poppy was in there.

A moment later, Millie handed him a lit lantern. "I'll inform Mr. Towers of what happened."

"*Only* Mr. Towers," Carlos warned her. "Don't let anyone else know about this until it's resolved."

"Aye, sir."

Millie bustled away, leaving Carlos alone.

Carlos sank to his knees, contemplating the rectangular entrance to the void beyond. There was no way he could do this.

The only time he'd been in the tunnels before, he'd been blindfolded, with Poppy leading him because he was too cobarde to look.

But if he didn't follow, Poppy would be lost forever. He remembered her describing how the tunnel that led to Pencliff Tower branched off a larger cavern, with a dozen more passages from there. She could be taken down any one of them, and then from there to a boat...and gone.

With a deep breath, Carlos stepped into the darkness.

The urge to turn right back around and run to the safety of the open air was overwhelming, but he clamped down on his emotions and took another deep breath, then another, until he realized his chest was heaving and the panic hadn't gone anywhere.

"Anda el diablo controlate," he told himself. If Poppy could navigate these caverns, so could he.

With the lantern held high, Carlos moved along the narrow, twisting passageway as fast as he could. The light was so dim that he could barely see a few feet in front of him.

"Don't blow out," he whispered to the lantern. "If you go out, I can't see anything." And that would end him.

The first several hundred feet were just a matter of bulling past his fear—the passage was an unbroken tunnel with no branches at all. A part of his mind (the part that was trying desperately not to panic) saw the markings of tools along the stone walls. Poppy was right that much of this tunnel was man-made, a deliberate effort to connect the house with the labyrinth below. And considering that smuggling and piracy had been rife in this corner of the world for centuries, that made sense.

Then, up ahead, he saw what he dreaded. A decision.

A second tunnel joined the main one. It was a little narrower, but not much, and it sloped downward more dramatically.

Something caught the light several feet down the main passage—a few little, soft glowing things. He hurried forward, then stooped down to see what it was, and picked up several tiny seed pearls strung together on a red thread.

Despite everything, he smiled. Poppy had left him a sign by ripping off some more of the little pearl beads from her dress. As long as he kept finding these, he'd know he was going the right way.

Moving on, he made sure to keep an eye on the floor, especially any time there was a branching passageway. Each time, he managed to find a few of those pearls ripped off and flung to the ground, indicating which way Poppy had been taken.

He really ought to marry the woman the first chance he got. She was too clever to let go.

Thinking about Poppy helped keep the worst of his terror at bay. He ignored the sense of the crushing weight of tons of rock above him, and the dampness of the air that seemed to inhibit easy breathing, and the absurd feeling that time had simply stopped.

When he'd been locked in that closet as a child, he experienced the same horror—the conviction that surely it had been hours and hours, or days, only to realize that mere minutes had passed. The caverns were worse. They'd been here for eons, and would exist until the end of days. Time just didn't matter here.

No. Think about Poppy. Time did matter, because she needed him now. And he'd find her as fast as possible, and when this was over, he was going to tell the whole world that she was his, and they'd get married, and live joyfully somewhere in the bright sun and fresh air, and he'd never set foot in a cave again.

A grand plan.

First, he had to survive the night.

Chapter 23

THEY WALKED, AND WALKED, AND walked. Rowe kept behind Poppy, who held the lantern to guide the way (being untied after he got her safely into the tunnels). The deputy gave her directions from time to time, and Poppy kept pulling at the loose threads on the bodice of her dress, spilling small quantities of seed pearls every time their path took them down a new tunnel. She wasn't even sure why she was doing it, because no one knew she'd been taken. But a Wildwood girl always had a plan, and plans kept panic from taking over. Poppy looked back over her shoulder each time she scattered a new bunch of pearls, but Rowe hadn't seemed to notice anything. But he didn't like when she surveyed him, and he waved the gun meaningfully to get her moving again.

Rowe forced her through what felt like miles of tunnels. How far away were they going?

"Is it much longer?" she asked when they entered the large cavern that had so many other openings along the walls. She plucked at the pearls on her dress, trying to make the gesture look like pure nervousness. When Rowe finally steered her through the next tunnel, she had to leave a trace…or no one would ever find her.

God, she hoped Carlos was having better luck than she

POPPY AND THE PIRATE 222

was tonight. Was he onboard the *Agustina* yet? Did the smugglers suspect that they were going to be ambushed?

"Not too far. Why? You eager to begin your new life?"

"Don't be vulgar," Poppy snapped. "I'm having a difficult evening as it is!"

"Sorry," Rowe said, rather surprisingly. "I'm just following orders."

"Well, isn't that a relief!"

"Look, you should have known what the risks were when you got into this. Did you really think that Drake was going to let a flighty woman walk around free, knowing that he was the head of a smuggling ring? We're wrapping matters up shortly, so Drake gave the order to get rid of you."

Poppy didn't try to explain to Rowe that she wasn't who he thought she was. First, he wouldn't believe her anyway, and second, she had a chance to learn more about this whole operation since he thought she'd already been involved for weeks.

"Is Dr. Drake *really* the man in charge?" she asked. "I mean, a doctor just doesn't seem…"

"I know. He's got the perfect image in Treversey. Quiet Dr. Drake. No one would dream he's got a second side as a criminal. But he's smart, knows the value of money, and he got all the gangs working under Spargo now. Everything goes through them. It's more efficient, and a lot safer. We pass the savings onto our London contact, and everyone benefits."

"London contact?"

"Ainsworth." Rowe blinked. "You didn't know? He didn't mention it while you were all up at that house together?"

Poppy remembered that she was pretending to be Elowen. "I was trying to keep my involvement a secret."

Rowe chuckled. "Lot of little secrets up there. Too many. It would have been easier if Ainsworth bought the place. But the Towers got the jump on us. Doesn't matter. Soon we'll control all of the Cornish cross-channel trade. We'll have landing sites on any beach or cove we need."

A short while later, she saw brighter light ahead, and then they were in a familiar place. Poppy looked around the cavern. It was the very same one that she and Carlos found that first night. But now it was crowded with more boxes and barrels. The deputy hailed a man sitting on one of the crates at the other end of the large cavern. "Sir! Got her, no problem."

"Who's this?" asked the smuggler, looking at Poppy.

"The signaler. Miss Metcalfe," Rowe said.

"Miss Metcalfe has dark hair, and is about five inches shorter than this lass." He glared at Poppy. "Who are you?"

Poppy sighed. "Does it matter at this point?"

"Not for you," said the man she recognized as Peter Spargo (thanks to seeing him through her spyglass the other day). "But if this idiot grabbed the wrong girl, it means that Drake's order still needs to be carried out. Rowe, get back through those tunnels and back to the house. Find Miss Metcalfe and get her down here."

"Wait," said Rowe, just catching up. "You're not Elowen Metcalfe?"

"Very good, Mr. Rowe," Poppy said drily. "I'm a different houseguest."

"But you were…"

"Enough, Rowe!" the other man growled, interrupting what was about to become a very awkward comment for Poppy. "Go back and get the right girl."

"What am I supposed to do? Sneak in and start opening bedroom doors?"

"Sounds like a plan to me. Get moving!"

Rowe retreated down the tunnel they'd emerged from. Poppy looked after him. "I know what bedroom he's looking for. Why didn't you ask me?"

Spargo snorted. "You'd probably have lied. And anyway, Rowe ought to sweat a bit, after stealing the wrong girl."

"I don't suppose you'll let me go."

"Sorry, lassie. You know too much. But I'll see that you're treated well until we part company."

"Oh, you mean when I'm sold?"

Spargo grinned, and she realized that he had no heart at all. "Practice your smile, lass. Men like a lass who can smile."

"I sincerely hope you drown someday," Poppy said sweetly.

He gestured to the crates. "Sit. I'm going to tie your ankle to that ring in the wall, so don't think you'll be strolling out of here."

"What is it this time?" Poppy asked, gesturing to the cargo. "Did you steal the Crown jewels?"

"I would if I could," Spargo replied. "This is all supplies from the army or navy. Not as exciting, but still quite profitable. Opium, guns, and gunpowder. And of course, now we can add you to the merchandise."

He used a heavy rope that stank of tar to secure her leg to the iron ring in the wall. If she had a sharp blade, she could probably saw her way through it. But she was armed with only her wit, and that was simply not going to be sharp enough tonight.

Spargo left her then, telling her not to be an idiot or he'd have to kill her.

"I'd send a man to keep watch, but your value would very likely decline after any of my men got a quarter hour alone with you," he noted, with a leer. "So I'll come back for you myself, and you'd best be grateful for it."

"I hope you catch on fire, fall off your ship, and *then* drown," Poppy amended, not feeling in the least bit grateful.

He raised his hand as if about to strike her, grinned when she shrank back. Then he turned on his heel and walked out, toward the beach.

With her ankle attached to the rope, Poppy had about ten feet of range. She examined the crates, and then a cluster of barrels, hoping to find an abandoned knife or something to use as a weapon. Instead, she saw something more dangerous. One of the three barrels was open. She smelled the contents, and her nostrils flared. Gunpowder! It must have been opened so the men could refill their own supplies before the risky smuggling run began.

Inspired, she plunged her hand into the barrel, spilling out some in her haste to gather what she needed. She bundled a bit of powder into her kerchief and tied it up. Then she tucked it into the pocket of her dress, a hazy, desperate plan forming in her mind.

She listened to the distorted calls of men coming from further up the passage. She knew she had to create some sort of distraction so she might be able to get away. But how could she do that when she had no weapon?

Just then, a light glowed ahead, dazzling her eyes even though it was only a single lantern flame. Her heart beat nervously. Had Rowe returned so quickly? No, that had to be impossible.

Hiding wasn't an option, so Poppy grabbed the lantern. If she had to, she'd hurl it at the next man who approached her.

But the man who stumbled out of the tunnel into the light wasn't Deputy Rowe. In fact, it was a sinfully handsome, vaguely piratical gentleman of her acquaintance.

Poppy stared at Carlos in amazement. He'd come all the way through the miles of narrow tunnels, in the dark?

"Carlos?" she whispered.

Carlos smiled slowly, and walked up to Poppy. "Did you miss me?"

"Terribly." She threw her arms around him, and said, "You walked the passageway from the house? By yourself?"

"Well, there was something I wanted in here," he replied. He put a hand on her head as he held her close for a moment, and Poppy told herself that everything was going to end well now. "Gracias a dios te encontré. We've got to get out of here. I clonked Rowe on the head when he came back up the tunnel." He wagged the gun that had belonged to Rowe. "And I heard Spargo leave. But soon this cave will be swarming with smugglers."

"I'm tied up," she said.

He nodded. "Pull up your skirt and then cover your ears."

Poppy raised an eyebrow but complied with the order. Carlos lifted the gun and fired. The rope pulling at her ankle suddenly went slack.

"Oh, my Lord. You *shot* the rope in two?"

"I'm in a hurry. Now come on. Someone will have heard that and they'll come to investigate. Let's be ready."

* * * *

As Carlos guessed, the sound of a gunshot from inside the cave was enough to bring one of the smugglers in to investigate. But he didn't think it would be quite so fast. Nor did he dare hope that it was Spargo himself who rushed in, pistol in hand.

"What the hell is going on here?" Spargo yelled. He stopped short on seeing Carlos. "You! For some random sailor, you tend to be underfoot."

"Thank you," Carlos said, as he lifted his own gun (well, Rowe's gun). "Since we can all kill each other very easily, I suggest we don't. Spargo, you return to the beach. I'll be taking the lady back to the house."

Poppy had wrapped her arms around him. She said nothing, but he could hear her heart beating in her chest, and he felt her rapid breath on his cheek.

"Don't worry," he murmured. His fear of the caves had somehow evaporated. He knew what he had to do now, and that made everything simple.

"She can't go anywhere," Spargo said, shaking his head once. "She knows too much."

"So my mother often said," Poppy muttered.

"Shush, darling," he told her, covering a smile.

Carlos heard a distant shout, and he prayed it meant what he'd been waiting for.

A moment later, a man came running into the cavern, yelling for Spargo. "Sir, we've been betrayed! There's a cutter sailing into the bay! It's got to be HM Customs! And the *Seadragon* can't fire cannon because no one's on duty for it. We're all unloading the crates!"

"Well, get someone on the cannons, you idiot!"

The underling ran off before Carlos could stop him.

Spargo snorted. "No one can run things without me. But it doesn't matter, the *Agustina*'s out there too. They'll take care of the cutter."

"They won't," Carlos said bluntly. "*Agustina*'s orders are to keep the *Seadragon* from leaving the bay."

"How the hell would you know that?"

"Because I'm the captain of the *Agustina*, and that's what I told her to do."

"*You're* the captain? You must really want those guns, eh," Spargo said, still not quite understanding the situation—which suited Carlos very well.

"I want the guns, and I want the girl. Now we're all going to walk out to the beach. Because if you want me to give a different signal to the *Agustina*, you'll need me out there, alive and amenable. Understand?"

"Aye," Spargo said, glaring at Carlos. "Let's go."

"It's a trick," Poppy whispered. "He's going to kill both of us the moment he gets the chance."

Carlos raised the gun a little, pointing it at Spargo's head. "Drop your gun to the ground...away from you. Do it now, or I'll shoot you."

"Wait! Don't do it." He dropped it, then put his hands up. "I'll tell my men to stand down. On my honor, I'll let you both go as soon as the shipment's unloaded and my men can get clear of the beach."

Poppy looked very suspicious. "And how do we know you'll keep your word?"

He grinned. "My honor doesn't mean much, does it? I like you, lass."

"I can't say the same."

Carlos narrowed his eyes. "You go first."

Poppy raised her lantern to illuminate the passage for Spargo.

Just then, the light flashed over Spargo's hand, setting the rings and jewels he wore to glimmering. And Carlos saw something he hadn't noticed before. On Spargo's pinky finger, he wore a heavy gold ring set with a rectangular garnet, with a gold cross set over the stone.

Carlos knew that ring. Mateo had worn it every day of his life. On the band, Carlos knew that he'd find three stars on each side, a symbol used by Mateo's family as a play on their name.

"I'll be taking that ring," he told Spargo, in a very quiet voice.

Spargo glanced down at it, then back up to Carlos. "It's not for sale."

"I'm not here to buy it, hijo de la semilla. I'm going to return it to the family of the man you killed for it. Mateo Vega."

All at once, Spargo put the pieces together. Finally.

But by then Carlos was already rushing toward him.

Bodies collided. Dimly, he heard a scream, and the light went out.

Carlos and Spargo each fought as if their lives depended on the outcome—which was exactly the case. Spargo first went for Carlos's gun, and nearly grabbed it. Carlos hurled it away into the darkness rather than let his opponent get it, or risk Poppy getting shot.

But he wasn't totally unarmed. He had a knife, and used it. Spargo let out a roar of pain when Carlos slashed the blade across him—was it his face? The darkness was total.

A fist slammed into his gut, and he winced. He barely dodged the next blow, but he swung an uppercut and felt the deeply satisfying crunch as his knuckles connected with Spargo's jaw.

The other man was momentarily stunned, and that gave Carlos just enough time to do what he needed to do, which resulted in Spargo howling in pain as Carlos cut off the last two fingers of Spargo's hand, seizing the ring that had come to signify all that he was fighting for.

"Carlos!" Poppy called out then, sounding terrified but also angry. "¿Necesitas que te alumbre?"

"Sí!" he called back, moving away from Spargo to avoid getting hit again.

She relit the lantern. Blinking in the sudden light, he

saw that he'd got turned around in the darkness, or Poppy had moved during the fight. Yes, Poppy was now standing by the beach tunnel. She held a lantern, and what looked like a wadded-up handkerchief. A barrel had been knocked over in the scuffle—though he didn't remember doing it—and some powdery substance was spilling out.

Spargo was on his knees, clutching one hand in the other, bright red dripping from his fingers. He glared at them both.

"Carlos, get over here now," Poppy ordered, sounding like a general. "Mr. Spargo, you can follow us if you like. But I should mention that the guns are both over there." She pointed to the other side of the large cavern, where the gleam of metal proved her words true.

"You're both going to regret this," he snapped. "The moment you set foot outside, my men will end you. Except you, girl. They'll keep you around for a bit."

"I see," said Poppy. She took another deep breath as Carlos joined her. "Well, then I don't feel so bad about this."

Before he knew what she was doing, Poppy lit the corner of the handkerchief on fire.

Spargo had jumped up and rushed to where the guns were lying, but he looked back over his shoulder when Poppy yelped in surprise as the cloth burned.

"This is gunpowder," Poppy announced. "Carlos, *run*." She tossed the flaming bundle on the ground at Spargo's feet, then bolted outside, Carlos right next to her. Spargo was yelling curses, about to rush into their tunnel…just as the fire touched the packed gunpowder.

The explosion pushed Carlos and Poppy down the tunnel like pebbles rattling down a pipe. Carlos grabbed her and covered her with his own body as they tumbled outside onto the beach. Above them a gout of flame roared out of the cave mouth, to the shock of the crowd of smugglers who half-surrounded them.

Then another explosion sounded—but not from the caves. Blinking in confusion, his ears ringing, Carlos looked up and across the water.

At first, he wasn't sure what she was seeing. The *Agustina* was in the bay, of course. Carlos had planned it that way. But the cannon fire hadn't come from her deck.

Another ship was sweeping into the bay as if a hurricane were propelling it. It was clear that the crew of the *Seadragon* hadn't noticed it until it was too late to flee.

Then the ship turned sharply and opened fire again, with three cannons aimed directly at the *Seadragon*. Shrieks of dismay were heard as several men jumped overboard.

Next to him on the sand, Poppy moaned.

"Poppy!" Carlos said. He pulled her up. "That was a lot more gunpowder than you needed. Are you all right?"

"I don't know," she said, looking stunned. "I do know that Spargo shouldn't have gone for the guns. It put him on the wrong side of the cavern. I did sort of warn him."

"You did splendidly, *querida*," he said, embracing her gently just in case she was injured.

"I still can't believe you walked that whole way alone and in the dark!"

He shuddered. "I know, and I don't want to think about it again." He patted the pocket where he'd tucked Mateo's ring, reassuring himself it had also made it out of the cave.

"You don't have to," she said. "It's over."

"I'm not sure of that. We are surrounded by a gang, and we have just killed their leader. I'll have to fight our way clear."

But in fact, there was little more fighting to be done.

Customs officers and a small militia of local men were swarming the beach, shouting for the smugglers to put down their weapons. The gang on the beach rushed around in total confusion, having no leadership to tell them what to do.

Meanwhile, the smugglers who jumped overboard got to the shore. However, all that accomplished was to make things easier for the uniformed men who had rushed down the beach. They herded each soaking wet smuggler out of the water before they could run.

One uniformed man approached Carlos and Poppy, and he suddenly recognized the face of Riding Officer Lowry.

The Customs officer did a double take on seeing Poppy, bedraggled but obviously a lady in her red evening gown.

"My goodness, Miss St George, what are *you* doing here?"

"I was in the wrong place at the wrong time," Poppy said, squeezing Carlos's hand to prevent him from jumping in. "One of the smugglers saw me earlier and decided I'd fetch a good price as a slave."

"Monstrous. Point him out when you see him, and I'll see that he faces additional charges."

"As a matter of fact, I know his name. It's Mr. Rowe, deputy to the magistrate." She didn't mention that he was likely unconscious in a cave at the moment.

Lowry's eyes widened, then narrowed. "I'll take care of it."

Carlos decided that he liked that young man.

They both watched as some of the Customs officers began hauling crates along the beach into one spot, where they'd be loaded onto the cutter.

Eventually, Collector Snell approached Carlos. Armitage walked beside him.

"Mr. de la Guerra!" Armitage said, on seeing them. "You're alive."

"Yes, though it was debatable for a moment. I trust Valentin and the crew of the *Agustina* did their part?"

"To perfection!" It was Snell who replied. "They lured the *Seadragon* into the bay with the promise of purchasing the guns, and then blocked the ship from leaving until the navy's ship could arrive. Spargo thought he had two deals done tonight. Buying the opium, then selling the guns. Instead, he lost both. As it should be. Where is he, by the way? I'd love to arrest him personally."

"Apologies, sir, but he's likely destined for a higher court now. His body is in the cave behind us. He got a little too close to a barrel of gunpowder and an open flame."

"Well, that's a shame. But it will save time in the long run." He turned to the magistrate. "I'll just go confirm that he's dead. Would you see that all the rest of Spargo's men are accounted for?"

Armitage nodded and hurried off.

"So Armitage was on our side?" Poppy asked skeptically.

"Yes, Miss…"

Carlos stepped up. "May I introduce you to Miss Poppy St George."

"A pleasure," Snell said, offering a courtly bow. "And to answer your question, Mr. Armitage acted as circumspectly as he could to bring closure to the issue of opium smuggling."

"So he wasn't in league with Spargo like Rowe was?"

"Not at all. He was chosen for the post precisely because he could be trusted not to join up with the smugglers. You see, Mr. de la Guerra, you actually wandered into an operation we've been monitoring since last year. Mr. Armitage first warned you off so you wouldn't muck anything up. Though in the end, it has all worked out. Now we have the smugglers and the contraband. All that remains is to identify the ringleader. Peter Spargo isn't the end of the chain."

"The one in charge is Dr. Burton Drake," Poppy blurted out. "And Mr. Ainsworth is their London contact for goods."

Snell's gaze leveled on her. "How might you know that?"

"Mr. Rowe, that deputy magistrate who kidnapped me, was quite talkative. Probably to show off."

"Very unwise of him, but helpful for us." Snell looked beyond them, and Carlos turned to see the remains of Spargo being hauled out of the cave. It really was all over.

"Ah, if it's all right with you, sir, I should take Miss St George back to the house," Carlos said. "It's been a very long night."

At the officer's assent, they walked quickly past the now-bound smugglers on the beach. Carlos led Poppy up the steps to the lawn of Pencliff House, where the first hints of dawn were coloring the sky.

Chapter 24

POPPY SIGHED AS THEY CLIMBED—all. the. way.— up the cliff stairs, and crossed the lawn to approach the house. "I don't think we're escaping detection this time."

"I do not intend to try," Carlos said. "After all, we're properly betrothed and we have nothing to hide."

"*Properly* betrothed might be a bit of an exaggeration," she said. "I do hope Blanche won't be too terribly disappointed that you're no longer on the marriage mart."

"She never had a chance." He stopped and turned to her, taking her hands in his. "I thought I'd lost any chance to win you after last year. Can you imagine how shocked I was to see you appear at this house?"

"As shocked as I was," she guessed, with a laugh.

"I told myself it was a sign. You're singular and rather sharp, but I need that. And I think it possible you might find me tolerable."

"Not the word I'd pick," Poppy said, looking at him. "But I don't want to flatter you."

He laughed. "We can discuss that later. For now, just admit you rescued me."

"I rescued you?"

"In more ways than one."

"Do you *want* to marry me?" she asked. "I mean, tru-ly?"

"Ever since you first threatened me at that party in London."

"Oh," Poppy said. "Well, all right then. I suppose I'll marry you after all." She tried to keep her tone careless and casual, but her foolish smile destroyed the illusion.

"You know, it occurs to me that I've got a cousin in Santo Domingo with a printing press, and he's always complaining that he can't get enough intelligent discourse to print steady issues of his newspaper, or the pamphlets advocating for independence. So what do you say? Want to join a revolution?"

"Your revolution? I'm not Dominican."

"Once you marry me, you will be, amor. All it really requires is fearsome intelligence, a love of justice, and the desire to defend people who cannot always speak up for themselves. And you have all of those."

She felt the warmth of his regard down to her toes. "Well, when you put it that way…"

"Good. That's settled," he said with a smile. "Now we just have to explain everything to everyone."

Not surprisingly, they were spotted well before they got to the door. Mr. Towers opened one pair of French doors and rushed out to the lawn, still in his dressing robe. "What in heaven's name has been going on? Millie woke me up with a mad tale of kidnapping and pirates and I told her not to read any more novels before bed. But she kept insisting and I got up to send for the magistrate. And did I just hear cannon?"

"You did," Carlos said cheerfully. "Smugglers were making use of your beach, but they have been captured, in no small part to the bravery of Miss St George here."

"Is that so?"

"Mr. de la Guerra gives me more credit than is due," Poppy said. "I merely reported an unusual occurrence, and he took care of the rest."

"Oh," Mr. Towers said. "And what, if I may ask, is the rest?" He looked very confused.

"The small matter of an opium smuggling operation," Carlos said.

Poppy could not reply because Miss Mist had darted across the lawn and meowed so loudly that Poppy had to scoop her up and reassure her that she was well and safe. The cat settled into her arms, purring contentedly.

Carlos was still explaining, "Thankfully, Customs and the local magistrate have the ringleaders in custody," Carlos continued. "It turns out that Ainsworth didn't just want to buy this property for the house and the lovely view... there's an extensive network of caves below, and one passage leads all the way to your basement.

"What?" Towers repeated, in total astonishment.

"Ainsworth pretends to be gentry—and his wife is gentry— but he has made most of his wealth from smuggling. He hoped to work himself onto the top of the chain here in Treversey, using Spargo as his pawn. Dr. Drake, however, was the real leader. He saw that Ainsworth was trying to become a more important part of the chain between here and London, and sold him out. Actually, Ainsworth is lucky we intervened when we did. Otherwise, Spargo was about to kill him and dispose of the body the way he has so many others."

"So it's over?" Towers asked anxiously. As he spoke, several more people started filing out of the French doors, drawn by the noise and novelty of the scene.

"Yes, it's over," Carlos said softly.

Poppy leaned into Carlos, hoping to convey some of her sympathy for the intense personal mission he'd just completed. He'd come to Cornwall to avenge his friend's murder, and now that was finally done.

"What a relief," Mr. Towers said as his wife joined them, clad in a morning gown with a riotous pattern of cabbage roses all over it.

"I will need a full accounting!" his wife said then. "Do not pretend that is the whole story!"

"Dearest," her husband began.

She pointed to Carlos and Poppy. "You two young people are...*glowing*. You're madly in love."

"Oh! Are you?" Mr. Towers stared at Poppy and Carlos, then he started to laugh. "You two stopped a smuggling ring and fell in love in the process?"

"To make a long story short...yes." Carlos cleared his throat. "Fortunately, Poppy has already agreed to marry me."

"Carlos!" Poppy almost shouted. "I wanted to tell my parents first!"

"Oh, this is too wonderful," Mrs. Towers cried. "I want to hear the whole story."

"Perhaps over breakfast?" Poppy suggested. "I'm *starving*."

"Indeed! I'll tell Cook we need sustenance as soon as possible."

About an hour later (during which Poppy was bathed and dressed so that she felt like a normal person again), she went down to the breakfast room. Everyone was there...with the exception of the Ainsworths.

Happily, sustenance was supplied in huge quantities. Poppy and Carlos found themselves besieged by more food than any human could eat. Soon the breakfast room was as lively as any ball, with chattering from incredulous guests.

Elowen beamed on seeing Poppy and Carlos safe. She

also seemed relieved her part in the smuggling could remain buried. Officer Lowry was there as well, having arrived to report the final details of the operation to the Towers (and to verify for himself that his beloved Elowen had not been troubled by the cannonfire).

Poppy was asked to recount Carlos's unusual proposal more than once, and she blushed each time, to the delight of Mrs. Towers. They received congratulations from the Metcalfe sisters and the Hobbsons.

Following breakfast, Carlos walked her back out to the terrace. Morning light restored all color to a world the moon had reduced to black and white. Poppy yawned. She hadn't slept all night long, though she hadn't noticed any tiredness before then.

Carlos stood beside her, watching the water. "I haven't been honest with you, Poppy."

"What do you mean?"

"I should have told you immediately when I met you that I intended to pursue you. My hesitation caused you a quite unnecessary amount of distress."

"Oh," she said. That confession wasn't what she expected. "Let us forget it. It was due to events beyond our control."

"I know we're engaged, but if you like, I can do all the things I meant to before. The courting, and the flowers and the meeting your parents and such."

"Those do sound nice, but I quite liked your unconventional courtship of the past few weeks—the skulking about, the explosion…and the kisses."

"The kisses were not explosive?" he asked, with false shock. "I'll have to try harder." He grinned, in a way that prefaced a terrible pun.

"Don't say it," Poppy warned.

"I just wanted to note that marriage to you might be

illuminating." He took her hands in his.

"Oh, please stop."

He leaned closer and said, "Sparks may fly."

"You're incorrigible," she said.

"You're incendiary."

Poppy winced. "What have I agreed to?"

"You agreed to marriage, because I set your heart ablaze."

"Stop, stop, stop. This is actually painful." However, she made no effort to pull away.

"Very well," he said. "I won't add more fuel to the fire."

"Carlos!"

"Should I put a damper on it?"

"Or I will," Poppy said, laughing. "I love you, but…"

He held her. "That wasn't so difficult, was it?"

"You mean all I have to do to stop your puns is to say *I love you*?"

"Try it," he encouraged her.

"I love you, I love you, I love you."

"And…I have nothing to say except that I love you as well."

Poppy smiled. "In that case, the marriage can go forward."

"Splendid. I'm burning to…"

"Wait, I love you!" she said.

"You're learning," he said, and kissed her. "And so am I."

Epilogue

ON A FINE AUGUST MORNING, Poppy woke up in her family's home in London. She lay in her own bed, in her own bedroom, and contemplated the early sunlight creeping its way along the wall.

It seemed incredible that she'd had such adventures this summer, or that her life had changed so dramatically within the span of a few months.

Carlos had (naturally) dazzled her parents when he'd met them. Poppy was a little dazzled herself when she heard him describing his home and all the luxuries Poppy could expect once she arrived in the role of Señora Poppy St George de la Guerra. Apparently, Carlos had been downplaying his status on the island. To hear him tell it, his family owned a large chunk of it, not to mention the shipping they controlled…a vital lifeline for any island nation.

In all, it seemed that Poppy more or less stumbled into a brilliant match. Everyone approved, the date was set, the details attended to…and now it was the fateful morning.

"Well, are you ready to get married?" Rose asked from the other side of the bedroom. The cousins had spent the previous night giggling and gossiping far too late, until they fell asleep, just like old times.

"I suppose I can't put it off any longer," Poppy joked, feeling a tinge of melancholy. She truly would be putting her childhood away forever.

"There's nothing to fear. Marriage is really quite wonderful if you have the right person at your side."

"As you do with Adrian."

Rose smiled. "I have no complaints. And he's delighted that Carlos was able to win you at last, because it means that we'll all remain linked, despite the distance between us."

"Of course we shall. I have already promised Mama that I'll visit as often as I can. Every year if possible."

"Oh, Poppy, don't make plans like that yet. You've got to settle in at your new home, and who knows? You may be breeding too much to set sail very often."

"Nonsense. We've decided to delay having any children until we're both ready. And that won't be for years. We got this whole matter of a nation's independence to settle first."

"But with you stepping up, that will be sorted in a few months," Rose said with gratifying confidence. "I overheard Carlos and Adrian talking yesterday at the house. Carlos seems to think that you will be like lightning to tinder, once you start writing for his cousin's paper."

"La Luz," Poppy said. "A good name. I just hope I can help make some kind of change." Carlos's cousin had already enthusiastically responded to the suggestion that Poppy write for La Luz, thanks to an essay she'd written—and Carlos had translated—and then sent in one of the dozens of letters back to Santo Domingo. His family and friends appeared to thrive on correspondence, which made Poppy feel quite at home.

There was a knock at the door. At Poppy's assent, Heather, Camellia, and Daisy all popped into the bedroom (they'd slept across the hall).

"Today's the day!" Heather cried. "Ugh, I can't believe you're moving to the Caribbean. It's literally half a world away."

"My soon-to-be husband does own a ship, you know," Poppy pointed out. "We can return to England whenever we need to."

"I do hope so," Daisy said. "It's all well and good for us to be madly in love with our spouses, but friendships are irreplaceable. We must never drift apart, even though miles will separate us from time to time."

"Well said," Camellia murmured.

Rose hugged Poppy tight. "Oh, I'm going to cry."

"Save that for the wedding ceremony," Heather advised. "Speaking of which, let's get you ready, Poppy. We're going to make you the most beautiful bride in all of England this year."

A couple of hours later, a polished Poppy arrived at the selected spot. By mutual agreement of all parties, the wedding was held at the Viscount Norbury's London home. Poppy's parents were quite happy with that option, since the idea of holding a wedding that included a duke, viscount, and earl on the guest list was a little unnerving for even the most successful of fabric importers.

In remembrance of the events that brought them together, Poppy wore a brand-new red dress with flowers embroidered all along the hem, and seed pearls sewn along the neckline and sleeves so thickly that the top of the dress resembled pearlescent armor. Her hair was pinned up, and gold ribbon had been threaded into it by Daisy, who also lent Poppy several diamond hair pins that sparkled in the light.

Poppy walked down the aisle, surrounded by friends and family, all of whom she wanted to kiss and hug and generally wish the world to. There were the Towers, and the Metcalfes, with a very attentive Mr. Lowry nearby. Daisy and her duke were seated in a place of honor, being the most high-ranking guests (after Poppy's parents, who needed no titles to earn their place at the front). Rose sat with Adrian, her happiness for Poppy radiating outward from her whole being. There was Heather and her Scottish husband (plus several siblings, for the MacNairs appeared to travel in packs). Camellia was there, sitting next to Mrs. Bloomfield, no doubt so they could share handkerchiefs as they waxed sentimental about school days. There were the men and women her stepfather employed, looking very much at home—despite the fact that the home belonged to a viscount. Poppy beamed at everyone, her heart overflowing.

When Carlos saw her, he looked stunned.

"What's wrong?" she whispered when she reached him.

"Nothing. It's just that I'm used to seeing you covered in dirt and salt water...and now you look like a queen."

She winked at him. "Well, I make no promises as to how our little revolution will end. Perhaps I'll claim your island for myself."

"You could," he breathed. "I love you."

"Oh, that's nice," she said, her heart fluttering. "I don't need to be a queen, you know. If I've got your adoration, I don't need anyone else's."

"We might have another ceremony in Santo Domingo," he warned in a low voice as they turned to the minister standing at the front. "According to their letters, my family is quite devastated to miss this one, and my parents will very likely want to see me married in a Catholic Church...even though we're already married."

Poppy waved her hand, dismissing the issue. "I'm

happy to marry you a thousand times. That implies a thousand wedding nights."

"You're so wise," he murmured, kissing her.

"That's supposed to happen at the end," the priest reminded them, with a chuckle.

"My goodness," said Poppy. "We certainly wouldn't want to do anything out of order."

"Or anything that might upset convention," added Carlos.

The priest sighed. "Are you two ready to be married or not?"

"Ready!" they said at the same time.

"Very well. Then let's begin."

And so they did.

Author's Note

THE TALE THAT POPPY RETELLS and acts out in the prologue is inspired by "The King and the Emperor," from the *Tales of Rabbi Nachman*. I first ran into the story in *The Serpent Slayer and Other Stories of Strong Women*, written by Katrin Tchana and illustrated by the incomparable Trina Schart Hyman). Tchana's version, called "The Rebel Princess," is the one that gives the names of Judith and Zev to the princess and prince of the tale (in Rabbi Nachman's telling, no one is named).

The character of Carlos was born and raised in what is now the Dominican Republic, though that name did not exist until 1844, after this novel takes place. Thus, he refers to his homeland as Santo Domingo, which was used to refer to both the city and the larger region around it. On the western half of Hispaniola was the colony of Saint-Domingue, which later morphed into the country of Haiti. The whole island was known as Hispaniola (and still is today). But to make things more confusing, the names of Santo Domingo and Saint-Domingue were *also* sometimes used to refer to the whole island, depending on whether the French or the Spanish were nominally in control of it at the time. No wonder the residents sought independence—they just wanted a name everyone could rely on.

For the Spanish lines and phrases in the story, I am very grateful to Stephanie Martin Llanes and her mother Anmarie Llanes for translating my words and supplying some great insults. Isn't learning fun? I am further indebted to Claudette Cruz from *The Editing Sweetheart* for additional translations. However, any mistakes made (no matter what language they're in) belong solely to me.

ABOUT THE AUTHOR

Elizabeth Cole is a romance writer with a penchant for history. Her stories draw upon her deep affection for the British Isles, action movies, medieval fantasies, and even science fiction. She now lives in a small house in a big city with a cat, a snake, and a rather charming gentleman. When not writing, she is usually curled in a corner reading...or watching costume dramas or things that explode. And yes, she believes in love at first sight.

CPSIA information can be obtained
at www.ICGtesting.com
Printed in the USA
BVHW081139260423
663000BV00003B/556